MW01138262

THE SOLARIANS

Norman Spinrad

ReAnimus Press

Breathing Life into Great Books

ReAnimus Press
1100 Johnson Road #16-143
Golden, CO 80402
www.ReAnimus.com

ISBN-13: 978-1490394978

First ReAnimus Press print edition: June, 2013

10 9 8 7 6 5 4 3 2 1

Norman Spinrad titles available from ReAnimus Press in print and/or ebook editions

BUG JACK BARRON
THE LAST HURRAH OF THE GOLDEN HORDE
THE IRON DREAM
THE VOID CAPTAIN'S TALE
GREENHOUSE SUMMER
CHILD OF FORTUNE
LITTLE HEROES
A WORLD BETWEEN
STAYING ALIVE
EXPERIMENT PERILOUS: THE 'BUG JACK BARRON'
PAPERS
PASSING THROUGH THE FLAME
FRAGMENTS OF AMERICA
THE CHILDREN OF HAMELIN
THE SOLARIANS
AGENT OF CHAOS
THE MEN IN THE JUNGLE
SONGS FROM THE STARS
THE MIND GAME
RUSSIAN SPRING
PICTURES AT 11
JOURNALS OF THE PLAGUE YEARS

Chapter I

IT WOULD be another uneven battle. Four to three, standard odds—in this case, in the Sylvanna system, it meant a fleet of eighty of the dead-black ships now crossing the orbit of the outermost planet in tight cone formation, base forward, flagship at the apex.

Fleet Commander Jay Palmer formed the Human Eleventh Fleet into disc formation, only three ships thick, the flagship in the third rank.

He sat in the command chair of his flagship; in front of him the Master Battle Grid, showing the Duglaari fleet as a cone of red blips, his own outnumbered ships as sixty golden blips, Sylvanna, a G-5 sun as a green globe; to his left, the Damage Control Board—sixty lights, now all green, showing all ships in fighting trim (amber meant a damaged ship that still had power, blue meant a dead hull or worse); to his right, the Computer Data Screens.

He was dressed in dull olive battle fatigues, devoid of brass, open at the collar and designed strictly for comfort. It was his job as a Fleet Commander to merge himself with his fleet, or, more properly, to make each ship an extension of his mind, a part of him. A good commander thought of his fleet as an integrated organism: the ships were the limbs, the pseudopods; the flagship, the computer-ship, was the brain; and he was the heart, the ego, the soul.

Separate earphones were plugged into each of his ears. The right earphone gave him direct contact with the chief computation officer. The left was the command circuit; the voices of the sixty individual captains.

A throatmike was secured to his Adam's apple. In his right hand was a two-position toggle switch—forward and he was speaking to the chief computation officer, back and he could command his sixty captains. A similar switch was in his left hand, but it had three positions: forward for the computation earphone, back for the command circuit, middle for both at once.

"Computation," Palmer grunted, "confirm numbers."

"Eighty Doogs," mumbled his right earphone. "Estimated contact time, one hour."

Palmer's gaunt face screwed into a frown. It was a face that would be handsome in repose, but now there were hard lines around the full lips, and three furrows in the high forehead.

He flicked on the command circuit. "Leave plane of ecliptic at ninety degrees Galactic North," he ordered. "Full speed."

He kept his large gray eyes glued to the Master Battle Grid. The disc of golden dots began to move upward, above the green median line that represented the ecliptic. A battle on the fleet level began as a contest of position. You must not let yourself be caught between the enemy and a sun, not when your fleet was the smaller one. The standard Duglaari tactic was to force a fleet back on the sun it was defending; if they were fast enough, they could box you in so that escape was impossible — superior numbers in front of you and a sun to your rear; there would be no place to go. The Fleet Resolution Field of the Duglaari was stronger — they almost always had more ships — and it would push the Human Fleet back, back into the stellar furnace, until the fleet would be forced to break formation, and fight on a ship-to-ship basis, hopelessly outnumbered....

Sweat gathered on Palmer's upper lip. The Human Fleet was rising above the ecliptic, but now the Duglaari Commander had spotted the maneuver, and the red cone was rising too, as the fleets closed on each other at terrific speed. It was like chess; the openings were more or less standard. If the Human Fleet could rise above the Duglaari, it could descend behind them, and then it would be the Duglaari fighting with a sun at their back, and while their total Fleet Field would still be the stronger, it would be fighting the pull of Sylvanna as well as the push of the Human Fleet Field, and the battle might be more or less even.

But the Duglaari were rising as fast as the Humans; in fact, Palmer's trained eye could see that they were rising about five percent faster. The Humans would not be able to rise above them.

Palmer snorted to himself. They were taking the bait. If they could be fooled long enough….

"Cut speed to three-quarters," he ordered. The Human Fleet slowed its rise; now it was clear that the Duglaari would rise above them, but Palmer hoped that it would be close enough so that the Duglaari commander would still believe that the Humans were trying to go *up* and around. If the Doogs could be conned into maintaining their rate of rise long enough, then….

Soon the fleets would be upon each other.

"Cut speed to two-thirds."

Again the Human Fleet cut its rate of rise slightly.

Palmer studied the Master Battle Grid carefully. The Duglaari were not slowing down! It was working! At the present relative rates of speed, the Duglaari would hold the space above them; the base of the cone formation pressing with its field on the face of the Human Fleet's disc, forcing it back and sunward.

But in another moment, the Duglaari would be committed to their rise; they were now travelling at nearly twice the speed of the Human Fleet, and they would never be able to turn in time....

Now!

"Kill forward speed!" Palmer barked. "Emergency power braking! Reverse direction one hundred eighty degrees! Drop! Drop! Drop!"

The Human Fleet stopped rising. It began to fall back down towards the ecliptic. Faster and faster it fell, through the ecliptic, and then down past it.

Frantically, the Duglaari slowed down, reversed direction and tried to follow the Humans down. But the Doog commander had reacted too slowly. He had actually lost the contest for position when he had failed to realize that the Human Fleet had been purposely slowing its rise.

Instead of the gap closing, it was widening.

"Ninety degree turn!" Palmer ordered.

The Human Fleet changed direction again. This time, it shot on a line parallel to the ecliptic, but below it, out away from Sylvanna, and underneath the Duglaari Fleet. It shot past the Duglaari, and now the Duglaari were between the Human Fleet and Sylvanna.

"Rise! Rise! Up! Up!"

The Human Fleet shot upward. The Duglaari Fleet braked its descent and tried to rise faster, but the Humans had the jump, and the Fleets had reversed positions.

The apex of the cone that was the Duglaari Fleet now pointed towards Sylvanna. Its base faced the face of the disc formation of the Human Fleet.

It had worked. The Duglaari were caught between the Human Fleet and Sylvanna.

Palmer switched over to the Computation circuit. "Do we have the power to force them back?" he asked, but he was pretty sure what the answer would be. The Resolution Field Drive was used to drive ships in normal space.

It resolved the electron spin of all masses within it into a unidirectional vector at right angles to its lines of force. In tight formation, the individual Resolution Fields of the ships were merged into one great Fleet Resolution Field, enveloping all the ships.

In addition to propelling the fleet forward, the Fleet Field would push anything in front of it in the same direction that the Fleet was moving—in this case, that *anything* included the Duglaari Fleet.

But the Duglaari had a similar field, and it was pushing against the field of the Human Fleet. There were three factors which would determine in which direction the two fleets would now move: the strength of the Human Field, the strength of the Duglaari Field, and the fact that the Duglaari Field also had to fight the pull of Sylvanna.

The Duglaari Field would be stronger than the Human Field by a factor of three to four, but perhaps when the additional factor of Sylvanna's gravity was subtracted from the Duglaari Field strength....

The computer now had the answer. "Negative," said the voice in Palmer's ear. "However, it could be worse. We balance them out now. We can't push them back, and they can't push us. Stalemate."

Palmer sighed resignedly. It was as he had expected. The Humans had won phase one of the battle—the contest for position. They had temporarily nullified the Duglaari's numerical superiority.

Now phase two would begin: the battle of attrition.

The first phase of a battle, the positional phase, was usually over in less than an hour or so; the second phase, the attrition phase, could drag on and on and on....

In the present positions, the field strengths of the two fleets stalemated each other. There was only one way to break that stalemate and force the battle to a decision—destroy more ships than you lost, so that your Fleet Resolution Field would then become proportionally stronger than the enemy's.

The choice of possible weapons in this phase of the battle was severely limited. Nothing with significant mass could pass from one fleet to the other—it would be caught in stasis midway between the two contending Resolution Fields. This ruled out all missile weapons. It even ruled out anti-proton busters, since the anti-protons which the busters projected had mass. Nuclear and thermonuclear explosives were out too, since it was impossible to set them off closer to the enemy than to your own ships.

That left only energy weapons operative.

"Computation," Palmer mumbled into the throatmike, "take over. Use pattern GN-64, to start with."

Palmer scowled. This was the part of a battle that he hated most. The only weapons that could be used with any effect now were the lasecannons, which projected heat beams of fearful intensity. But, like any other energy weapon that had ever been invented, the beams had to be kept locked on an enemy ship for long seconds for them to burn through the metal of the hull and do any real damage.

He studied the Master Battle Grid. The ships within the Duglaari cone were beginning to move within their formation in complex, seemingly random patterns. The idea, of course, was to prevent the Humans from keeping a lasecannon beam locked on a ship long enough to do any damage. The gold blips of the Human Fleet were performing a similarly complex dance of death.

The patterns looked random, but they were not. They couldn't be, for, in addition to avoiding lasecannon beams, the ships of both fleets also had to remain tightly integrated into their respective Fleet Resolution Fields, else the field would be broken and the un-integrated fleet routed.

This was far too complex a task for any living organism, even a trained and experienced Human or Duglaari fleet commander, to perform. It was all done by the Fleet Computers, which conned both fleets during this phase of the battle.

Palmer could pick which of the literally thousands of preprogrammed patterns the computer would use at any given moment; he could switch the chosen pattern at any time, but that was the extent of his control over his fleet now.

And he didn't like it one bit!

A Duglaari beam glanced harmlessly across one of the ships in the front rank, and detectors howled. Now a Human beam bounced off a Doog ship in the base of the cone; in a fraction of a second, the Doog was no longer there, and the lasecannon beam lanced harmlessly off into empty space.

The computers, damn 'em, were feeling each other out, trying to rationalize the enemy's "random" movements into predictable mathematical patterns.

Palmer, like most fleet commanders, hated the computers. For one thing, they robbed him of complete control of his fleet; for another, the Command Computers, back in the Olympia system, were losing the goddamn war. The Duglaari computers were better than the Human ones, and there were more Doogs than men.

Mankind was facing extinction, and the computers had regularly announced that fact for the past three hundred years.

One of the green lights on the Damage Control Board went amber. The Duglaari were figuring out pattern GN-64.

"Switch to GP-12," Palmer ordered.

Now the Duglaari computer would have to crack the new pattern before it could damage another ship, and....

There!

One of the red blips flared purple and went out. Its power was dead. *Scratch one Doog!*

Now the Duglaari would change patterns.

This could go on for a long, long time. As soon as one fleet's computer caught on to an enemy's pattern, the opposing commander would switch to a new pattern, and the computer would have to begin anew.

There would be no great conflagration destroying scores of ships in a few minutes of red-hot action. There would only be a slow chipping away—a Doog ship here, a Human ship there—until the stalemate in field strengths was broken.

If it was broken. Palmer remembered the story of the battle of Bowman. Fifty Humans, fifty-eight Doogs. Neither side had gained a significant advantage, the Humans destroyed one Doog ship for every Human ship lost, and the battle wore on for well over a standard day. In the end, every single ship in both Fleets had been destroyed.

It was sheer idiocy.

Jay Palmer knew very well what he *wanted* to do. Break formation suddenly, make an all-out, do or die attack on the Doog flagship, the computership. If you could knock out the flagship, destroy the computer, the battle was all over. Then the enemy couldn't evade your lase-cannon beams and maintain its Fleet Field at the same time.

But, he knew, even if such a tactic succeeded, he would be court-martialed afterwards. The war, and every single battle in it, was fought under the rigid control of Computation Command. Any commander who thought he could outthink computers would be busted to permanent latrine orderly. *If he were lucky.*

Another light on the Damage Control Board went amber, then blue. And then another!

Damn! Damn! Damn!

"Switch to GN-41".

On and on it went, hour after hour. Space gradually became littered with the corpses of ships, with shards of metal, clouds of debris where a powerplant had been hit by a heat beam, exploding a ship.

Lasecannon beams lit up the blackness like linear novae, and the battle wore on, the ships within the formations continued their dances of death.

Palmer was bathed in sweat, his hair was wet and matted. It seemed to him as if he had spent his entire life in the command chair. Feeling was gone from his buttocks. His throat was raw from rasping commands.

They had gone through hundreds of patterns, and the Duglaari had done the same.

Grimly, Palmer studied the Damage Control Board. Ten of the lights were now amber, another seven were blue. Seventeen ships out of commission.

The Duglaari had only lost fourteen.

Palmer knew that he was losing the battle. The point of no return had not yet been reached; by using emergency power, the Human Fleet was still holding position, but if the Doogs got, say ten ships ahead, then phase three would begin, and....

"Computation," Palmer rasped wearily. "Extrapolation, please."

"Chances of Duglaari victory: seventy percent," said the voice in his ear. "Human victory, twenty-three percent. Stalemate, seven percent."

Palmer signed. He made up his mind—when the chance of Duglaari victory reached eighty percent, he would break contact and flee. *If not....*

If not, the Duglaari Fleet would keep getting proportionally stronger and stronger. Since the Humans had forced the Duglaari into the sunward position, it would not be over quickly—the Doogs wouldn't be able to simply push them into the sun. Instead, the cone of the Duglaari Fleet would hollow out into an empty hemisphere, the hemisphere would advance and envelop the Human Fleet. Then the Duglaari would form a globe, with the Human Fleet in the center.

The stronger enemy Fleet Resolution Field would surround the Human Field; the Duglaari generators would press irresistibly inward, the Human Fleet would be crushed and compacted until ships collided, until there was nothing left but a huge, tightly compacted mass of mangled metal—and dead men.

In the beginning of The War, three hundred years ago, such battles to the death had occurred, with horrid regularity. It had cost many ships and men to learn the lesson: if you can't win, *retreat*. Get out with as many ships as you can. Heroics only meant that the imbalance in men and material between Human and Duglaari would grow that much worse.

Eighty percent would be the point of no return.

"Switch to GN-7."

At least the number of patterns was virtually inexhaustible....

But two more lights went amber. Then blue.

"Switch to GN-50."

Damnit, the Duglaari computer was learning to crack the patterns faster. Maybe, in some weird Duglaari mathematical system, the Human patterns fell into some master pattern of their own. Maybe that was one of the reasons that the Doogs were better....

No! No! Not *better*. Maybe more advanced, maybe a bigger, older civilization, but not *better*....

Another light went amber.

"By all the cowards of Sol!" Palmer swore. "Switch to GN-13."

Almost immediately, the amber light went blue. The Duglaari computer had adjusted again, and this time almost as fast as the pattern had been changed! *It's hopeless....* Palmer thought bitterly.

"Switch to GN-69," he muttered into the command circuit.

"Commander Palmer! Commander Palmer!" It was the voice of Twordlarkin, the chief computation officer. Palmer had a pretty good idea of what was coming....

"Commander, the latest extrapolation is eighty-three percent chance of Duglaari victory. My official recommendation at this time is immediate retreat. We can expect the beginning of an engulfing action shortly, otherwise, and we will be unable to successfully resist it."

Palmer swore, taking care to switch Twordlarkin out of the circuit first, though. *Official recommendation!* An "Official Recommendation" from a chief computation officer was a command in everything but name, even to a fleet commander. The Navy runs the ships, so the saying went, but the computers run the War. Only one thing could save a fleet commander who ignored a computation "recommendation" from a court-martial—victory.

Fat chance of that. The hell of it was that Twordlarkin was right. Sylvanna was lost. Still, a combat officer should at least have the right to order his own retreat.

Palmer reactivated the computation circuit. "Very well," he grunted. "Recommendation acknowledged and approved." He switched over to the command circuit. The standard retreat tactic should work this time, he thought, since at least we're not caught between the Doogs and Sylvanna....

"Fleet Commander to all ships. On my mark, reverse Resolution Field Generators one hundred eighty degrees. Five... four... three... two... one... *mark!*"

Suddenly, every remaining Human ship reversed its generator. Instantly, the Human Fleet Resolution Field was reversed, and the disc formation of Human ships shot outward at tremendous speed. For now, instead of opposing the outward thrust of the Duglaari Fleet Resolution Field, the Human Fleet was suddenly riding it, adding its power to the power of its own Field. As a result, the outward acceleration was twice that that either of the fleets could manage by itself.

For a few brief moments, the Human Fleet continued to open up the gap between itself and the startled Duglaari. Then the Doog commander reacted, reversing *his* Fleet's Resolution Field, so that the Human ships were no longer riding it. Impelled now by the greater power of its larger Fleet Field, the Duglaari Fleet was beginning to close the gap. It would be a race to the outskirts of the Sylvanna System, a race for life.

Palmer glanced hurriedly at the Master Battle Grid, then switched on the Computation circuit. Computation had *some* really vital uses, after all.

"Do we have a big enough jump, Twordlarkin?" he said. "Will we be able to beat them to the orbit of Sylvanna VIII?"

There was a long, tense minute of silence as Twordlarkin put the problem, involving distance, initial acceleration, relative speeds and closing speed to the Command Computer.

"Affirmative," Twordlarkin finally said. "They cannot catch up to us before we cross the orbit of Sylvanna VIII."

Palmer heaved a deep sigh of relief. The battle was over now. The Duglaari Fleet would not be able to catch up until the Human Fleet had crossed the orbit of Sylvanna VIII, the outermost planet, and once the Human Fleet left the Sylvanna system, it would be able to translate safely into Stasis-Space.

Stasis-Space was not the mythical "hyperspace" of the ancients. It was not an abnormal condition of space at all; it was a bubble of time. Within the bubble, time was many, many times faster than outside, while spatial properties, aside from some weird optical effects, remained essentially normal. A ship in Stasis-Space did not exceed the local speed of light, but, in relation to normal time, time in the bubble was contracted, so that the bubble itself disappeared from the normal timestream, and reappeared light years away, in a matter of hours, by "normal" reckoning. An inverted Stasis Field was erected within the outer Stasis-Field of each ship, so that the crewmen lived within the normal timestream and did not age abnormally.

Since ships in Stasis-Space carried their own timestream with them, they could not even be located by other ships.

The Human Fleet, what was left of it, would get safely back to the great base in the Olympia system....

Palmer checked his Damage Control Board. Thirty-two of the original sixty lights were still green. Thirty-two ships had gotten away safely....

"How many Doogs destroyed?" he asked Computation glumly.

"Eighteen," was the answer.

Twenty-eight Human ships traded for eighteen Duglaari.

Twenty-eight ships, *and* the system of Sylvanna.

Somewhere out there, safe in their bubble of time, were the Duglaari troopships. Now the Duglaari could safely bring them into the Sylvanna system....

Palmer tried not to think of what would happen in the Sylvanna system now. There were fifteen million Humans in the Sylvanna system.... They were as good as dead.

No, he thought bitterly, not as *good*. Not nearly as good....

Not nearly.... He remembered Brycion, the planet where he had been born, the planet where he had spent the first five years of his life, the planet where his parents had died, and he saw, through the eyes of his childhood, what was about to happen to Sylvanna.

There were fifteen million people in the Sylvanna system and perhaps enough ships for a hundred thousand of them to flee before the Doog troopships arrived. That was the mathematics of chaos and riot and terror.

He dimly remembered what had happened when the Doogs had driven the defending human fleet from the system of Brycion. There had been close to a hundred million humans in the Brycion system and ships enough for a hundred thousand to escape. A thousand mad, terrified people fighting for each berth, with only hours to go before the Doogs arrived.

Palmer's memories of that time were confused and fragmentary, but mortally vivid. He remembered a human sea flowing out over a deepspace field, toppling ships with the sheer weight of stampeding humanity, he remembered fires, and shooting and senseless, futile fighting in the streets.

He remembered his father and his mother, fighting their way, block by block, to the deepspace field. He remembered being herded aboard a ship with what seemed to him at the time a million children.

But most of all, he remembered the last he ever saw of his parents, a glimpse out the viewport just before the ship lifted off for Olympia and relative safety....

A maddened, seemingly endless mob was roaring across the open concrete towards the ships. A thin circle of men and women, mostly parents of the children the ships were to carry to safety stood between the mob and the ships, buying with their lives the time needed for the ships to lift off.

He saw his father, and his mother too, firing coldly into the terror-maddened mob, and the leading wave of the endless human sea about to engulf them in its deadly embrace....

Then, mercifully, the ship had lifted off, and Palmer never knew for sure whether his parents had been torn to pieces by the mob, or whether they had survived to face the Doog occupation.

Ever since he had been old enough to understand, Palmer had hoped that his parents had died then and there, torn to pieces by men turned into animals. Horrible as such a death was, the people who died before the Doogs landed were always the lucky ones....

Palmer tried to turn his thoughts away from Brycion and the past. Now there was Sylvanna, and the present....

Soon the Doogs would bring in the troopships and occupy the three inhabited planets of the Sylvanna system.
There would be no great conflagration, no mass slaugh-
ter, no bloody extermination of human beings. That
would be a waste of time and energy and material, and
the Doogs were too efficient to waste effort on a pogrom.

The humans would simply be herded into small,
crowded reservations, and the Sylvanna system would be
repopulated by Duglaari.

The humans within the reservations would be left
strictly alone, to fend for themselves—minus medicine,
food, clothing, machinery, even water.

The Duglaari would simply keep them penned up like
wild animals until they finally killed themselves off fighting for what little food and water there might be in the
reservation areas.

The Duglaari were not needlessly cruel.

But they were not needlessly merciful, either.

Chapter II

TO THE people of the Human Confederation, the solar system of Olympia was almost a capital, and to Jay Palmer, it was almost a home. By some by-now-untraceable quirk of history, Olympia had received the lion's share of wave after wave of refugees. Since most of these refugees were children, the government of Olympia had become a kind of massive foster-parent, and since the chief business of the human race was the war for survival against the Duglaari, all these war-waifs were, with their own enthusiastic approval, pointed towards military careers throughout their rattier abbreviated childhoods.

From this position as the number one supplier of officers and non-coms to the human fleets, Olympia had naturally evolved into a garrison system. There were three inhabited planets in the Olympia system: Olympia II, a small Mars-sized world with a medium-thin atmosphere, was a huge drydock and armory world; Olympia IV was a tiny, frigid, airless rock, but as such it was an excellent location for the cryogenic computers that formed the Chief Computation Center of the Confederation.

And Olympia III, a temperate, Earth-type planet, had become the nerve-center of the Confederation, the headquarters of the closest thing that there was to a united human government—the Combined Human Military Command.

Jay Palmer had grown up in this garrison system and spent what leaves he had in the Official Liberty Cities of Olympia III, and as unlovely as it was, Olympia was home.

Palmer had left the battered remnants of his fleet in the drydocks of Olympia II, and had caught the first shuttle for Olympia III. As he stepped through the airlock of the shuttle and onto the debarkation ramp, the warm, fragrant air of Olympia III reminded him that it had been a long time since he had had a leave, or even a moment to wish for one. There were pleasures to be had in the Official Liberty Cities, the usual soldier's pleasures and quite suddenly Palmer felt the weary, stale aftermath of battle wash over him, the slackness that comes after a long period of high tension, and he knew (hat what he needed most now was a short period of unwinding, a real bender, and then a long, long sleep.

But that would have to wait. This shuttleport was not in one of the Liberty Cities. It was directly outside Pentagon City, the Headquarters of the Combined Human Command, and the first order of business was not liberty, but a painful debriefing session with High Marshal Kurowski himself.

As Palmer stepped down the ramp and onto the concrete apron of the shuttleport, the solid, geometric massiveness of Pentagon City loomed above him, almost stupefying him, though he knew the place about as intimately as anyone could.

The shuttleport was right outside one of the entrances to the city, and from the field, the seemingly endless wall, stretching vertically for five hundred feet and horizontally past the horizon in both directions made Palmer feel like a microbe on a slide, looking up into a strange world whose scale was beyond his comprehension.

There was nothing else like Pentagon City anywhere else in the Human Confederation or in the Duglaari Empire. Or, as far as anyone knew, in Fortress Sol itself.

Pentagon City was the largest single building in the known Galaxy.

It was built in the shape of a pentagon, for some mystical reason lost in the mists of antiquity, ten miles on a side, five hundred feet tall. The walls were a hundred feet thick, im-pervium-reinforced concrete, and there were no windows. The whole building was air conditioned and artificially lit. It even kept its own time. Nothing short of a direct hit with a fusion bomb could touch it, and there were subterranean redoubts beneath it that could survive even that.

Palmer walked slowly across the field towards the nearby entrance to the city, his gaze fixed upwards at the endless expanse of smooth, featureless wall. It always seemed to him that Pentagon City had come in his mind, and in the mind of many others, to symbolize the Confederation itself, in the way that the Pyramids had symbolized the forgotten civilization of the Nile back on mysterious Earth.

Although no one he knew considered Pentagon City anything but ugly, everyone had a weird kind of affection for it. It was a kind of beloved monstrosity, a monument to the present instead of the past. It was the Confederation's monument to itself, the most massive and total shrine to the military mind that had ever been built.

It almost made Palmer feel that any race which could produce such a building-city should surely be able to defeat the Duglaari Empire. *Almost....*

Palmer presented his credentials to a guard at the entrance, and after an inspection that was little more than a formality, he was admitted to the outermost ring of the City. Although it was called Pentagon City, and although upwards of fifty thousand men actually lived within its walls, it was not set up like a City at all. It was simply a gigantic office building. It had fifty above-surface levels, twenty subsurface levels, and a hundred concentric rings of corridors on each level.

Palmer was now in the outermost ring of the ground floor level, Level One. The walls of the corridor were studded with doors to offices, as far as the eye could see, and further. The corridor itself was as wide as a small street, and to complete the city-effect, the center of the corridor was filled with scores of men zipping by on tiny one-man scooters. More scooters were parked against the walls.

It would have been totally absurd to expect anyone to be able to find his way anywhere in the vast maze that was Pentagon City by himself. Not only was the scale of the building too great, no one could possibly remember where more than a few dozen of the thousands of rooms and offices were.

Therefore, the corridors were supplied with nearly a hundred thousand tiny one-man scooters, all circuited in to one master computer located deep within the subterranean bowels of Pentagon City.

Palmer threaded his way to one of the unoccupied scooters, sat down, snapped on the safety belt, and punched "L-50, R-1, 1001" on the row of buttons mounted on a pedestal on the front of the scooter, where the manual steering controls would normally be. "L-50" meant level fifty, the top floor; "R-1" was ring one, the innermost of the hundred rings; "1001" was the office number of High Marshal Kurowski. Had Palmer been headed for an office whose coordinates he did not happen to know, he would've looked them up in the directory chained to the seat of each scooter.

Palmer pushed the power bar forward. The scooter shot along the corridor for about half a mile, till it came to one of the radial passageways that led from the perimeter of Pentagon City to the center.

It turned into the radial passageway and accelerated. Palmer watched the signs at the turnoffs flash by: Ring hundred... ring ninety... fifty... thirty... twenty... ten... five....

At ring one, the scooter turned off, and boarded a small elevator, which automatically shot upward, controlled by the same master computer as the scooters. Level ten... twenty... forty....

At the fiftieth level, the elevator came to a halt, and the scooter took over again, finally depositing Palmer neatly outside room 1001.

The lettering on the door said simply: "Coordinating Commander-in-Chief." Kurowski's name was absent for reasons of economy—Supreme Commanders came and went with such dreadful rapidity that there was no point in wasting the paint.

Palmer announced himself to the grid on the door, and a moment later, the door opened, indicating that Commander Palmer was to come in.

Kurowski was seated behind a frighteningly uncluttered and huge duroplast desk. At his right elbow was an intercom; at his left, a box of cigars.

The entire rear wall of the office was a huge political map of the known Galaxy. The Duglaari suns were four hundred and twenty malignant red dots arranged in crescent formation between the Human Confederation and the center of the Galaxy. The Human Confederation suns, two hundred twenty of them—no, thought Palmer, *now two hundred nineteen*—were an ellipse of gold dots partially embraced by the horns of the red crescent.

At the far end of the ellipse, out towards the rim, was a great glowing green sphere that dominated the entire map. That rich green color could mean only one thing to a human being, no matter what planet he had been born on—the mysterious, sealed-off ancestral home of the human race, Fortress Sol.

Kurowski's furrowed old face creased into a sardonic smile as he watched Palmer stare at the map. No one could help but be moved to reverie at anything that brought Sol to mind. That was one of the reasons that the map was there; with the map at his back, Kurowski might absorb some of that awed respect accorded Sol.

"Sorry, sir," Palmer said, saluting. "It's just that...."

Marshal Kurowski nodded his large, white-maned head. "I know, Commander, I know," he said. "One reason I have that map is to remind me of Sol. I think too many people these days don't take The Promise seriously." He waved Palmer to a rather hard and uncomfortable chair in front of the desk.

Palmer sat down, still finding it hard to take his eyes off the map. He remembered that Kurowski was a Believer, the first Believer to be Supreme Commander in a decade, so they said....

"Well, Commander Palmer," Kurowski said sharply, "tell me about Sylvanna."

Palmer resisted the urge to look away from the High Marshal, and stared straight into his cold blue eyes.

"There's not really very much to be said. We lost the system, and we lost twenty-eight ships. We destroyed eighteen Doogs. I have no excuses to make, sir. We were outnumbered, as usual, and we were forced to retreat, as usual."

Kurowski forced a thin smile. "At ease, Commander," he said. "I'm not putting you on the carpet. Hell, man, if you had pulled off a miracle and held the system, they would have brevetted you to Marshal on the spot, awarded you the Confederal Medal of Honor and probably made *you* the Supreme Commander-in-Chief. We haven't had a victory in seventeen years, and if we cashiered a fleet commander every time we lost a battle, we'd have no commanders left at this point."

Palmer fidgeted in the hardbacked chair. "Sir," he said, "as I've said in the past, I think we'd have a better chance if we didn't rely so heavily on computation. Take Sylvanna. At the beginning of the battle were able to force the Doogs into the sunward position. If I had been allowed to break formation and attack the Doog computership in the rear, with say half my forces, we might've been able to knock it out, and then we'd still be holding Sylvanna now, instead of...."

Kurowski sighed heavily. "Don't be juvenile, Commander," he snapped. "You know as well as I do that even I can't make a move in violation of computation 'recommendations.' I don't like it any more than you do, but even High Marshals aren't immune to courts-martial."

"But sir, even Computation admits that best estimates show that in another century and a half, we'll have lost The War, and the Doogs will completely wipe us out. What do we have to lose?"

"Don't you believe in The Promise?" Kurowski asked.

Palmer started to mumble the conventional reply. Then something made him stop. "Sir? May I be completely frank? I mean, I know that you're a Believer, and no disrespect intended.... That is...."

"Come on Commander, spit it out!" Kurowski barked. "You're entitled to your opinions, and by damn, *I'm* entitled to hear them."

"Very well sir. The plain truth is that I *don't*. After all, we haven't heard a peep out of Fortress Sol for nearly two hundred and seventy years. I think that The Promise was just a way of rationalizing Sol's cowardice when they pulled out of The War. I don't believe in secret weapons until I see them. If they really haven't abandoned us to the Doogs, why don't they *do* something? Why do they keep the Sol system completely closed off to us? How do we know that they haven't just made a deal?"

"A deal? With whom? *The Doogs?*"

"Yes, sir. Why not? The Duglaari agree to leave Sol alone, and in return, Sol pulls out of The War, and closes itself completely to all interstellar contact. They throw us to the wolves, and save their own skins."

"You ever talked to a Doog, Commander?"

"No sir."

"Well," sighed Kurowski, "if you had, you'd know why what you suggest is totally impossible. The Doogs started this war with one objective, and one objective only: to completely eliminate the human race. Down to the last planet. Down to the last man. The Doogs..., well they may be mammals like us, they may breathe the same air and thrive in the same temperature range, but their minds work on totally different premises. To them, there are only two kinds of organisms in the Universe: Duglaari and vermin. *We* are vermin. Would we make deals with cockroaches? If there's one thing we've learned in three hundred years, it's that you just can't negotiate with the Doogs."

"Well then, why *did* Sol pull out of The War? If they really face extermination too, why don't they fight? Why did they quit and leave us with nothing but empty words? 'We will turn inward and build for Man a fortress in his home system, an impregnable redoubt that will, when the time is right, send forth its hosts to destroy the might of Duglaar, completely and forever.' Even the language sounds phony. Sure, they've built a fortress, but not for Man. For Solarians only."

Kurowski shrugged. "I don't know all the answers," he said. "Who does? All we really know is that thirty years after The War started, there was some kind of lightning revolution on Earth. We don't even know what the revolutionaries stood for, it was all over so fast. The leader, MacDay—all we know about *hint* is that everyone who met him was completely awed by him, and found his motivations completely beyond comprehension. He pulled Sol out of The War, issued The Promise, sealed off the Sol system, and that's the last we've heard from Sol for nearly three hundred years. The way I see it, you have two alternatives. You can believe in The Promise, and then you have the hope that someday, somehow, the tide of The War will turn. Or you can believe that The Promise is just so many empty words, in which case you must resign yourself to the idea of Man's eventual extinction at the hands of the Duglaari, since all our computations assure us that we cannot win. Most people prefer hope to resignation."

"Sir," said Palmer softly, "do you *really* believe that the Duglaari are *better* than we are?"

"I certainly do not!" roared Kurowski. "It's just simple mathematics. Three hundred years ago, when our races first met, Man held two hundred fifty-eight systems. The Doogs had three hundred and sixty. Man had had interstellar travel for a hundred and thirty one years; the Doogs had had star-ships for nearly three centuries. There were about a hundred billion Men, and almost two hundred billion Duglaari. They were an older race, a bigger race, and they had a big head start. That doesn't mean they're any *better* than us, Commander! I don't want to hear *that* again! An individual man is in every way a match for an individual Doog. They just had the good luck to evolve a little bit ahead of us. That's all it is—luck, and more planets, more ships, more men."

"Sol understood that pretty quickly, didn't it?" Palmer said bitterly. "They realized that they were the furthest of all Human systems from the Duglaari. So they figured that we colonials could hold them off for a few centuries, with our planets and our ships and our blood, while they sat on their fat cans and piously prayed for a miracle."

"Commander," Kurowski said testily, "we *all* know that The War is just a holding action, but we've *got* to believe that Sol is doing something. If we don't, we might just as well lay right down and die. We...."

The intercom buzzed insistently.

"Damn," Kurowski grunted, and picked up the receiver.

Palmer watched as the High Marshal's face passed from a scowl to puzzlement, to what was plainly numb amazement.

Woodenly, Kurowski hung up the receiver.

"Sir...?"

"That was Detection Command," Kurowski whispered hoarsely. "They've just picked up a strange ship that came out of Stasis-Space past the orbit of Olympia DC. It's not one of ours."

"A Doog? One Doog attacking Olympia?"

"It's not a Doog," Kurowski said softly. "They've made contact with the ship's captain...."

The High Marshal swiveled in his chair to stare dazedly at the map behind it.

"The ship claims to be from Fortress Sol," he said.

Being the nerve center, the heart of the Human Confederation military effort, the system of Olympia was guarded by three full fleets of a hundred ships each. Moreover, each of the three inhabited planets in the system was further protected by swarms of intrasystem ships. Beyond that, Olympia III was a vast garrison, containing the greatest concentration of troops in the Confederation.

A Duglaari attack on Olympia was unthinkable, at least at this stage of The War. It would be a suicide try, and the Doogs were far too methodical and calculating for that.

Nevertheless, the Human Military Command was not about to take the strange ship's declaration that it was from Fortress Sol at face value. The whole thing might just conceivably be some far-fetched Duglaari trick. No one had seen a Solarian ship, no one had even heard the voice of a single Solarian for nearly three centuries, and somehow, no matter how unlikely it was that the ship was really a Doog, it was far more unlikely that the ship was really from Sol.

It was exactly as if the ship's captain had blandly announced that he was the Messiah, Jesus, Mohammed and Buddha all rolled up into one neat package.

Indeed, to most of the Human Confederation, Fortress Sol came pretty close to being just that. Mankind was a race doomed to extinction, with the added advantage that it knew it. Decade after decade, the number of Human-held systems dwindled and the size of the Duglaari Empire waxed. The Doogs had a third more ships, nearly twice the population. Better computers and more of them, and a monomaniacal urge to completely destroy their competitors, namely the human race.

Man had one hope, and one hope only, however vain and superstitious that hope might be—*Fortress Sol!*

Sol was the one unknown factor in the carefully calculated pattern of the Human-Duglaari War. Behind the screen of ships and mines that destroyed anything attempting to cross the orbit of Pluto, *anything* might be a building—a weapon that knocks off whole solar systems like clay pigeons, said some; an impenetrable shield of invulnerability, said others; an unbelievably huge armada of robot ships; Conversion Bombs; a virus deadly to Doogs but harmless to men—the catalogue was limited only by the ability of frustrated men to imagine superweapons.

And now, after two hundred and seventy years, the hosts of Fortress Sol had at last broken their isolation and sent... *one ship?*

The Human Military Command was taking no chances. The Solarian ship was escorted all the way to Olympia III by sixty warships armed to the teeth and ready to shoot at the slightest hint of a trick.

The moment it landed at the deepspace port outside the south wall of Pentagon City, it was surrounded by a full division of troops, including twenty tanks, and even three unwieldy portable lasecannons.

High Marshal Kurowski awaited the Solarians at the far end of a corridor of armed soldiers, whose presence was only partly ceremonial. Kurowski was flanked by the Chief of Computation, Lauris Maizel, and Gaston K'nala, the Systemic Defense Commander. Directly behind these three were eight Theater Commanders, and behind them were the seven Fleet Commanders who happened to be in the Olympia system at the time, including Jay Palmer.

There was something about the whole scene that Palmer could not help finding scandalously entertaining. Behind him was the titanic bulk of Pentagon City, in front, acres of soldiers in olive battle fatigues, tanks, lase-cannons.... And all of this military might surrounding one very small ship colored the luminous grass-green of Fortress Sol.

Palmer could not conceive of *anything* emerging from that ship that would not be a ludicrous anticlimax.

And then a port opened and six Solarians stepped out.

The troops seemed to quiver imperceptibly. The assembled dignitaries wilted ever so slightly. High Marshal Kurowski ran his tongue tentatively over his lips.

Palmer felt the... *otherness*. There was an aura about the Solarians that was instantly apparent but impossible to define. They seemed six ordinary human beings, three men, three women. Two of the women—the busty blond and the tall, willowy redhead—might be called striking, but not super-normally so. The third woman was a quite plain-looking, mousey-haired girl. Two of the men were also quite ordinary looking: a slight, sandy-haired man well under six feet; a darker, chunkier man with a thin black moustache. The third man was somewhat more impressive—tall, very well-built, with huge luminous green eyes set deep under craggy brows, and a large expressive mouth—but he too was nothing supernormal.

They were dressed in simple green tunics; the men wore low boots, the women sandals. The men's tunics were cut loosely, the women's tight enough to be interesting without being in bad taste.

Everything, every major and minor detail about the Solarians was quite ordinary.

Except the total effect.

They moved as if they owned the Universe, as if they had casually inherited it generations ago. They smiled to themselves as they surveyed the military display before them as if it were a pageant of particularly clever trained monkeys. The group of Solarians radiated a calm confidence that was far beyond arrogance.

They sauntered casually up to where the official party stood, and yet the very casualness seemed to convey the power of a full-scale military parade.

"I am High Marshal Luke Kurowski, Coordinating Commander-in-Chief of the Combined Human Military Command," Kurowski said stiffly and uneasily.

The Solarian with the great green eyes parted his full lips in the ghost of a grin.

"I am called Lingo," he said. "Dirk Lingo."

"You are the captain of the ship?" Kurowski said. "You are in charge?" It immediately seemed a ludicrous question to Palmer. The man called Lingo radiated authority as a star radiates light.

"I am Leader," Lingo said. It sounded unmistakably like a title. "Robin Morel," he said conversationally, smiling at the redhead. "Fran Shannon." He waved his hand in the direction of the mousey-haired girl. "Raul Ortega," Lingo said, nodding at the man with the black moustache.

"And this is Max Bergstrom and Linda Dortin," he said, giving the blond girl and the sandy-haired man some kind of cryptic signal with his eyebrows.

Max Bergstrom and Linda Dortin ran their eyes slowly over the official party, in a strange kind of unison, as if they were reading some secret language engraved on the men's foreheads. Palmer could see a puzzled uneasiness ripple in waves across the face of the official party as the gaze of the Solarians passed over them.

Then they were looking straight at him.

He noticed that both pairs of eyes were virtually identical—large, calm and brown, with tiny flecks of blue in the irises. A curious tension flickered across his mind. Then something in his head seemed to laugh warmly, and finally something sensuous and languid stroked his mind, like the hand of a woman caressing a kitten....

Then the two Solarians averted their eyes and the feeling was gone.

"W-Welcome to Olympia," stammered Kurowski dazedly.

"Thank you," said Lingo, staring up at the bulk of Pentagon City with a wry grin on his face. "This... ah... edifice is most impressive. A fitting monument to... er... a certain" mentality. We have nothing like it in the Sol system."

It did not at all sound like a compliment.

"May I ask just why you've come here, after three centuries of isolation?" asked Kurowski, recovering some of his martial stiffness. "Surely not just to offer opinions on architecture?"

Lingo laughed. It was a deep, musical laugh, full of complicated and disquieting undertones.

"Why, why do you think we've come?" he said. "To win The War, of course."

"To win The War?" grunted Kurowski dubiously. "Just the six of you?"

"Just the six of us," said Lingo evenly. "More simply would not materially affect our mission."

"You expect us to swallow that?" snapped Kurowski. "After three centuries of doing nothing, after three centuries of leaving us to the mercy of the Doogs, after three centuries of.... Sol has the gall to send *six people* to tell the Confederation how to fight The War? Six...."

"Marshal Kurowski," interrupted Lingo, "are you winning The War now? Since you are not, any change will only improve your chances."

"And just what do you propose to do?"

"We have a plan," said Lingo. "And we have the means to

carry it out. Or perhaps I should say we *are* the means of carrying it out."

"And just what is this plan?"

Dirk Lingo smiled disarmingly. "Surely," he said, "there are better places to discuss such matters than standing on a landing field. Also, I think this is a matter for your final authority to consider.... Some Council, or Executive Board, or....?"

"I could call a General Staff meeting," Kurowski suggested grudgingly.

"That should do nicely," replied Lingo. "Shall we go inside?"

And without waiting for an answer, Lingo turned his back on Kurowski and walked towards the entrance to Pentagon City with the other Solarians in his wake. He did not bother to look back to see if the High Marshal and the official party were following.

But they were.

Palmer and the other lesser officers trailed after them, in something of a fog, much as Kurowski trailed after Lingo and company.

As a junior officer aspiring to higher rank, Palmer knew a virtuoso performance when he saw one. In a few short minutes of perfunctory conversation, Dirk Lingo had, with nothing to back him up at all, established himself as Kurowski's equal in rank, at the very least. And he had done it as if it were merely his natural due, as if it were the most natural and obvious thing in the Universe for an unknown Solarian to treat the Coordinating Commander-in-Chief of the combined military forces of the entire Confederation like... like a junior Fleet Commander!

Chapter III

THE GENERAL Staff Meeting Room (L-38, R-4, Room 173) was suitably impressive. The ceiling was a huge duplicate of the wall map in Kurowski's office. One entire wall was draped with a huge Confederation flag—a five pointed yellow star in a blue field. A huge crescent-shaped duroplast table, with built-in autosecs and a recessed viewscreen filled the better part of the room.

High Marshal Kurowski sat in the geometric center of the table. Flanking him, in descending order of precedence towards the end of the table were the Chief of Computation, the Chief of Intelligence, the Prime Logistics Officer, the Chief of Psychological Warfare, the Civil Coordinator, and the eight Theater Commanders—no one under the rank of full General.

No one, that is, except Commander Jay Palmer, who was perched nervously on the edge of a chair at the extreme left end of the table—a position of zero precedence, protocol-wise—and who was dazedly trying to figure out exactly what a lowly Fleet Commander was doing in such exalted company.

The only thing he knew for sure was that his presence, like the meeting itself, was Dirk Lingo's doing....

As the Solarians and the official party had been about to enter Pentagon City, Palmer, who had been respectfully trailing behind the high brass, who in turn were confusedly following the Solarians, saw that Lingo had stopped, turned, and said something to Kurowski. To judge by the High Marshal's expression, he was exasperated by whatever the Solarian had said, and so it was with considerable uneasiness that Palmer approached him when the High Marshal called him over.

"This is Fleet Commander Palmer," Kurowski said to Lingo, studiously ignoring Palmer and pointedly not introducing the Solarian to him.

"How do you do, Commander Palmer," Lingo said pleasantly. "Sorry about your Fleet."

Palmer started. It was not at all like Kurowski to talk so loosely about a recent defeat with someone as questionable as Lingo.

Then he saw that the High Marshal was at least as upset as he was.

"Mr. Lingo wanted to meet you," Kurowski said quickly, trying to brush aside the mysterious breach of security. "I don't have the faintest idea why...."

"Just thought it would be a good idea to meet a field officer," Lingo said. "Someone below General Officer rank, someone fresh from battle...."

"How in hell did you know that?" Kurowski finally exploded. "You couldn't...."

"Let's just call it an educated guess," Lingo said with a little shrug. "The important point is that I feel that it is necessary that a representative field officer be present at the General Staff Meeting, and that Commander Palmer will do as well as anyone else."

"That's out of the question," Kurowski snapped. "No one under the rank of General is ever admitted to a General Staff Meeting. It's against all the...."

"I don't hold the rank of General," Lingo said, a slight chill coming into his voice. "Neither do any of my friends. Does that mean that the meeting has to be called off?"

"Of course not," spluttered Kurowski. "That's an entirely different matter. You're not under Confederation discipline. Commander Palmer is. No junior officer...."

"Commander Palmer will attend the meeting," Lingo said very quietly, "or there will be no meeting." There was a calm, confident, not-quite-arrogant finality in Lingo's voice.

"But...." Kurowski muttered, obviously looking for a way to back out gracefully, rather than under duress.

Lingo smiled. "If it will make you feel any better, Marshal Kurowski," he said, warmth suddenly returning to his voice, "why not consider Commander Palmer *my* guest at the meeting? That should satisfy your sense of protocol."

"Very well," Kurowski said stiffly. "Commander Palmer, you are dismissed until the General Staff Meeting."

As Palmer saluted, and turned to leave, Lingo stared directly at him for one frozen moment. The Solarian's greatgreen eyes seemed to be laughing at some private joke. Finally, Lingo gave him a crooked grin and an almost imperceptible wink. Somehow, he could not imagine why, that look had reminded Palmer of the strange, calm staring expression in the eyes of Max Bergstrom and Linda Dortin as their gaze had passed over him for that brief moment on the landing field....

And now, as he sat in the General Staff Meeting Room, his thoughts once again returned to that strange moment on the landing field, when he had felt that gentle probing of his mind behind two pairs of calm brown eyes. That must've been how Lingo knew about Sylvanna; Palmer thought suddenly. Some kind of telepathy!

He was uneasily sure that whatever Lingo's real reason for insisting on his presence had been, it was somehow connected with that fleeting moment of mental probing.

Palmer had the feeling that he was being used as a pawn, and he did not like it one bit. He stared uneasily at the six hardbacked chairs that had been set up for the Solarians, facing the inner curve of the table.

Finally, Kurowski nodded to the General Staff, and pushed a button on the intercom in front of him, signaling that the Solarians were to be sent in. The General Staff stood up, not in token of respect for the Solarians, but so that *they* could sit down first, thus establishing their precedence over Lingo's group.

The Solarians ambled into the room, with their already-familiar air of easy arrogance. Lingo glanced at the standing brass. His eyes seemed to twinkle with some secret amusement. Then, before Kurowski could say a word, Lingo abruptly sat down. His companions seated themselves flanking him.

The General Staff remained standing for a long, confused moment.

Then Dirk Lingo waved his hand negligently. "Sit down, won't you, gentlemen?" he said pleasantly.

Palmer manfully suppressed a laugh. It was just too much. Lingo had done it again, and with foolish ease.

Kurowski flushed as he seated himself ungracefully. "I think the first order of business should be a short briefing for the benefit of our Solarian friends on the present state of The War," he said, trying to regain the initiative. "After all, they have been *out of contact* for so long. If you will look above you, you will see a political map of the known Galaxy, showing Duglaari suns in red, the Human...."

"We are familiar with such maps," said Lingo sharply. "Please proceed."

Kurowski momentarily lost his temper and shot Lingo a truly poisonous look. Then he recovered his composure.

"Very well," he said. "As you can see, the Doogs have approximately four systems to every three of ours. They have a roughly similar advantage in ships and personnel.

Enough so that we are losing The War—our most recent computations say that we can hold out for but another century—but not enough to enable them to strike any one decisive blow. It is a war of attrition, slow, methodical, logical, like the Doogs themselves. It...."

"All this is ancient history, Marshal Kurowski," snapped Lingo. "Such information is of little use to us, since all it amounts to is a statement that we are losing The War. And for the same reasons you have been losing it for the past three centuries. May I suggest that we could all save considerable time if Raul simply asks a few questions. He's our Game-master."

"Your *what?*"

Lingo smiled. "Gamemaster," he said. "Let us say, for the sake of simplification, that it is merely our term for strategist. Raul?"

Once again, Palmer was moved to envious admiration. Lingo had wrested control of the meeting from Kurowski and laid it in the lap of the dark man with the moustache without even raising his voice!

"Right, Dirk," said Ortega crisply. "I think only three questions are really necessary. First, who plans overall strategy for the Human Confederation?"

"*I* am Commander-in-Chief," said Kurowski stiffly. "I...."

"Just a moment, Marshal Kurowski," interrupted Maizel, the Chief of Computation. "I think it is accurate to say that the Command Computation Center on Olympia IV computes the overall strategy of The War."

"So the computers still control overall strategy," muttered Ortega, with an air of obvious distaste.

"Of course," said Maizel. "The Doogs have an advantage in planets and ships. Therefore, we must at least use what resources we have to maximum efficiency, which means tight computer control of all aspects of The War."

Ortega snorted. "They haven't learned a damn thing in three centuries," he muttered to Lingo. "MacDay was right. Question two," he said, turning to Maizel and Kurowski. "Do all computations still show that even with one hundred percent efficiency in utilizing resources, the Duglaari will eventually win The War?"

"We've already told you that," snapped Kurowski.

"Then why in blazes do you continue to use the computers to run The War?"

Palmer felt like standing up and cheering, and he could see that even Kurowski was similarly pleased. Ortega had put the unvoiced feelings of all field commanders into one short, unanswerable question. Why not gamble, if all computations say you must lose anyway?

But Maizel had an answer, the old, infuriating stock answer. "Because," he said, "at least by using our resources to maximum efficiency, which can only be achieved by computer control, we can draw The War out to its maximum possible length, thus maximizing the probability of developing some new weapon that will overcome the inherent numerical superiority of the Doogs, and...."

"In other words," said Ortega, "the longer an ostrich keeps his head in the sand, the better his chances of surviving?"

Lingo smiled magnanimously. "You must excuse Raul," he said. "Like all Gamemasters, he is prone to reduce things to the simplest possible terms. Which sometimes results in painful bluntness. However, I must point out that his analysis is essentially correct. Have you never considered abandoning the computers and trying something too daring for a mere machine to conceive?"

"You mean try suicide," sneered Maizel. "It is only the computers that let us stand off the Doogs in the first place."

"What about simply playing a good hunch?" suggested Ortega.

"You're out of your mind," shrilled Maizel.

Lingo and Ortega sighed knowingly and resignedly to each other. "Oh well," muttered Ortega under his breath, "it *was* worth a try."

"Are you trying to tell us that we can't win The War after all?" said Kurowski. "Is that what you broke three centuries of isolation to do? To come here and simply throw the...."

"Not at all," soothed Lingo. "As a matter of fact, we've brought you that for which you have been so irrationally waiting—the Secret Weapon, the factor that will suddenly turn The War around."

"You have?" said Kurowski, obviously wanting desperately to retain his fast-dwindling belief in The Promise. "What is it?"

"Us," said Lingo, smiling blandly.

"You?"

Lingo gestured to Max Bergstrom and Linda Dortin.

"You are thinking," said Bergstrom, in a flat monotone, "that Solarians have developed delusions of grandeur in their isolation. You are thinking that perhaps Commander Palmer was right—perhaps The Promise was merely a lie to conceal cowardice, perhaps...."

"How can you know that?" gasped Kurowski. "No one heard that conversation but Palmer and me...."

"You are thinking," said Linda Dortin, picking up smoothly from Bergstrom, "that it is impossible for us to know about a private conversation that occurred while we were still in space. You are thinking that the only way we could possibly have this information is if we were reading your mind.... That only telepaths could be doing what we are doing...."

"And of course you are right," said Lingo.

"You're... you're all *telepaths?*"

"No," said Lingo. "Just Linda and Max. We all have our own Talents, and it would be pointless to have more than two telepaths in a Group."

"That's the secret weapon?" said Kurowski. "Telepathy? It may have its uses, but how can we fight the Doogs with it?"

"It is only *part* of the weapon," Lingo said. "Perhaps a further demonstration...?" He chuckled to himself. "Linda, perhaps... ah... Commander Palmer would favor us with a little dance?"

"What?" shouted Palmer.

Then he felt something giggle in his head. His limbs were moving of their own volition. He was climbing up onto the table. He was standing on the table-top. His feet began to move rhythmically. His fingers began to snap.

Commander Jay Palmer began to dance a jig on the conference table.

"Stop it, Palmer. I order you to stop!" roared High Marshal Kurowski.

"I... I *can't*, sir..." moaned Palmer, still dancing furiously, "I can't!"

"Enough," ordered Lingo.

Quite suddenly, Palmer's body was his own again. Numb and blushing, he crawled back to his seat.

"As you have seen," said Lingo dryly, "telepathy implies certain... ah, other powers besides the ability to read minds. As in many other areas, communication implies *control.*"

"You mean you can teach our troops to use this technique?"

"Hardly," said Lingo. "This is a Talent; you either have it, or you *don't*. No, our plan calls for more direct action. You saw how it was possible to control Commander Palmer. Imagine having the Kor of All the Duglaari under similar control."

"The *Kor?* You mean you propose to go to Duglaar?"

"You are getting the picture."

"I'm getting the picture, all right!" snapped Kurowski. "You're out of your minds! You could *never* get to Duglaar in one piece. There are so many ships guarding the Dugl system that a microbe couldn't slip in. It's a physical impossibility to come out of Stasis-Space within a solar system, so you'd be forced to proceed from beyond the orbit of the outermost planet to Duglaar itself under Resolution Drive. You wouldn't have a chance. They'd blow you to bits before you got within the orbit of Dugl VI!"

"You are right," said Lingo. "There is no way of *forcing* ourselves into the Kor's presence. Nevertheless, there is a way of penetrating to the Council of Wisdom."

"*And that is?*" snorted Kurowski.

"We surrender the Human Confederation to the Duglaari Empire."

"*What?*" screamed the entire General Staff in virtual unison.

Lingo laughed. "Relax, gentlemen," he said. "I don't propose to actually surrender the Confederation, merely to use such a supposed mission to receive an audience with the Kor."

"They'll never go for it," said Kurowski. "The Doogs aren't interested in negotiated surrender. They're out to exterminate us completely, and they'd never bother to offer terms."

"Who said anything about terms?" said Lingo. "We'll simply surrender unconditionally rather than go through the wasted effort of continuing to fight a war we can't win. *Efficiency.* No human would think that way, but that's exactly what the Doogs would do in our position. The efficient thing. The Doogs worship logic and efficiency, as you gentlemen should know, having tried diligently to emulate them for three centuries."

"Perhaps it just might work..." mused Kurowski.

"What you are thinking," said Max Bergstrom, "is that all that would be risked in such an attempt is six otherwise useless Solarians."

Kurowski blushed, and tried to blurt a denial, but Lingo cut him off.

"Come, come," he said, "you needn't be ashamed of the thought. It *is* a calculated risk, and you are right—we are useless to you here. But there *is* one additional detail that you have overlooked. We would need an official of the General Staff along, to make it look good. Say... the Commander-in-Chief...?"

"If you think that I'm going to risk my neck in this harebrained...."

"Relax, Marshal Kurowski," said Lingo. "I have anticipated your reluctance, and I have an alternate suggestion. Why not send along a junior officer instead, someone more dispensable? Of course, you would have to make him a temporary Ambassador-Plenipotentiary and raise him to the rank of General...."

Kurowski licked his lips. "You mean someone like, say a *Fleet Commander?* Someone like Commander Palmer?"

"Precisely."

"Wait a minute!" cried Palmer, "I...."

"*Commander* Palmer, shut up!" barked Kurowski. "*General* Palmer, I hereby appoint you Ambassador-

Plenipotentiary of the General Staff and attach you to duty aboard the Solarian ship."

"But Marshal Kurowski...." began Palmer.

"I think that there is no point in further discussion," interrupted Lingo. "We are all quite tired, and we'd like to leave for the Dugl system tomorrow morning. Commander... er, *General* Palmer, you will please report to the ship at eleven hundred tomorrow. If you will excuse us, gentlemen...."

And with that, Lingo and the other Solarians simply got up and walked out, like a royal family terminating an audience.

Only after the meeting had broken up, and Palmer was alone with his thoughts, did he realize what Lingo had done.

It was all a super-snowjob. Lingo had dominated the meeting from beginning to end. He had controlled things so completely that he had accomplished what no one had been able to do for three centuries — he had gotten the General Staff to permit a major move *without consulting the computers.*

And the General Staff had swallowed the Solarians' plan without thinking. Because, if you had time to think about it, the plan was a patent absurdity. Even if they did get to see the Kor, which was highly doubtful despite Lingo's glibness, even if they did get control of the Kor's body, what then? What could they possibly make the Kor do that would change the course of The War without getting the Kor deposed? Make him do a jig?

No, the Solarians were up to something. Palmer didn't know what it was, but he didn't like it.

And all he *did* know was that he was stuck right in the middle of it!

Palmer walked slowly across the deepspace field towards the Solarian ship, his clothing bag slung over his shoulder, practicing the difficult task of keeping his mind blank. It was important not to think of... of what was in the bag... because if the Solarian telepaths could read his mind....

Kurowski had had plenty of second thoughts, at Palmer's final briefing, once he had had the time to really think about what was proposed.

"Of course it sounds funny," Kurowski had said. "We both know that the chances of your ever reaching Dugl are very slim indeed. I'm not trying to kid you, Palmer. But there are at least two very good reasons why we must let them try whatever they're going to try. First of all, and you as a field officer should certainly appreciate this, we've *already* gained something by all this."

"What do you mean, sir"?

"Think, Palmer, think! The mere fact that the General Staff agreed to let the Solarians try this plan immediately, *without consulting the Command Computers first*, established a precedent. Even if this mission fails, even if you... ah... don't come back, this may enable us to go against computation again in the future. It means a possible chance to restore command to those who deserve it.... field officers like you and me, not old fossils like Maizel. And of course, hare-brained as it seems, the Solarian plan might just succeed, in which case, certain defeat becomes victory. What've we got to lose?"

"Just one very junior Fleet Commander," Palmer sighed resignedly.

"No sir,... *Jay*," Kurowski said solemnly. "I promise you one thing: whatever happens, the rank of General is yours permanently. If you do make it back, it will be made a regular appointment, and if... well, if you don't make it, the rank will be made permanent posthumously. We owe you at least that much."

"Thank you sir," Palmer said, without displaying any great enthusiasm. "But I still don't see what the Solarians can really accomplish even if they are able to control the Kor."

"I would suppose," Kurowski said, "that they would make the Kor give orders that would cause the Duglaari to lose as large a portion of their forces as possible. It's common knowledge that if the Doogs lost, say three or four thousand ships, we'd be on at least an even footing with them. In fact, the odds might very well end up being in our favor. After all, in this kind of war, it's ships that count. Why, if I could, I'd trade even the Olympia system itself for the destruction of three or four thousand Doog ships. Why do you think the Doogs have never tried an all-out attack on Olympia — or Sol itself for that matter? Because they're too smart to risk the ships they'd need to succeed."

"All that's true, of course," Palmer said. "But I still don't see how the Solarians hope to pull anything like that off, and I'm *sure* it's a mistake to trust them."

"Trust them?" Kurowski said. "Who said anything about trusting them? Why do you think I'm risking a man as valuable as you on a mission like this? We could just as well have brevetted a green lieutenant to General, after all. I want a man along who can make quick judgments. Lingo is in command of this mission, but I'm empowering you to abort it at any time you see fit. If you suspect that a fast one is being pulled, you are empowered to take over the ship and order immediate assistance from any and all Confederal ships in the area. You will use force if you have to, and if all else fails, you must be ready to destroy the ship and sacrifice yourself if the occasion demands it.

See to it that you are properly equipped and armed. And since you may be searched, I want you to take a standard bag of your clothing over to the Intelligence Lab. They'll hide enough weapons and explosives in your kit to meet any emergency."

Kurowski stood up and extended his hand. "Good luck, General Palmer," he said.

Palmer hitched his clothing bag a bit higher on his shoulder. It contained quite a hidden arsenal: a blaster, a derringerlase, a stungun, even a neonuclear timebomb disguised as a shaver. Smaller weapons, and enough components to duplicate the larger ones were sewn into the cuffs and seams and linings of the spare clothing. The Solarians might discover some of the weapons in a thorough search, but never all of them....

The Solarian ship looked almost disappointingly normal from just outside the airlock. It was, of course, much smaller than the battlecruisers that Palmer was used to, and it was colored a luminous green, but a cursory inspection showed him the usual Resolution Field Generator projectors and the customary Stasis-Field antennae at nose, tail and midsection.

The airlock door opened, and Dirk Lingo stepped out. Palmer tensed and tried to make his mind blank as he saw that Max Bergstrom was following Lingo. The Solarians lowered a ladder to the ground.

Palmer hoisted the clothing bag higher still on his shoulder, and mounted the first rung of the ladder.

"Just a moment, General Palmer," Lingo said. "Max...?"

Palmer willed his mind to go blank. Don't think of the... he told himself. Don't think of what's in the.... *Don't! Don't!*

Now Bergstrom was fixing him in that calm, even, brown stare, and Palmer could feel probing tendrils skirting the edges of his mind.

Don't think of the weapons! he told himself. Don't even think of *not* thinking of them... Laaaaaa.... Laaaaa.... Ooooooh.... Palmer tried to fill his conscious mind with nonsense syllables, mental static, as he felt Bergstrom probing, gently but irresistibly into his consciousness.

He seemed to feel a puzzlement in his mind, a puzzlement that he suddenly realized was Bergstrom's, not his. Laaaa... Ooooooh... Eeeee... he thought desperately with the surface of his mind.

But Bergstrom was not put off by the surface static. If anything, it seemed to pique his curiosity, and Palmer felt him reaching deeper and deeper into his mind, rifling his memories of the past day like a man skimming through an encyclopedia. He felt himself remembering Kurowski's final briefing, against his own will, and he found himself also forced to remember the instructions of the Intelligence Lab officer....

Then the ordeal was suddenly over, and he felt that his mind was once again his own.

Bergstrom turned to Lingo with a little grin. "Everything but the kitchen sink, Dirk," he said.

Then he turned to Palmer. "You had better leave that bag here," he said. "That's quite a collection of hardware."

"What are you talking about?" Palmer said lamely. "I...."

"Don't you feel just a little silly trying to lie to a telepath?" Bergstrom said quietly. "I'm referring to the blaster, the stun-gun, the derringerlase, the...."

"All right, all right," grunted Palmer. "You win. But at least let me take some of my spare clothing along," he said quickly, opening the bag.

"Which uniform did you have in mind?" Bergstrom said with a grin. "The one with the gas pellets sewn into the cuffs, the one with the flamegun parts sewn into the jacket lining, or maybe the one with….?"

"All right…" sighed Palmer, resignedly. "I think you've made your point." He threw the clothing bag down on the field in disgust, and began to climb up the ladder to the airlock.

It just wasn't fair! How in hell could anyone get anything past a telepath? he asked himself angrily.

Although he did not feel Bergstrom reading this in his mind, the Solarian was grinning broadly.

"No hard feelings, General," Lingo said as he closed the airlock door behind him. "Don't take it so hard. You had every right not to trust us, and therefore every right to try and smuggle weapons aboard. It's only natural that you don't trust us…."

"And also only natural that *you* don't trust *me?*"

Lingo laughed. "Exactly," he said. "So you lost this friendly little game. Who knows, maybe you'll win the next match. No hard feelings?"

Palmer shrugged. "No hard feelings, Lingo," he said.

"Would you like to see how we Solarians con a ship?" Lingo said. "You should find it most interesting. Perhaps a bit frightening, but *most* interesting. Let's go to the control room."

The control room was like nothing Palmer had ever seen on a ship before. There were four pilot's chairs in the hemispherical room, but two of them were dummies, strictly for passengers.

The other two seemed little more than dummies themselves. One had a small panel of dials and gauges in front of it; the other was equipped with switches, levers, pedals, and what looked like an honest-to-God *steering wheel* off a groundcar!

And that was *it*. No computer panel, no punchboard, no navigation console, no nothing.

Fran Shannon was sitting in the chair with the dials. She smiled at Palmer absently.

"Fran's our Eidetic," said Lingo, which explained exactly nothing. He motioned Palmer to one of the dummy seats and sat down in the chair with the controls.

"One of my lesser Talents," said Lingo. "I'm an Absolute Space-Time Sensitive. It's something like absolute pitch in music. I can sense proper trajectories, accelerations, course deviations, and so forth. Far superior to a computer."

Palmer shrunk back into his chair. "You mean you're actually going to con this thing *manually?*" he said weakly. "The ship's computer doesn't handle lift-off?"

Lingo laughed resonantly. *"Ship's computer?"* he said. "This ship doesn't have a computer. We have found that what the ancients always said is really true: the human mind is the best computer of all, provided it is properly utilized. If it has the Talent for the particular job. And, as I said, piloting is one of my Talents. As the ancients used to say, I fly this ship by the seat of my pants."

Palmer moaned softly.

"Screen on," said Lingo, throwing a switch.

Palmer gasped. The entire hemispherical wall-ceiling of the control room was one huge continuous viewscreen. It was like sitting in a chair on top of a flagpole; bare sky overhead, the field below. It was dizzyingly real.

"I *told* you you might find it a bit frightening," said Lingo good-naturedly. "Grid for lift-off," he ordered.

A red line appeared in the "sky" running around the circumference of the room. A yellow line appeared at right angles to it.

"Artificial horizon and gravity-normal," Lingo said. "Ready for lift-off."

Lingo busied himself with the controls. The Resolution Field was on. The ship began to rise, faster and faster. Now Palmer could see the ground falling away beneath them. It was like being tied to the *outside* of a ship.

The ship wobbled, and Palmer knew that a three degree wobble for more than a second would more likely than not send them crashing back onto the field. That was why a computer *had* to handle lift-off.

But, incredibly, Lingo was correcting the wobbles as fast as they came. It was an obvious impossibility, but he was doing it. They didn't crash. Instead, they kept rising and accelerating, and Olympia III became a curve, and then a disc, and they were in orbit.

The stars were swimming all around them. It was like floating in space in a spacesuit. Palmer closed his eyes, to ease his growing vertigo.

Despite his better judgment, he opened them a moment later, and to his surprise, the vertigo was gone, and he was enjoying the sight.

"Grid for this locus," Lingo said.

The red and yellow lines were replaced by a gridwork of white, dividing the field up into squares, each of which represented one degree of the hemisphere.

"Let's have Dugl," Lingo said.

Fran Shannon stared blankly into the field of stars, thousands upon thousands of them, red, green, yellow, blue. Then she threw a red circle of light around a very faint yellow sun near the center of the hemisphere with an indicator on the panel. Lingo pressed a button, and a slightly larger red ring appeared at what Palmer guessed was the geometric center of the hemispherical viewscreen.

"Close enough for now," said Lingo. He manipulated the controls and the ship began to accelerate, faster, faster, faster....

Palmer lost track of time. The vista of stars, the ship's steady acceleration, were hypnotic.... Hours and hours passed as the Resolution Drive accelerated the ship to near-light velocity. He must've dozed off, for the next thing he remembered was being awakened by Lingo's voice.

"Okay. We're beyond Olympia IX. Ready to begin final corrections for entering Stasis-Space."

"Wait a minute!" shrieked Palmer. "You can't just go into Stasis-Space without a computer fix!" It was sheer insanity! Fortunately, it was impossible to come *out* of Stasis-Space within a solar system—the mass pressure of the star held you inexorably in Stasis-Space until you were a safe distance away. But it was all too possible to turn *on* a Stasis-Field generator too close to a star-sized mass. Not only would such a generator explode, leaving what was left of the ship stuck in Stasis-Space forever, but the stresses would trigger a nova in the sun itself. That was why all solar systems, Doog and Human alike, were so heavily patrolled—theoretically, one suicide ship could destroy an entire solar system. However, at least at this stage of the War, such a danger *was* purely theoretical. A ship on such a mission had to approach its victim star on Resolution Drive, and a single ship on Resolution Drive was completely vulnerable to the ubiquitous systemic patrols.

But now, for no sane reason at all, Lingo was going to expose Olympia itself to the danger of a possible nova. It was madness to take such a pointless chancel to turn on the generator without an accurate fix from the ship's computer insuring that the ship was far enough away from Olympia....

"Remember?" laughed Lingo. "This snip *has no* computer. But it's really quite simple. All I have to do is center Dugl in the red circle. It represents the line of I flight of the ship."

Lingo manipulated his levers and pedals and steering wheel. The small red circle with the yellow star that was Dugl within it began to creep closer to the larger circle in the center of the viewscreen as Lingo adjusted the ship's attitude in space. Now they were touching....

And now Dugl was centered in the larger red circle, within the smaller red circle, like the bullseye of a target.

But if Lingo is wrong, if we're too close, Palmer thought, then Olympia's the target.

"Lock controls!" said Lingo. "Turn on Stasis-Field!"

Palmer held his breath. Abruptly, the star-studded field that was normal space vanished, and Palmer found himself in the swirling, pulsating formless maze of colors that were what the distorted time of the Stasis-Field made of the visual universe.

But the generator had not blown. Lingo had done it. They *had* been far enough out! Olympia was still safe....

And they were on their way to Duglaar!

Chapter IV

"WELL, General Palmer," said Lingo, "as you can plainly see, the generator hasn't blown. We're still here, and so, presumably, is Olympia."

"I only hope it wasn't just dumb luck," said Palmer grudgingly. "I still say it was a stupid risk to take."

Lingo climbed nimbly out of the pilot's seat. "Had it really been a risk," he said, "I'd certainly agree with you. Causing a sun to go nova is hardly a joke. But you don't think it a risk when you entrust such a dreadful responsibility to a computer, to a mere machine. We just happen to place more trust in the human mind than in electronics. After all, when you come right down to it, even the best computer is no more than an extension of the human mind."

"That's a pretty superficial way of looking at.... Palmer began. But Lingo cut him off with a wave of his hand.

"It's going to be a long voyage, my friend," he said. "We'll have plenty of time to argue later. So let's not waste *this* argument right at the beginning. The others are probably already in the common room. I could use a drink. How about you?"

The common room just did not seem to be on a spaceship. The walls were paneled in pine. The floor was covered with a soft green carpet. The furniture was hefty, mostly made of genuine wood and leather, and incredibly opulent. Along one wall of the large room was a bar that would've done the General Officer's Club back in Pentagon City proud. Another wall was practically all viewscreen. There was a great clutter of equipment in one corner of the room: a hi-fi, a smell-organ, what looked like a therimin, and half that were totally unfamiliar. There with real paper-paged and cloth-bound books

What looked almost like an elliptical pool-table sat in the center of the room, but in place of pockets there were what looked like canisters of multicolored sand.

Palmer stood there for long moment as drinking it in. This room must've cost more than the rest of the ship put together! He thought.

Dirk Lingo signaled to Raul Ortega, who was standing behind the bar. "How about a Nine Planets for the General?" he said.

Ortega busied himself with bottles, glasses, tubes and mixing spoons.

"This is... ah... quite a layout for a spaceship," Palmer said. "Not exactly what I'm used to."

Robin Morel, who was lounging disconcertingly in an overstuffed chair, laughed musically. "War is hell, General," she drawled.

Ortega had completed the Nine Planets, whatever *that* was. He handed Palmer a tall frosted glass filled with nine different levels of liquid: ice-blue, brown, purple, aqua, maroon, brickred, green, yellow and orange.

"One for each planet of the Sol system, Ortega said, giving Lingo a conspiratorial wink.

Palmer eyed the huge drink dubiously It looked very formidable.

"Sip it slowly," suggested Fran Shannon who had entered the room with them. "One level at a time."

Palmer lifted the glass to his lips and sipped tentatively. The first level was bitingly cold. Pluto, I suppose, he thought, trying to remember his Solar geography The next four levels were also bitingly cold, but in gradually decreasing intensity. The sixth level seemed somehow sandy, old and dry — Mars, he guessed. The seventh level was soothing, warm and mild. It could only be Earth. The eighth level was hot head off.

The final level nearly took the top of his head off.

"Wow..." he muttered hoarsely, numbly aware that he had somehow finished the drink.

All the Solarians were in the room now, and they were grinning and nodding to each other.

"That Raul is some bartender," said Max Bergstrom. "If you really feel brave, have him mix you a Supernova sometime."

Palmer shook his head slowly. The an impossibly long time. "I think I've had quite enough for now," he said giddily. "What in the Galaxy was in that thing?"

"It'd take all day to explain *that*, General," Ortega said with a wry grin.

"Call me *Jay*" Palmer said impulsively. He was beginning to feel very lightheaded and weak-kneed, as if he had been drinking steadily for hours.

"I hope that drink was... ah, non-toxic," he said dizzily, plopping himself down in the nearest chair. As he said the words, he had meant them as a flippant remark, but by the time he had finished the sentence, which seemed to him interminable, he was seriously wondering whether the drink might not actually have been poisoned. After all, the Solarians just could not be trusted....

"Don't worry, Jay," Robin Morel said with a little laugh, "it only *seems* lethal."

Palmer's head was really beginning to whirl now. He was losing all sense of time now. It was even becoming hard to tell just how many Solarians were in the room with him now. There seemed to be hundreds of them. The air seemed to have a body and flavor of its own, and it was flowing languidly like thick syrup. Palmer had never even come close to being this drunk before, and he was not sure that he liked it. He felt all right now, light-headed, euphoric, a bit giddy, but the thought of staying in this state for hours was rather frightening and more than a bit nauseating.

Either Bergstrom had read his mind, or the others had read his face, for the Solarians were all laughing, and Ortega was practically roaring.

"Don't worry, Jay," Lingo said. "This too, shall pass."

Linda Dortin seemed to drift over to the hi-fi, and pleasant, soft, rather vague music began to fill the air. Fran Shannon sat down at the smell-organ, and began to play.

The room was transformed into a garden in the springtime. There was a warm, heavy, constant background odor of freshly cut clovered grass. Against this background, Fran played constantly shifting, ephemeral whiffs of flowers—roses, lilacs, morning glories. The smell patterns seemed to ebb and flow in a strange kind of unison with the notes of the music.

Palmer's head felt as if it were going to explode. A part of him was relaxing and enjoying the strange, all-enveloping synthesis of intoxication, odors and music. Never had he been so taken out of himself....

But that was the trouble. He had never drunk anything remotely like that Nine Planets, and he couldn't know what its real effects might be. He had the Solarians' word that it was harmless, but just how much was that really worth? Maybe they intended to keep him in this stupefied state permanently.... Maybe the drink had other properties that would rob him of his will.... And maybe, despite what Robin had said, the drink might just have been poisoned after all.

Palmer dimly realized that this train of thought might be considered paranoiac, and even *that* might be caused by the drink. The trouble was, he had no usable criteria to measure the situation against. If the Solarians were really trustworthy, then it was simple foolishness to worry drink, but if they were plotting some king of treachery, then the foolish thing had been taking the drink in the first place....

Palmer was not really a drinking man, but like all soldiers on liberty, he occasionally had a few more drinks than he needed. At such times, he had known what it was like to be more intoxicated than you want to be, to sit around hoping that you won't be sick, and stoically waiting for the effects of the alcohol to wear off.

He felt that way now. He did not feel sick, nor maudlin, nor frightened, but he had had enough and he was no longer enjoying the intoxication. He simply wanted it to end.

The trouble was that he had lost all sense of time. He had not the slightest idea of just how long he had been drunk, and what was much worse, he had no idea of how long the effects of the Nine Planets would last.

He felt himself at the center of a warm, vague, pink fog. It seemed to him that he had been befogged for as long as he could remember, and it seemed as if he would be drunk forever....

Then, quite suddenly, the mist began to lift, to melt away like cotton candy in warm water.

With amazing rapidity, he was all at once stone sober.

To his great and wondering surprise, his head was clear and his vision sharp. There was no headache, and no dullness. In fact there was no morning-after feeling at all. He felt as if he had just had eight hours of perfect sleep. He even felt hungry.

"Aha," said Ortega. "I see that it's worn off. That's the beauty of a Nine Planets. The first seven levels are increasingly strong intoxicants. The eighth level is a delayed action sober-izer, and the last is an energizer. A binge, a good night's sleep, and wide-awake in the morning in less than twenty minutes!"

"*Twenty minutes?*" exclaimed Palmer. "Is that all it was?"

"That's all," said Ortega.

"How do you feel?" Lingo asked.

"I feel great!" exclaimed Palmer. "In fact, it gave me quite an appetite."

"Purely intentional," said Linda Dortin. "Dinner is about to be served." She pushed a button behind the bar, and a section of wall opened, revealing a large dinner table with seven settings—cloth napkins, ornate china, genuine silverware—already layed out on it, and seven comfortable-looking lounge chairs.

Palmer and the three male Solarians sat down at the table, and Palmer expected the women to sit down too, since the room was obviously completely equipped, and they would surely have an autoserver.

But instead, the girls went to another section of the wall. A button was pressed, and a panel slid open, revealing a tureen of steaming soup, slices of melon, a roast, and assorted side dishes.

To Palmer's amazement, they began serving the meal gracefully by hand.

Why, this went out with rockets! he thought. Yet there was something soothing and graceful about this kind of meal, and the women seemed to enjoy it too.

"Almost like one of those ancient family meals you read about," Palmer said.

"Close," said Lingo. "You know, there was a time when 'family' included three or four generations. In those days, each meal was really quite a complex social event.

Of course there were plenty of disadvantages. A man was tied to his extended family, often for life, and if they were a bunch of obnoxious louts who he couldn't stand—well, that was just too bad."

"But I suppose it did give people a sense of belonging," mused Palmer. "I mean, I can almost feel what it must've been like. This is all somehow... comforting."

"Yeah," cracked Ortega. "But those old families could also tear each other to tiny little pieces. Trouble was, that the social structure threw people together on a purely chance basis. And involuntary groupings always mean trouble."

"Ah, you're just a professional cynic, Raul," said Fran Shannon. "Why it must've been very romantic in the old days."

"Sure, sure, *very* romantic. Did you know that those *romantics* used to go around *murdering* people just because they found their wives with someone else?"

"Oh, come off it Raul," laughed Fran Shannon. "You're just making that up!"

"*Oh?*" said Ortega, with a little grin. "Not only am I not making it up, but that sort of thing is *still going on*, on the planets of the Confederation, isn't it Jay?"

Palmer flushed. "Of course it is!" he blurted. "Ah... I mean, if you mean what I think you mean. Er... none of you people are... ah... married?"

"Yes and no," said Ortega.

"*Yes and no?*" exclaimed Palmer. "You either are or you aren't!"

"*No*, then, according to your way of thinking," Lingo said. "But kind of *yes* according to ours. We're all married to each other, in a sense. We're all important to each other. In many ways, we function like what you would call a family. But on the other hand, we're all completely independent individuals, and we're perfectly free to form whatever relationships we care to outside the Group."

Palmer shook his head. It was quite beyond him.

"For instance," said Robin, "you're not a member of our Group, but there's no reason in particular why you should have to sleep alone all the time, now is there?"

"There certainly is!" blurted Palmer. But as all six Solarians burst into good-natured laughter, he began to wonder just what it was.

Ortega was puttering about the bar. Fran Shannon was off in a corner of the common room reading a book. Max and Linda were....

Palmer, sitting in a lounge chair, with Lingo and Robin in chairs flanking him, could not figure out what Linda and Max were doing. They were sitting on the couch, staring into each other's eyes, not moving a muscle and not uttering a sound.

Palmer glanced at Robin, caught her eye, glanced over to Max and Linda and then back at Robin. It was clearly a question.

Robin laughed and smiled warmly at him. "Don't ask me," she said. "I'm no telepath. They're... well, they're communing with each other in a way that only two telepaths can, and two telepaths that care for each other, at that. Personally, well I'd rather express my affection in less cerebral ways." And she winked at him.

Palmer squirmed uneasily in his chair and glanced at Lingo to see if he had caught it. Lingo was staring pointedly off into space and grinning to himself, as if at some private joke.

"What do you think, Jay?" Robin said.

"Huh? About what?"

"About affection. Don't you think that people should show it if they like each other? I mean in the most natural way. Which, for a man and woman is…." she stared long and frankly and steadily at him. Palmer glanced nervously at Lingo, who was still pointedly ignoring the conversation.

"Well sure, if two people are in love they should…. I mean, abstinence for its own sake went out with the Age of Freud."

"No, no," Robin said. "I don't mean love, I mean *like*. Don't tell me you believe that a man and a woman have to be in love with each other before they…."

"Of course not!" Palmer said. "There's nothing wrong with sex for its own sake, either. It's the most natural…."

Robin laughed. "I don't mean that either!" she exclaimed. "Don't you understand what *like* means? It means not being in love with someone, but not being totally indifferent to them either. I'm in love with Dirk, for instance. But… that doesn't keep me from *liking* you, now does it?"

The words were ambiguous, but the warm, close, deep look certainly was not. Palmer felt himself unwilling to return the stare and uncertain as to how he felt about it. After all, he thought, Lingo is sitting right next to us.

He glanced at Lingo. This time Lingo looked back. There was neither anger nor jealousy on his face. He merely seemed highly amused at something. Palmer could not imagine what.

"You *do* like me, Jay?" Robin said. "I mean, you don't find me ugly, or stupid or boring?"

"Huh? Why of course not. Why should I? Of course I like you, Robin."

She laughed softly, and stared at him again, arching her eyebrows up and down in one quick meaningful stroke.

He understood the question, but he didn't quite know how to answer it, and what was worse, he didn't know how he *wanted* to answer it. So he pretended that it had never happened.

Lingo gave vent to a quick, stifled grunt that sounded like a manfully muffled laugh. He glanced over to Robin, shrugged, and motioned to her with his hand.

She shrugged back, smiled pleasantly at Palmer, got up, walked over to Lingo's chair and sat down in his lap.

Lingo laughed, kissed her lightly on the nose and said, "You must be losing your touch, Robin."

"Can't win 'em all," Robin said, kissing him back.

Palmer got up in embarrassed confusion and walked over to the bookcase, where he pretended to become absorbed in one of the volumes.

A few minutes later, Max and Linda disengaged their stares, and, without a word being passed between them, both got up. Max walked over to Fran Shannon, said something to her, and they walked out of the common room together.

Meanwhile, Linda had whispered something in Ortega's ear, and they too left together, arm in arm.

Palmer lay uneasily, but in a way gratefully, on his cabin bunk. The cabin was somehow a relaxingly pleasant contrast to the rest of the ship—a small, plain cubicle with bunk, table and locker, much like any other cabin on any other ship. It was Spartan, and hence reassuringly familiar.

It had been quite a trying day, all things considered. The more he saw of the Solarians, the less he seemed to understand. In their natural habitat, they seemed even stranger than they had on Olympia III....

Palmer shook his head. Are they simply a degenerate bunch of hedonists? he thought. He had never seen such incredible luxury on a spaceship before, and on a mission like this, it seemed almost criminal.

Am I being unfair, though? Palmer asked himself. After all, when you come right down to it, what's the point in asceticism for its own sake?

But what really troubled him was the pattern of relationships among the Solarians—if there *was* a pattern. At times, they seemed almost like a family... But then there was that business about not sleeping alone.... And the business about "like" versus "love"....

And Robin.

The way she looked at me... he thought. An invitation if I ever saw one. And Lingo was right there. But he didn't mind at all.... And then, all of a sudden they start acting like an old married couple. And the way Linda and Max spent all that time just staring at each other, and then each of 'em goes off with someone else. It just makes no sense.

There was nothing naive about Palmer; he had certainly not spent all his nights alone, or even always with a woman who was really important to him. One either had a serious relationship with a woman or a casual one. Either was "quite normal, depending on the circumstances.

But how could there possibly be a middle ground?

Yet to the Solarians, there obviously *was* some kind of middle ground between the casual and the serious. There had to be some rules, at least of taste, if nothing else, in the Solarian culture, but Palmer was unable to see them.

It was all totally maddening. I'd have an easier time understanding six Doogs, he thought.

This was going to be one long trip.

Palmer stood uncertainly just outside the entrance to the common room. Rationally, he knew that there was no reason for him to be leery of facing Lingo or Robin, but his mind was having trouble convincing his viscera.

He shrugged resignedly, and stepped through the entranceway. A sudden twinge, almost an unpleasant kind of wistfulness quivered through Palmer as he entered the common room. The Solarians were clustered around the strange elliptical table. They were talking animatedly, laughing, smiling. The group radiated a bubbling sense of camaraderie, fellowship, warmth.

Palmer recognized the unpleasant feeling for what it was: loneliness, estrangement. And envy. These people had a *something*. Something that was shared, without being all-enveloping, something that enabled them to pass the long weeks of the voyage to Duglaar pleasantly and zestfully, with neither boredom nor sheer hedonism.

They had *roots*. Each one had roots in the other five, and Palmer knew with certain conviction that as long as this group was together, any place in the Galaxy would be home to them.

But a professional soldier, he thought bitterly, has no home. And while he felt the warm pull of the Solarian group, he could not forget for a moment that these people were Solarians, strangers from the hermit system of Sol, whose motives and aims could neither be understood nor trusted.

But still....

"Ah, Jay," said Lingo. "This should interest you. A fascinating game. Take a look."

Palmer walked over to the elliptical table. Seven little piles of what looked like seven different hues of colored sand had been laid out on the surface of the table. A transparent plastic plate covered the table-top about an inch and a half above the piles of sand.

"What is this thing, anyway?" he asked.

"A telekinesis table," said Robin Morel. "Only a few people like Max and Linda have a real telepathic Talent, but everyone has *some* latent telepathic ability. This set-up is designed to let the average person play around with his latent psi faculties."

"How does it work?" asked Palmer.

"The surface of the table is virtually frictionless," said Ortega. "The colored 'sand' is really tiny balls of colored steel, micro-polished so that they have the lowest possible frictional coefficient. Then the transparent top-plate is sealed over the table-top, and the air in between is evacuated, creating a reasonably good vacuum. So rolling friction and air resistance are as close to zero as possible, thus minimizing the amount of psychokinetic force needed to move the 'sand.' And of course, the individual balls have very small masses. I've only an ordinary amount of psi myself, but watch! I'll use the green pile."

Ortega stared intently at the table-top. As Palmer watched in amazed fascination, the pile of green particles slowly began to flatten out until it was a rough circle, only one particle thick. Gradually, the circle began to change, and after several minutes, the rough initials "R. O." had been formed by the green particles.

"Not bad for an amateur," said Max Bergstrom. "Of course Linda and I can work this gizmo with our minds tied behind our backs."

Suddenly, the red pile began to move as if each of the individual particles were an energetic little insect. In seconds, a red heart was formed on the table-top.

The yellow pile snapped into the shape of an arrow, which pierced the heart. Some of the yellow grains jumped to the surface of the heart and formed the legend "M. B. 1 L. D."

"Oh really!" grunted Ortega, wrinkling his nose.

Everyone laughed. Even Palmer found himself joining in.

"Come on, you try it now, Jay."

"I really don't think I...."

"Oh, come on!"

"Well..." said Palmer dubiously, "just what am I supposed to do?"

"Just think at the sand," said Ortega. "Try the blue pile."

Palmer shrugged, and stared intently and somewhat self consciously at the pile of blue particles. Move! Move! he thought, come on, damn you, flatten out!

Nothing much seemed to happen. A few individual particles at the apex of the pile trickled down towards the edges. Palmer concentrated intently for several minutes. Perhaps there were a few more particles at the periphery now than when he had started, and maybe the pile was minutely flatter, but....

"Very good for the first try!" exclaimed Robin Morel as Palmer finally looked up from the table.

"Really?" he said, with genuine pleasure.

Robin smiled warmly at him. *"Really,* Jay," she said. "Lots of people can't even move a single particle the first time. Maybe we've got a latent telepath among us."

Palmer laughed almost boyishly. These people really did seem genuinely interested in him, in a completely wholehearted and unaffected manner. Maybe....

"Maybe we've been misjudging the Confederation all these years," said Ortega. "Maybe the Confederation planets are just loaded with Talents." He said it in a completely light-hearted manner, but somehow the words completely punctured Palmer's bubble of elation. These people *were*, after all, Solarians, and they were on what could prove to be a deadly mission to the Human Confederation. They *had* deprived him of his weapons, and they were just not to be trusted. It would be madness, possibly treason, to let himself become a part of this group, no matter how attractive the prospect was made.

"Something wrong, Jay?" asked Robin.

"Ah... no.... I think I'll... uh... go read a book."

He left the Solarians and went over to the bookcase. As he puttered aimlessly among the books, he felt their eyes upon him, even as they continued their psi games. It was horribly uncomfortable. The covert glances made him feel more an outsider than ever, and worse, they made him feel that it was entirely his fault.

But worst of all was what was expressed in those fleeting glances. For it was not annoyance, but pity.

It was impossible to sleep. He sat tensely on the edge of his bunk, confused and undecided.

Palmer could sense that the Solarians were offering him *something*, but it was a something he did not really understand. Yet most of him wanted it very badly. He had grown to manhood in a civilization that had been at war for three centuries. He was a soldier, and, he knew unselfconsciously, a good one. He never remembered wanting anything else. It seemed though, that there *was* something missing from his life, something whose absence he had not even suspected until he had met six people who had it... even if he still didn't know what it was....

But then there was the mission, perhaps the most important mission in the history of the Confederation. What were the Solarians really up to? Was their goal really the same as the Confederation—to win The War—or were they somehow out merely to save Fortress Sol at the expense of the rest of the human race?

Under other circumstances, he might've felt free to simply become a part of their group, but could he afford to trust them that far, not knowing the real nature of their mission?

On the other hand, perhaps becoming part of the group was the only real way of learning anything. After all, if he showed them that he trusted them, might not they begin to trust him?

Unless they *did* have something to hide.

It was just all too much for....

There was a knock on the door.

"Come on in," Palmer said, rather reluctantly.

It was Robin Morel. She opened the door, stepped inside, and sat down beside him on the bunk. She studied his face for a long moment.

"Something's bothering you, Jay," she said.

"This isn't exactly a pleasure-jaunt," he snapped, far more sharply than he had intended. He was becoming uncomfortably aware that this was one attractive woman.

"I mean something else," she said softly. "There's this hostility between you and the rest of us. We can feel it, and I'm sure you feel it too. The mission would go a lot more smoothly if it weren't there."

"You expect me to trust you? Did you trust *me*? You took away all my weapons, didn't you? Do you call that trust?"

"A man who's armed to the teeth isn't exactly acting friendly either," Robin said with a little smile.

"Touché," Palmer replied, in a somewhat better humor. "So let's agree that we don't trust each other."

"It doesn't *have* to be that way."

"I don't see how it can be any other way," Palmer said. "I'm a Confederal officer, and you're Solarians. We've been cut off from each other for three centuries, and not by *our* choice."

"But we're both fighting the same enemy, aren't we?"

"Are we?" snapped Palmer. "We've been holding off the Duglaari with our ships and lives for three centuries. What've *you* been doing?"

"Fighting the same battle in a different way," Robin said evenly. "Of course you won't really understand until you let yourself become a part of our Group. Why not give it a try?"

"Give *what* a try?" Palmer said defensively.

"Give *us* a try. We're human beings, not monsters. We want to be your friends. In a way that you can't understand yet, we want to be more than your friends."

"Just how do you mean that?" he said, with an exaggeratedly blank expression on his face.

Robin laughed. "Perhaps not *quite* the way you think I mean it," she said. "Although there is no reason for you to sleep alone unless you want to."

"I thought you and Lingo...?"

"Sure," she said, "but we don't *belong* to each other. A human being isn't a piece of property, Jay."

"You mean he wouldn't be jealous? There wouldn't be any bad blood between us?"

"Why should there be? Would you be taking something from him? Would there somehow be less of me for him? It's not as if I were in love with you, the way I am with Dirk. He knows that. Besides, it would all be within the Group."

"You say that as if it meant 'all within the family'."

"In a way it does," she said. "A Group is like... well, if you've never been a part of one, there's no way to really tell you. It's a little like a family, but there's no head of the household. It's a relationship of complete equals. And people only become a part of a Group because they want to. They're free to form whatever outside relationships they like, and there are other relationships within the Group, like Dirk and me, or like Linda and Max who are even closer. Yet it's all part of one harmonious... Jay, there's just no way to describe it to an outsider. You've got to *feel* it."

Palmer felt the attraction of what she was describing, not because he understood what she was saying—for he but dimly grasped the concept—but because of how she said it. Letting himself go, becoming a part of this Group thing, he somehow felt would be like coming home. Although he had never really had a home....

And yet, might not this be exactly what they *wanted* him to feel? Might not the whole thing be a trap? Certainly the bait was attractive enough....

"What do you say, Jay?"

"I'll sleep on it," he replied.

"Alone?" she asked with a little smile.

"Alone."

Chapter V

AFTER Robin had left his cabin, Palmer sat tensely on the edge of his bunk, unable and unwilling to go to sleep.

How long have I been on this ship? he asked himself. It seems like years....

Palmer grimaced. Now that he thought about it, most of his life had gone by like hours—fight, retreat, liberty, fight. In a war that lasted for centuries, the life of an officer was year after year of endless repetition. There had been more novelty in the past two days than in the last two years. It was just too much to digest in one piece....

There was Robin... and the Solarians... and the mission. Most of all, certainly most important of all, was the mission. But what *was* the mission? Kurowski's orders were to play along with the Solarians unless they appeared to be pulling a fast one. Then, thought Palmer, I'm suppose to take over the ship, or destroy it as a last resort.

But how do I do that, when I've lost all my weapons, and when I'm dealing with people who can read my mind and control my body?

Wearily but restlessly, Palmer got up and began to pace the floor of the cabin. It all boiled down to whether or not the Solarians could be trusted. They seemed like the friendliest people in the Galaxy, there was a warmth about them, an ease, an openness that Palmer had never experienced before. There was a complete lack of jealousy, and an apparent willingness to share... *just about anything*. Ordinarily, he would've been more than happy to call such people friends... or something more than friends.

But these were the same people who had invaded the privacy of his very mind, who had dragooned him into a supposed mission whose outcome seemed a certain and meaningless death. Whatever they might be as human beings, they were still *Solarians*. And Fortress Sol was synonymous with secrecy and the unknown. In what unguessable ways might the people of Sol have changed in three centuries of isolation?

In their personal lives, the Solarians were alien and incomprehensible in so many ways... Wasn't it reasonable to assume that their political motivations might be equally alien?

Palmer sat down on the bed again, and began to undress. One thing, at least, was clear—he had to find out more. He had to learn the truth about Fortress Sol and the Solarians' mission before he could even hope to act.

Perhaps, he thought, perhaps the easiest way would be to let myself go, to become a part of their Group?

He grinned wryly to himself. Letting himself go with Robin might not exactly qualify him for hardship pay either.

Raul Ortega was alone in the common room, leaning on the bar and sipping a tall drink as Palmer entered.

Ortega nodded, and poured another tall red drink from a frosted pitcher that rested on the bartop. "Have one, Jay," he said.

Palmer walked over to the bar and picked up the drink. He eyed it suspiciously and twirled the glass slowly in his hand.

Ortega laughed. "It's just plain old red wine this time," he said. "Nice and cold."

Palmer took a tentative sip. "Wine all right," he said. "And pretty good wine at that."

"Nothing but the best," drawled Ortega. Then, with sharp suddenness, "Why don't you trust us, Jay?"

"Why should I?" Palmer snapped. "You read my mind against my will. You confiscate my weapons. You dragoon me into a suicide mission. And to top it off, you're Solarians, and no one's been permitted in the Sol system for three centuries. What reason can you give for my trusting you?"

"You're still alive," Ortega said quietly.

"What is that supposed to mean?"

"Think it over," Ortega said. "You've been disarmed. Max and Linda can read your mind and control your body any time they want to. There's not a thing you can do to harm us, while we can do just about anything we want to with you. There's your reason to trust us."

"That's a reason to *trust* you?" Palmer exclaimed.

"Best reason there is," Ortega said, taking a long sip of wine. "You've got absolutely nothing to gain by *not* trusting us. You can't do anything to harm us, and you might as well face the fact that we can do just about anything we want to you. So what can you gain by not trusting us?"

"That's pretty fine reasoning," Palmer said. "What it boils down to is that my only choice is whether I'm going to be a prisoner or a willing guest."

"Right on the button," Ortega said. "We're offering you friendship, real friendship, Jay. Accept us for what we are and this will be a much pleasanter trip. Don't fight it, Jay. All you stand to gain is insomnia. Give us a try."

Palmer shrugged and took a long drink of wine. "You know, Raul," he said, "you may have a point." Maybe not the point you think you have, though, he thought.

Palmer smiled with careful boyishness at Robin Morel across the dinner coffee. He had made up his mind. He would not remain aloof from the Solarians; he would go along with whatever the Solarians liked, up to a point. At least until he knew enough to decide what the Solarians were really up to, and whether or not they could really be trusted. It was clearly his duty to infiltrate the Group.

And besides, it might not be such unpleasant duty at that.

"What's the grin for, Jay?" asked Lingo conversationally. "You and Robin...?"

"Certainly not!"

"Not yet, anyway, Dirk," Robin said.

Palmer flushed, and everyone laughed. After a moment, he forced himself to laugh with them.

"I think that's the first time I've seen you laugh," Lingo said. "It suits you well. There's been too much tension on this mission. We all...."

"Robin spoke to him about all that last night," Max Bergstrom said.

"How did you....?" Palmer blurted in astonishment.

Bergstrom grinned and tapped his right temple with a fore-finger. "And *you*," he said, "have decided to give us a try. Welcome to the Group."

"Doesn't anyone have any privacy with you telepaths around?" asked Palmer, forcing his voice into a tone of geniality that he did not really feel.

"All the privacy you want," said Linda Dortin, "and not a drop more or less."

"What does *that* mean?"

"If you'll think about it," said Lingo, "the existence of a telepathic minority implies some very delicate social problems. As does the existence of other Talents. If it weren't for the Organic Group, well...."

"Organic Group?"

"That's what the six of us are, Jay," Lingo said. "An Organic Group. The human race has always had individuals with unusual talents, it's always encompassed great differences among its members. There's far greater variation within the human race than among the Doogs. But until very recently, this has worked largely *against* mankind, because the tendency was always for similar human types to cluster together in mutual hostility against the other human types. The basic unit, for instance, has always been the family. And of course, a 'family' could be defined as a group of people with very similar genetic makeup. Likes always tended to group together, in small groups and in larger ones — the smallest being the family, and the largest the nation-state, of which planetary governments are merely the most recent form."

"I never looked at it that way," mused Palmer. "You mean that nation-states are just extensions of the family?"

"What else? The larger units of a social structure are always determined by the nature of the basic unit."

"And 'race' is just an extension of the idea of a clan!" exclaimed Palmer. "Sure…. it's so obvious, that…."

"That's why the human race has never been united," Lingo said. "Even the Confederation is just a collection of sovereign solar systems. If the Doogs didn't exist, neither would the Confederation. It would fall apart, because the basic social unit is the family."

"What does all this have to do with telepaths?" asked Palmer.

"Imagine," said Max Bergstrom, "if all telepaths — and there axe millions of us in the Sol system — considered ourselves a race, a clan, and considered everyone else…."

"Enough!" shuddered Palmer. "I get the point!"

"You get *part* of the point," said Lingo. "Telepathy isn't the *only* Talent. Take the six of us: two telepaths, Max and Linda. Raul is a Gamemaster…."

"Gamemaster? I've heard that word before. At the General Staff meeting. It means strategist, doesn't it?"

Ortega laughed. "The same way that 'soldier' means 'hired killer,'" he said.

"You see, Jay," said Lingo, "being a Gamemaster is not something you can just learn. It's a genuine Talent, an instinctive, at least partly hereditary genius. Like telepathy. Raul has the instinctive ability to conceive of military and geopolitical struggles, like the war with the Doogs, as if they were but a game of cards or chess."

"You mean he's a human Strategy Computer, the way you're a human ship's computer?"

Lingo laughed. "You'll find this hard to take, Jay, but a Gamemaster is far superior to any strategy computer, even the Computation Center on Olympia IV. For in addition to dealing with objective data, he takes into account subjective factors, such as the psychology of the opponent, the idea of bluff, a thousand subtle factors that computers will always be blind to. They can build computers that can play a good game of chess—since chess is a game of logic—but no computer will ever be able to compete with a good human gambler at cards."

"And there are millions of us, too," said Ortega. "What if *we* considered ourselves a race apart?"

"And Fran is an Eidetic," Lingo said. "She has total recall; she's a walking almanac, encyclopedia, memory bank. Robin is something far more subtle—a specializing non-specialist. For want of a better term, we call that Talent being a 'Glue.'"

"So the entire Sol system is inhabited by people with all these greatly different Talents?" said Palmer.

"You're getting the point," said Lingo. "As the human race evolves, the differences among its individual members become *greater*, not less. Specialization becomes more and more pronounced. And if the race continued to be organized on the basis of nations, clans, families of like clustering together...."

"The human race would explode!"

"Exactly," said Lingo. "The Organic Group is a new basic unit, based not on the similarity of its members, but on their *differences*. It's not merely a good idea—it's an evolutionary necessity. People with very different Talents and natures come together in the *basic* unit. And of course, with the basic unit built upon this kind of functional cooperation, the whole civilization is stable and unified."

"But how can you come to any decisions with such a set-up?" asked Palmer. "What, after all, can hold such dissimilar types together?"

"This will be the hardest thing of all for you to swallow, Jay," said Ortega. "But the fact is that *Leadership* is also a Talent, like telepathy or Gamemastership. Dirk is our Leader. Just as he wouldn't think of trying to function as a telepath or an Eidetic, none of us would think of trying to be Leader."

"'And this is what I'm getting into,' you are thinking," said Linda Dortin. "Of course you're staggered. Your entire civilization is built on a different basis than ours. But we understand... after all, how can telepaths fail to empathize? We realize how hard it will be for you. And we'll help you as much as we can. Right now, you want to be alone to digest all this, eh?"

"Yes," whispered Palmer, and to his own surprise, he was not at all resentful that Linda had read his mind and spoken his thoughts for him. He recognized it for what it was—not prying, but a single act of kindness.

As he left the table, Robin said "I'll look in on you, Jay, when you want me to."

"How will you know?" He stopped himself. Of course, she would know if he wanted to see her. He understood something of the ethics of telepathy now. Max and Linda would read his thoughts only when it was necessary for the good of the Group.

Or when he wanted them to.

The only word for it was *alien*, Palmer thought, as he paced the narrow space between his bunk and the locker. It was alien to the very basic premises of the only civilization he had ever known.

Become a part of *this?* Trust people from a civilization as alien as *that?* Was it possible, even if he wanted to?

It was one thing to accept the Doog's alienness — they were, after all, a non-human civilization. But the Solarians were human beings, which somehow made them even more alien than the Duglaari.

And yet, he asked himself, must *alien* always equal *evil?* Must different always mean wrong?

Was it not possible for an alien social structure to be better? Might not the humans of Fortress Sol be *more* human than the humans of the Confederation, and not less?

Was there any objective way of knowing? If there wasn't, there would never be any possibility of trust between the Confederation and Fortress Sol, any more than there could be peace between Man and Doog. But the Solarians *were*, after all, human beings, weren't they? Men... and women....

Perhaps if Robin....

He felt something smile warmly within his mind, and he knew that Robin would now be on her way to his cabin.

A few minutes later, she opened the door. It was, he realized, not necessary for her to knock.

They sat down on the bunk, and she smiled at him, the warm, inviting smile of a beautiful woman. And yet he could not help thinking of her as a beautiful, desirable, *alien* woman.

"Feeling better?" she asked, with a little twist of her head which made her soft red hair bounce provocatively. He was inanely aware that he was alone with a beautiful woman, a woman that was at once desirable and alien, warm and chillingly strange.

"If anything, I feel worse," he said. "More confused."

"About us? Or about yourself?"

"Both, I suppose," he answered. "There's such a difference between us. I have no way of understanding you, I mean *really* understanding. At least Max and Linda are telepaths; they can get inside of me. They can know what I am, what my motives are...."

"They *could*," said Robin, "but they wouldn't. It's just not done, any more than you would peek into someone's boudoir without permission."

"That's *some* comfort, anyway," Palmer said, "but not very much. I still can't understand you people. It's as if you were a bunch of Doogs."

"Believe me, Jay, the two of us have much more in common than either of us do with the Duglaari. Doogs are basically logical; humans are illogical, or better, *alogical*. Our two cultures, after all, do share millenia of the same history. We *are* the same race, and we *do* have a common enemy."

She laughed. "And of course, I've got a lot more in common with you biologically than any Doog."

He gave her a half-serious leer. "And how am I supposed to take that?" he asked.

She stared at him with sly shyness. "How would you like to take it, Jay?" she said.

"How would *you* like me to take it?" he said, with a little grin.

She laughed. "Don't you really know?" she said. She reached out slowly and stroked his head, entwining her fingers in his hair.

He put his left hand on her shoulder, lightly and hesitantly. Then he reached up and ran his right thumb slowly and languorously across her forehead.

"I suppose I do," he said, drawing her to him.

Robin Morel rolled over on the bunk, propped herself up on her elbows, smiled up at Palmer who was leaning against the headboard and said "Well, am I really so terribly alien?"

Palmer forced a grin. "No…" he mumbled.

"Well then what's the matter, Jay?"

"This mission may take weeks," he said. "I mean, the seven of us will be cooped up on this little ship for a long time…."

"So?"

Palmer grimaced. "Well… uh… *Dirk.* I mean, you and Dirk…. The situation could get awfully sticky if Dirk and I were feuding."

"Why should you want to feud with Dirk?" Robin said.

"I don't. But that doesn't mean that he may not want to feud with me."

Robin sighed. "I thought we went through all that. Look, let's get one thing straight — Dirk is my man. You're *not* competing with him, and he's not competing with you. I like you, but I don't feel the same way about you as I do about Dirk. I know it, Dirk knows it, and I certainly hope that *you* know it. There's no cause for any jealousy."

Palmer scowled. "That's all very well for *you* to say, Robin," he said, not unkindly, "but you're not a man. Men feel different about that kind of thing. You know, two deer knocking their antlers together and all that kind of thing. I know that if I were Dirk...."

"But you're *not*, Jay," Robin said. She gave him a little smile. "And you're not a deer, either. Neither is Dirk. We're human beings, not animals. Know what I think you're *really* afraid of?"

"What?"

"That Dirk *won't* be jealous."

"Huh?" Palmer grunted uneasily. "What is that supposed to mean?"

"I think you know what it means, Jay. Be honest with yourself. It's not your fault that you feel that way. Your whole culture has conditioned you to it. Admit it, Jay. If you can admit it to yourself, you can face it and overcome it."

"I don't know what you're talking about," Palmer protested, perhaps a bit too strongly.

"You really want Dirk to be jealous," Robin said.

Palmer squirmed. "Why should I want that?" he said. "I've got nothing against Dirk personally."

"Of course not. That has nothing to do with it. But in your culture, men have been taught to measure themselves against other men. If Dirk *is* jealous of you, then it means that you're one up on him. But if he isn't, it means something very bad—that you're not even enough of a man to make him jealous of you."

"That's a horrible way of looking at things!" Palmer snapped. "That's looking at life as if it were one endless dogfight...."

"You're right," Robin said quietly. "But honestly, isn't that the way you've been looking at it all along? I've told you that Dirk wouldn't be jealous, and Dirk has as much as told you. So doesn't this pointless competitiveness have to be coming from inside *you?*"

Palmer was silent for long moments. It was hitting home. I don't really want to take her away from Lingo, he thought, and Lingo must know it. So why should I be jealous of him, or he of me?

Yet when he looked at his own feelings, he was forced to admit to himself that he *would* feel some kind of deep sense of inferiority if Lingo was not jealous at all, almost a sense of insult. It would be as if Lingo were to say "You're not enough of a man for me to even worry about."

It hurt to admit it, but Robin was probably right.

"Maybe... just maybe," he muttered, "maybe you've got a point."

She smiled up at him, and layed her hand gently in his. "I know it took a lot of guts to admit that, even to yourself," she said. "And *that's* what really makes a man a man, not butting antlers together. If you've really learned that, Jay, I think you can really begin to understand that there can be people who are different from you, whose entire culture and psychology and values are built on entirely different premises, and yet who are not really alien, not *less* human than the people of the Confederation but *more* human."

"You, eh?" he said quietly. "Well, you might just be right. Let's go on up to the common room. As long as we're being so honest, I've got to admit that I won't be really convinced that Dirk won't take a swing at me until he *doesn't.*"

Lingo gave Palmer a knowing smile as he and Robin entered the common room together. Bergstrom was there too, and Palmer flushed and gave the telepath a dirty look that was a half-question.

Lingo caught the look and laughed warmly. "No, Jay," he said, "you've been enjoying complete mental privacy, and you'll continue to enjoy it for as long as you want to. Of course, if there is any... uh... particularly pleasant experience that you want to share with the entire Group, Max and Linda *can* link all our minds together. But that kind of thing is always strictly voluntary."

"You don't... er, mind?" Palmer blurted "I mean...."

"Why should I?" Lingo said, giving Palmer a smile of deep and genuine friendship. "I haven't lost a thing, and I can see that *you've* gained a lot. Why shouldn't I be happy for you? You're feeling ten times better than you did, more relaxed, calmer. I can see it myself. It sticks out all over you."

"I don't think I look any different," Palmer mumbled.

"Jay, to a trained eye like mine, it's written all over you. For instance, your muscles are all more relaxed—I'll bet your neck size, for one thing, is at least a sixteenth of an inch smaller now than when you came aboard. You're walking differently too—more flatfooted; before, you were way up on the balls of your feet. In dozens of little ways, you're different now. More relaxed, less tense, less hostile."

Palmer laughed nervously. "But you scare me more than ever, Dirk," he said, and he meant it more seriously than not. Only after Lingo had pointed them out, did he notice the changes in his posture and muscle-tone. It must be part of what they called the "Leadership Talent." How many more unknown abilities did these Talents imply?

"You still find us pretty alien," said Bergstrom, "which is understandable. But I think you've come to realize that *alien* doesn't have to mean wrong. A subtle change, but a significant one. And we can prove it to you. Come on over to the telekinesis table."

Bergstrom, Lingo, Robin and Palmer gathered around the table.

"We know a hell of a lot more about *what* telepathy can do, than we do about *why*," Bergstrom said. "But we do know that state of mind and emotional calmness do affect performance, somehow. You remember, when you tried the 'sand' before, you were only able to move a few grains. Raul, who has only the minimal amount of latent telepathic Talent that you do, was able to spell out his initials. Of course, some small part of the difference was simply practice, but the fact that Raul felt a part of an Organic Group was what really made the difference. There is something about degree of involvement in a Group that effects performance."

"Go ahead, Jay," Robin said. "Try the green grains. Just try to flatten the pile out. You're in for a little surprise."

Palmer grinned self-consciously, and fixed his attention on the conical pile of micro-polished steel balls. One, two, three, four grains trickled down the slope of the pile. Five... nine... fifteen....

He strained his mind as hard as he could, willing the particles of steel to tumble down the slope, somehow drawing on the desire of the others to have him succeed. Twenty-five... thirty... fifty....

Palmer exhaled deeply, in exhaustion and satisfaction, and looked up from the table.

The green pile was nearly flat.

"I'll be damned!" he muttered. "It works!"

Robin kissed him with great mock ceremony on both cheeks. "I hereby dub thee honorary Solarian and member of our Group," she laughed.

Palmer grinned and made a little mock bow. He really did feel accepted, though, and he found himself accepting the acceptance.

Yet there was something very peculiar about the whole thing. An Organic Group was apparently a very tight-knit social unit. In a very real sense, these Solarians were a *family*, or at least the Solarian equivalent.

So why should they be so willing to accept an outsider into the Group? Why should they, moreover, go to such pains to see to it that the outsider *did* join the Group?

There *had* to be some ulterior motive. But what? It couldn't be fear — there was obviously nothing he could do to harm them, not with two telepaths around. It had to be something involved with the mission itself. But what was the *real* mission in the first place?

Personally, his attitude towards the Solarians had softened, but the original mystery remained.

Palmer strolled in the corridor past Lingo's cabin. He noticed that the door was open. Lingo was sitting in a chair, reading a book. He was alone. Maybe this was the chance he had been waiting for....

"Dirk?" Palmer said, stepping inside. "Got a moment?"

"Sure, Jay," Lingo said, laying the book down open on his lap, "Sit down."

Palmer sat down on the edge of the bunk.

"I'll be honest with you, Dirk," he said. "Personally I like you, but I still don't trust you, and I don't trust what you're doing. Not that I don't trust you personally, but I don't trust the motives of Fortress Sol."

Lingo smiled. "In your position," he said, "I'd feel the same way. You're a soldier, and according to what Max and Linda read of your mind, a damned good one. By now, you must know that we knew quite a bit about you before that General Staff meeting, and we wanted you to come with us on this mission all along. As I say, though, I can sympathize. After all, if it came down to it, the Confederation would gladly sacrifice Fortress Sol to win The War, wouldn't they?"

Palmer squirmed uncomfortably. He knew it was the truth.

Lingo laughed. "Don't let it bother you," he said. "The Confederation would be *right*, if it had the opportunity to make such a choice. As some ancient once said: War is hell.' What's really bothering you is...."

"Is that I think you could be on your way to Duglaar to make a deal with the Kor," Palmer blurted. "Now I've said it, and I'm glad to have it out in the open. After all, it makes sense. The Doogs agree to let Sol alone, and Sol agrees to stay out of The War, maybe publicly declares its neutrality. You know that if Sol openly declared that the Confederation could never expect The Promise to be fulfilled, all the fight would go out of us. With the way our propaganda has stressed the myth of Sol, the Doogs must know it too. Wouldn't letting one lone human system survive be a price the Doogs would be willing to pay for such an easy victory?"

Lingo grimaced and shook his head. "You don't understand Sol, Jay," he said, "and you certainly don't understand the Duglaari."

"How could we?" snapped Palmer. "You left us to fight and die, to make all the sacrifices, while you sat safe and isolated...."

A dark shadow crossed Lingo's face, and bitter lines came into his mouth. "So *you* made all the sacrifices, eh?" he said savagely. "We've had it easy, huh? Yet you've seen an Organic Group, and you know that Sol has undergone a great social change. You think such changes come about painlessly? MacDay understood the nature of The War, all right. He was a great man, how great you can never begin to imagine. He saw that Mankind was logically doomed. The Doogs had *everything* their way. Not just material and population advantages—they had forced Man into fighting The War on Duglaari terms completely. Their superior computation made the entire Duglaari Empire one hundred percent efficient. Man had to achieve the same efficiency or be swept from the Galaxy in decades, not centuries. So they tried to make men into better Doogs than the Doogs. Not better men, Jay, better *Doogs*. They turned The War over to Computers, *like the Doogs*. They began fighting in a perfectly logical manner, *like the Doogs*. But the Duglaari are a perfectly logical race, and Man is basically *alogical*. Man can *never* be a better Doog than the Duglaari. This is what MacDay saw—that the entire war effort was futile, that it was doomed from the beginning."

"We all know that," Palmer said. "But *some of us* haven't just laid down and waited to die, some of us are at least *trying!*"

"Bah!" Lingo spat, his eyes shooting fire. "Only a fool dedicates himself to a lost cause. MacDay was no fool— he saw that there *was* still one great unknown in The War—the *why* of it! Why did the Doogs start The War? Why did such a completely logical race throw its entire might against Man, when all logic showed that Man could never beat them, that men were no real danger, that the Duglaari Empire was growing at a rate *twice* that of the human race, that if they simply isolated Man for a few centuries, they would outnumber us not four to three, but four or five to one? Yet they *did attack! Why didn't they wait?*"

"I... never thought of that. It seems so obvious, yet...."

"Of course you never thought of it! No one else did. There was only *one*—MacDay! He knew the answer, the obvious answer: the Duglaari are *afraid* of Man, deathly, mortally afraid!'

"What?"

"Think, man, *think!*" Lingo cried, pounding his fist on the open book in his lap. "The Doogs are one hundred percent efficient. Yet even the most casual study of human history shows that, under great enough stress, men can become *more* than 100% efficient! When he is not busy denying his own nature, Man can literally do the logical impossible. History proves it. Man's basic nature is *alogical!* Men will try things that no Doog would attempt, because the Doog would *know* that they were impossible. Yet men will try *anyway*, and sometimes, despite all odds, he will succeed! *This* is what the Duglaari fear. They fear it because they can never understand it. That's why they *must* consider us Vermin.' Because to them, we must either be vermin... *or gods!*"

"But... but how does that explain MacDay's isolating Sol?"

"Remember, Jay, you're talking about one of the greatest men who ever lived. MacDay saw that *Man too* was afraid of his alogical nature. Like the Duglaari, he couldn't understand it either, and so he has always feared it, and tried to deny it. MacDay had a definition of Man as 'the only animal who can never understand himself.' Intelligence fears that which it can't understand.... All human societies have tried to deny Man's alogicality. MacDay knew that Man's only hope was to form a new society, one that would *develop* Man's alogical nature, one that would be thoroughly *human*, as the Duglaari Empire is thoroughly *Doog*. He was too much a part of his people to see what that society would be like, but he knew that Man had to have it or perish.

"So he seized power, and isolated Sol. And then he systematically went about tearing the social order to pieces! All computers were junked. All government, save enough military organization to maintain isolation, was abolished. MacDay threw Mankind off a cliff, into chaos, hoping that he would find a way to fly before he hit bottom. It was the bravest thing any man ever did. The suffering was unimaginable. You cannot begin to comprehend the horrors that were purposely loosed. MacDay *knew* how terrible it would all be. He also knew he would never live to see the outcome, that he would never know whether he would be remembered as a hero, or as the greatest monster in human history. Yet such was his courage, that he did it anyway."

Palmer was shaken to the core. The truth was far more terrible than the enigma had ever been.

"And... and it worked?" he muttered.

"It worked," Lingo said. "Out of the chaos and madness, a new society slowly arose, based on the Talents, based on the Organic Group. It stabilized less than a century ago. There were things that had to be mopped up, things I don't want to even think about. Not until now was the new society ready to do battle with the Doogs. But now we *are* ready. This mission is the first step."

"And this mission... it's not what you told the General Staff, is it? It's something... *inhuman?*"

"No!" exclaimed Lingo. "It's something *totally* human. The strategy of the Confederation is what's inhuman."

"But you won't tell me what it is, will you?"

"No, Jay," said Lingo, his face softening with a strange wistfulness that seemed almost regret. "I know how hard this is on you, but you are not yet ready to understand.

What we are going to do is alogical. You would not understand it; you could only fear it. I can only ask that you trust us. Think of what Sol has gone through to bring this mission about Please, Jay, *please* trust us."

Palmer no longer felt that nagging suspicion of the Solarians' motives. There was no room left in him for that; he was filled with something far stronger: awe... *awe and fear*.

"I'll try, Dirk," he said, "really, I'll try"

"Good, Jay. I...."

"Dirk! Dirk!"

It was Ortega, sticking his head through the door. "We're within the Duglaari Empire now," he said.

Lingo stood up. "Come on, Jay," he said. "We're going to the control room. It's time to come out of Stasis-Space."

Chapter VI

FRAN SHANNON was already seated in one of the pilot's chairs when Lingo, Ortega and Palmer reached the control room. Lingo sat down in his seat and motioned Palmer to one of the dummies, which had been rigged with a microphone from the master radio panel. Ortega took the seat beside him.

Lingo turned on the great hemi-spherical viewscreen, and they were floating in the swirling maelstrom of colors that was Stasis-Space.

"Are you sure we're within the boundaries of the Duglaari Empire, Fran?" Lingo asked.

"Positive," she replied. "We're less than a quarter of a light year from one of their peripheral suns."

"Raul," said Lingo, "you think there'll be a Doog patrol this far out from their central suns?"

"About a ninety percent chance that there will," Ortega said. "Remember, the Duglaari have been on the offensive throughout The War. No human ship has penetrated much beyond the periphery of the Duglaari Empire. So we can figure that they'll concentrate most of their patrols around the periphery of their territory, with the rest of their defensive forces concentrated around the individual solar systems."

"Well, even so, I'd say that our chances of encountering an interstellar patrol are near zero," Lingo said. "So our best bet is to head for that nearby sun Fran mentioned."

"Right, Dirk," Ortega said. "If we get near the outskirts of the system in normal space, we're bound to encounter a Doog systemic patrol."

"Fran, exactly how far are we from that Doog system now?"

"Approximately .221 of a light year, Dirk."

"Close enough," said Lingo. "Prepare to enter normal space."

Palmer could contain himself no longer. "Are you all out of your minds?" he shouted. "What in blazes are you doing?"

"Getting ready to come out of Stasis-Space, Jay," said Lingo evenly. "Didn't you hear me?"

"Can't you think of a pleasanter way to commit suicide?" Palmer snapped. "If we show ourselves this close to a Doog sun, we'll certainly run into a heavily armed patrol!"

"Of course we will, Jay," said Ortega. "That's exactly why we're doing it."

Lingo threw a switch, and the piebald chaos of Stasis-Space was gone. The star-studded blackness of normal space appeared in the viewscreen. A great yellow sun outshone all the other stars, though it was not close enough to show a disc.

"There she blows," said Ortega. "The Doogs favor G-type suns, same as we do."

"Grid, please," Lingo said. Fran pressed a button, and the gridwork of white lines appeared, superimposed on the image of the space surrounding them. The large red circle indicating the ship's line of flight appeared in the exact center of the great viewscreen, and Fran threw a smaller red circle around the Duglaari star with her indicator.

Lingo turned on the Resolution Drive. He adjusted the ship's attitude in space so that the smaller circle surrounding the Doog sun was centered in the larger circle indicating the ship's line of flight. They were headed straight for the Doog sun!

"Lock controls," Lingo said. "Switch on beacon."

"Beacon!" shouted Palmer. "Beacon? Will someone please tell me what's going on? Is everyone crazy? We're heading straight for a Doog system and you turn on the ship's *beacon?* You'll have every Doog ship in the area down on us!"

"That's the whole point," said Ortega. "Naturally, they'd detect us sooner or later anyway, but the beacon'll make it surer and quicker."

"But this is insane! What's preventing us from going all the way to Dugl itself in Stasis-Space? We'd be unde-tectable in Stasis-Space, instead of being sitting ducks, the way we are now."

"Use your head, Jay," Ortega said. "Olympia is the capital of the Confederation, right? It's guarded by a tre-mendous concentration of ships. What if a Doog ship ap-peared at the outskirts of the Olympia system all of a sudden? What do you think the Olympia Systemic De-fense Command would do?"

"Are you kidding? They'd blast it to very small pieces, of course! What do you think they'd do, let it get close enough to Olympia to turn it nova by turning on its Sta-sis-Field Generator?"

"Exactly," said Ortega. "And do you think Dugl will be any less heavily guarded? Do you think the Doogs will be any less trigger-happy? Do you think we'd have any chance at all of getting within two billion miles of Dug-laar without being blown to bits?"

"But... but that's what I've been saying all along!" ex-claimed Palmer. "We don't have a snowball's chance in hell of getting anywhere near Duglaar in one piece! Now you're admitting that the whole mission is impossible?"

"Not at all," replied Ortega. "Merely that...."

"No time for explanations now, Raul," interrupted Lingo. "Look!"

A tiny, dim speck seemed to move perceptibly near the yellow Duglaari sun.

"They're really on their toes, aren't they?" Lingo said. "Let's have a close-up, Fran."

Fran did something with her controls, and the viewscreen surrounding them flickered out for a moment. When the screen went on again, the Doog sun showed a perceptible disc.

And directly ahead of them, was a cloud of tiny lights.

"One... two... twelve... fifteen.... Twenty Duglaari ships!" Ortega said. "Headed straight for us, and closing fast."

"All ahead, full!" said Lingo. "Jay, pick up the mike!"

Numbly, Palmer gripped the microphone. "What're you doing?" he muttered confusedly.

"No time to explain now," Lingo said. "You promised you'd try to trust us, Jay. You've got to do it right now. Here's what I want you to do: tell 'em who you are, and that we're on our way to Duglaar to surrender to the Kor. Keep repeating it. They're in radio range now."

"But...."

"Please, Jay!"

Palmer shrugged resignedly. Okay, he thought, I'll have to trust you now. What else is there to do?

"This is General Jay Palmer, Ambassador-Plenipotentiary of the Combined Human Military Command. We are on our way to Duglaar to surrender the Human Confederation to the Kor. This is General Jay Palmer, Ambassador-Plenipotentiary of the Combined Human Military Command...."

Faster and faster, the Duglaari flotilla came at the Solarian ship. Faster and faster, too, the Solarian ship sped, straight at the Duglaari ships. The closing speed was tremendous, and growing every moment, as both continued to accelerate.

"... We are on our way to Duglaar to surrender to the Kor. This is General Jay Palmer...."

Now Palmer could see that the Doog flotilla had arranged itself in a great hollow hemisphere — terminal battle formation. If the Solarian ship continued on its course, it would be caught in the hollow hemisphere; the hemisphere would become a globe, and they would be squashed by the Doog Fleet Resolution Field....

"Ambassador-Plenipotentiary of the Human Confederation. We are on our..."

The Doogs were almost upon them! The individual ships could be clearly made out now, squat and black and deadly. In a few more minutes, the hemisphere of Doog ships would reach out for them like a monstrous amoeba.

Lingo pressed a button, and after about a minute's hesitation, as the Stasis-Field Generator warmed up, the Doog flotilla was suddenly gone. The stars too, were gone. Space itself was gone, and they were safely back in Stasis-Space.

Palmer sighed deeply in relief. Lingo had snapped them back into Stasis-Space just in time. Another minute or so, and....

"Okay, Jay," Lingo said. "You can relax for a while."

"*Now* will someone please explain why we took such a crazy chance?" Palmer asked.

"Can't you figure it out, Jay?" Ortega said. "We *can't* just pop up outside the Dugl system. Our chances of getting to Duglaar that way would be exactly zero. What we're doing is risky, but it's the only way. We've got to prepare our reception. We've got to make the Doogs curious enough so that they won't blast us the moment we arrive at Dugl. We've at least got to get them to establish contact before they start shooting."

"That's a tall order," Palmer said. "Curiosity is not exactly the Duglaari strong point. They play it safe. And the safe thing for them to do is to blast us out of space and not leave enough left to ask questions of later. You really think appearing like this and announcing ourselves once will get them to hold their fire at Dugl?"

"No," said Ortega. "That's why we've got to do it two more times."

"*What?* But the next time, the Doogs will have been already alerted! It'll be even more dangerous!"

"We've got no choice," Ortega said. "We've got to show them that this appearance was no fluke, that we're *purposely* putting ourselves at their mercy. And to do that, we've got to stick our necks out twice more."

"And what chance will we have of getting to Duglaar, even if we do get away with this game of cat and mouse?" Palmer asked dubiously.

"Not too bad," Ortega said calmly. "Maybe as good as fifty-fifty, if we play things right."

Palmer clutched the microphone grimly. They had reached another Duglaari system. Now they were ready to pull the lion's whiskers a second time. What would the Duglaari have waiting for them *now?*

Lingo pressed the button, and once more, they emerged into normal space.

"There they are!" Lingo exclaimed, pointing to a formation of Doog ships that began to change course in their direction even as he spoke. "That's no patrol, that's a full

Fleet! They're in radio range already, and they're closing fast. We don't have much time. Go ahead, Jay!"

"This is General Jay Palmer, Ambassador-Plenipotentiary of the Human Confederation. We are on our way to Duglaar to surrender the Confederation to the Kor...."

As he spoke, he kept a careful eye on the Doog Fleet, closing with them at ever-increasing speed. There was something strange about the Doog formation. They were awfully close, close enough so that they should already have formed the Fleet into hollow hemisphere formation, in preparation for the englobement action.

But instead, the Doog formation was a flat, one-ship-thick disc, the face of the disc facing straight at them.

".... We are on our way to surrender the Human Confederation to the Kor...."

Suddenly the face of the Doog formation erupted in gouts of flame. Palmer had time to see that a fusillade of missiles was headed straight for them, its speed the sum of the speeds of the Doog Fleet and the missiles' own propulsion systems.

"Get us out of here, Lingo!" Palmer roared. "Now."

"Wha—"

"Hit the button!"

Lingo took one look at Palmer's face, and obeyed the command. He pressed the button that started the Stasis-Field Generator. There was a long minute's delay as the Generator warmed up.

And a tremendous flash of light as the entire barrage of missiles exploded simultaneously, sending a tremendous wavefront of hard radiation straight for the ship at the speed of light.

Then the Doog sun, and the ships and the deadly blast of radiation were gone, and they were safely in Stasis-Space.

"Boy, that was close!" Ortega said. "Another few seconds, and...."

"I still don't quite know what happened, Jay," Lingo said. "How did you know that they were going to use missiles with proximity fuses? I thought they'd either try to englobe us, or actually hit us with a barrage."

Palmer grinned wryly. "Just the voice of experience," he said. "They weren't quick enough to englobe us last time, so it figured they would try to do something faster than an englobement—which an attack with contact-fused missiles is *not*. As soon as I saw those missiles, I knew that they would try to get us with the radiation from a shaped explosion. Remember, a wavefront like that travels at the speed of light, much faster than the missiles themselves could close the gap."

Ortega grimaced. "I wonder what they'll have waiting next time," he said.

"After what happened, you *still* insist on sticking our neck out a third time?" Palmer said, as Lingo once again prepared to plunge the ship into normal space.

"You know that we have to," Ortega said.

"One thing I just don't understand, Raul," said Palmer. "Why didn't we just tell them that this ship is from Sol? Sol's a magic word, even to the Doogs. And especially if their subconscious motivation is fear. Why keep taking crazy chances?"

"Good thinking, Jay," Ortega said. "You're learning, but you haven't learned it all yet. Our identity is our ace in the hole, and we've got to save it for the last hand. The Doogs we're playing cat and mouse with now are very junior commanders. Their orders are to destroy *all* hostile ships, and Duglaari obey orders—*period*. It wouldn't do us any good to tell these Doogs we're Solarians. Our only hope is to get to Dugl in one piece and tell the Duglaari Systemic Defence Commander *there* who we are. Look at it from the Duglaari point of view. They'll know the ship is coming, at Dugl. So they'll have one of their top military men in command of our reception committee. What I'm hoping is that when we tell *him* that we're from Sol, he'll have enough independent authority to hold his fire while he checks with Duglaari—maybe even with the Kor himself. And then, if the Kor is curious enough....

"Makes sense," Palmer said in admiration. Certainly no strategy computer would've been able to reason along *those* lines, he knew. A game of cards, a gamble— something no computer would understand. And the stakes were their lives, and perhaps the fate of the entire human race.

It was a good plan, *if* it worked. The only trouble was that it required another deadly game of cat and mouse. And this time, no doubt, the Doogs would be ready for them.

"Ready to go into normal space," Lingo said. He pressed the button.

Stars appeared. They were in normal space again. In the center of the viewscreen blazed a great yellow sun....

Off to one side of the sun, a point of light suddenly blossomed, then another and another, growing with lightning speed into great blinding pillars of light, straight at them in a terrible, searing, all-enveloping flash of....

Suddenly they were gone. The ship was back in Stasis-Space.

Lingo exhaled heavily, throwing back his head. Ortega whistled in relief.

"What was it?" muttered Palmer.

"*That* was closer than I care to think about," Lingo said. "Mines. Robot mines armed with lasecannon. We use 'em ourselves to cordon off Fortress Sol. They've probably got all kind of detectors—at least ours do. Radar, heat sensors, radioactivity detectors, laser rangefinders, visual pick-ups—you name it! They zeroed in on us in about a minute. The only thing that saved us was the fact that they were several light-minutes away, which gave me just enough time to put the ship into Stasis-Space before the lasebeams hit."

"Now what?" asked Palmer.

"Raul, can we skip it and go right on to Dugl?" Lingo asked.

Ortega stared into the now-comforting chaos of Stasis-Space. "Not a chance," he said finally. "If we go straight to Dugl, they're almost certain to believe that our first appearances were some kind of mistake. And if the Doogs here know we fled the robot mines, they'll leave the mines on automatic at Dugl, and then our chances will be totally non-existent. We've *got* to find some way of communicating with the Doogs here, despite the mines. Question is, how? I...."

"Wait a minute!" cried Palmer. "I think I have it! It's a long shot, but.... Those mines will report contact, won't they?"

"Ours do, anyway," said Ortega. "I think we can assume that the Duglaari robot mines will do the same."

"So there'll be a Duglaari patrol out to investigate, right?" said Palmer.

"Go on, Jay."

"Well, this is going to be pretty hairy, but if we can come put of Stasis-Space *behind* the first Doog patrol, then the Duglaari ships will screen us from the mines. They must have some device which prevents them from firing on their own ships, and if the Doog ships are between us and the mines.... Of course, there'll probably be a second wave of Doog ships, and we'll be sandwiched between them, but we ought to have a minute or so before we have to go into Stasis-Space, if it's timed just right...."

"Man, that's using your head!" exclaimed Ortega. "Maybe you've got it in you to become a Gamemaster."

Palmer grinned. "After all," he said, "I was a pretty good Fleet Commander before I became an expendable General."

"Dirk, you think you can do it?" Ortega asked.

Lingo pursed his lips. "I hope so," he said. "Anyway, we're going to try it. Let's see... the Doog patrol should be on its way by now.... Fran, give me an estimated time on our crossing the Doog patrol's trajectory, assuming that we continue in Stasis-Space at our current heading, and assuming that the Doogs started out from the orbit of the outermost planet, say three minutes ago."

Palmer winced. The idea of submitting such a problem to a human being went against his grain. It was strictly a job for a ship's computer.

But Fran Shannon was the closest thing to a computer that the Solarian ship had. She leaned back inertly in her seat, staring off blankly into space, and although she moved not a muscle, Palmer could sense the furious activity going on in her Eidetic brain.

Finally she looked up.

"Come out of Stasis-Space exactly five and a half minutes from now, Dirk," she said. "Of course, there's no way to be sure, since we're cut off from all external observations when we're in Stasis-Space, but that's the best estimate I can give you."

"It had better be good enough," Lingo said grimly. "Jay, get ready at the mike. You're going to have to do some mighty fast talking."

With thirty seconds to go, Lingo began a countdown. "Start talking as soon as we're out of Stasis-Space, Jay," he said. "Don't even wait to see if the Doogs are there. Twenty-five... twenty... fifteen... ten... five... three... two... one...."

Lingo pressed the button, and they were in normal space.

"This is General Jay Palmer, Ambassador-Plenipotentiary of the Combined Human Military Command...."

As he spoke as rapidly as possible, Palmer could see that there was a flotilla of Duglaari ships between them and the robot mines. It had worked!

"... On our way to Duglaari to surrender the Human Confederation to the Kor...."

He glanced in the direction of the Doog sun, and... there was another formation of Doog ships headed outward! They were boxed in, all right. The inner Duglaari ships fired a salvo of nuclear missiles. They had spotted the ship already! In about a minute and a half, the missiles would be on them!

"This is Ambassador Palmer..." he continued, trying to speed up the set speech as much as possible.

Now the outer Doog flotilla must've spotted them, for they had stopped, turned, and were hurtling towards them. They too let loose a barrage of missiles. The Solarian ship was between two opposing waves of nuclear missiles, like a fly between two immense clapping hands....

"... to the Kor...."

"That's all, brother!" cried Lingo, stabbing the button.

They were back in Stasis-Space. And they were in one piece!

And Ortega was laughing.

"You've got one strange sense of humor, Raul," Palmer said. "We come within seconds of being pulverized, and that's funny?"

"No... no..." roared Ortega. "The Doogs! The outer Duglaari ships fired a salvo of missiles at us; so did the inner Doogs. We're not there anymore, but those missiles sure are! They're headed straight for the two Doog fleets!" He clapped his hands together. "*Pow!*" he cried. "I suppose only a few missiles will really get through, but those Doog commanders reacted a little *too* quick. They're going to have some mighty fancy explaining to do about why they shot up each other's fleets!"

"My heart bleeds for 'em!" said Palmer.

"Well, thanks to you, Jay," said Lingo, "we've won the cat and mouse game handily. But that's only round one. Next stop—*Dugl!*"

Chapter VII

EVERYONE was gathered in the control room. Lingo and Fran were in their control seats. Robin Morel and Linda Dortin sat in the dummies. Max Bergstrom stood next to Linda and Ortega and Palmer flanked Lingo.

This was it.

The long voyage was moments away from being over. When Lingo presses the button, Palmer thought, we'll be right outside the Dugl system. He glanced at each of the Solarians in turn. Max and Linda were wrapped up in each other. Fran Shannon studied her control panel. Robin's lips overlapped slightly as she stared at the base of Lingo's head. Ortega was gazing blankly into the meaningless chaos of Stasis-Space, his mind busy elsewhere.

Lingo's eyes were on his instruments; his finger poised over the button that would snap them back into normal space.

Much to his own surprise, Palmer felt a wave of affection for the six Solarians sweep over him. He recognized the emotion; he had felt it many times before, just before going into battle with his old Fleet. It was the tight-knit comradeship of men who have faced death together before and are about to face it again; the silent, unspoken group loyalty of a battle-blooded crew.

Whatever was going to happen, whatever the rest of the enigmatic Solarian plan might be, he and the Solarians had faced the Doogs together, and, fighting together, they had survived. Whatever the vast gap in their cultures was, they were all human beings, and they were going to the very midst of the enemy, alone and together.

In a sudden burst of insight, Palmer understood what it must be like to truly be a part of an Organic Group. It was this pre-battle feeling, this closeness forged by the imminence of mortal danger, this unvoiced mutual trust and dependence, not for a moment, not only in the face of death, but always and forever. It was something very alien.

But it was *good*.

"Okay," said Lingo, a microphone in one hand, the other poised over the button, "this is it."

He pressed the button and they were in normal space.

The first thing that caught Palmer's eye was Dugl. A yellow sun, slightly smaller than Sol, with six planets. The second planet of that inconspicuous little star had spawned an incomprehensible race, an empire dedicated to the extermination of all men everywhere. Either the children of the second planet of Dugl must perish, or the children of the third planet of Sol must face extinction.

The second thing he saw was ships.

Hundreds of ships; the bulgy, dead-black, somehow-unlikely-looking warships of the Duglaari Empire. They were arranged in an immense hollow hemisphere between the Solarian ship and their home sun.

Palmer gasped in dismay. There must be three full Fleets combined in that formation, he thought. Three full Fleets combined into one super-Fleet, with a Fleet Resolution Field that could crush this one little ship into a tiny ball of fused metal in less than a minute, if it ever englobed them.

Lingo stared coldly at the great hemisphere of ships, the mike in his hand activated, but his voice silent.

Like a great, grabbing amoeba, the Duglaari Fleet began to move.

Straight for them, it came, accelerating under full Fleet Resolution Field power, faster and faster, straight at them, until it was a vast wall of ships, filling the entire field of vision of the huge hemispherical viewscreen. Closer and closer, expanding towards them like the vast cloud of superheated gas and deadly radiation of ah exploding star.

Finally, Lingo spoke. His voice was filled with a cold, terribly inhuman, preternatural power.

"Soldiers of the Duglaari Empire! This is a peaceful mission. This ship carries an Ambassador-Plenipotentiary from the Human Confederation come to discuss surrender with the Kor of all the Duglaari. This is a peaceful mission; we have no desire to fight."

A new note of ghastly, contemptuous arrogance came into Lingo's voice, as if he had suddenly been possessed by some omnipotent demon.

"Do not disturb the peace of this mission," he said, speaking as if it were an order. "You attack this ship at your own peril. We bear an Ambassador from the Human Confederation, yes. But this is not a Confederal ship.

"This ship is from Fortress Sol"

Palmer stared at Lingo in rapture. There was a terrible quality of *command* in that voice, the kind that men follow to the death, the kind no one can but obey. It certainly awed *him*. But how would it effect the Doogs?

For a few moments, the Duglaari Fleet continued its inexorable engulfment. Then it slowed, and finally it stopped. The great Duglaari Fleet hung motionless in space, dead still and silent.

The hush in the control room seemed one with the stillness outside.

Ortega stared at the immobile Duglaari warships, black and menacing. "Well," he finally said, "we're obviously still alive. I think we can assume that the Doog commander is talking it over with Duglaar, and probably with the Council of Wisdom itself. Question is, will the Kor be curious enough now to let us through?"

"Don't you think Dirk layed it on a bit thick, Raul?" Palmer said. "After all, it was all a bluff. Wouldn't the Kor be prone to call it, more than anything else?"

"You're thinking like a human being, Jay," said Ortega. "You're attributing human emotions to a Doog. Talk that way to a man and he'll probably take a swing at you. But a Doog will weigh the situation logically. One: we've engaged in two skirmishes already, and we've made no hostile move. Two: we're sticking our heads in the lion's mouth deliberately — they could destroy us any time they want to, and we must know it. Three: Dirk's manner of speaking completely contradicts points one and two. Therefore, no logical conclusion is possible. This should bother the Duglaari no end, because the concept of bluff is something they just don't have. And the Doogs are very cautious types. I don't think they'll want to destroy an enigma until they understand it. At least, let's hope so...."

"Look!" cried Robin.

One of the Duglaari ships was breaking formation and moving slowly towards them.

"Looks like the flagship," Palmer muttered.

"This is it."

The Duglaari flagship stopped about halfway between the Doog fleet and the Solarian ship.

Suddenly a voice came in over the radio, a strange, flat voice, curiously devoid of overtones and emotionally dead:

"Sol vermin that to Dugl itself do come, there their surrender to the will of the Kor to make, this ship to Duglaar follow must you, there your fate from the Council of Wisdom to learn."

"We're in!" shouted Ortega and Lingo.

"Yeah," grunted Palmer dubiously. "But the question is, in *what?*"

The Duglaari flagship began to accelerate inward towards Dugl. Lingo activated the Solarian ship's Resolution Field Generator, and the ship followed in the Doog flagship's wake, taking care not to lag too far behind nor to approach too closely.

They had only been under way for a few minutes when Palmer saw that the huge Duglaari Fleet was also beginning to move.

"Look at that, Lingo!" Palmer said, pointing to the Duglaari Fleet. The great hollow hemispherical formation of Duglaari ships was creeping up behind them. Now the great ring of ships that was the leading edge of the hemispherical formation had actually passed them and was closer to the flagship than they were, so that the Solarian ship was now cupped deep within the great hollow of the Duglaari formation like a pea at the focus of a radar dish.

"You know what this means?" Palmer said. "It means that they can englobe us any time they want to now. In a matter of less than a minute—we'd never have enough warning to warm up our Stasis-Field Generator in time. We're completely in their power."

"Of course," said Ortega. "Did you expect them to let us into the Dugl system under any other conditions? They're playing it completely safe, just in case we got any ideas of trying to nova Dugl by turning on our Stasis-Field Generator. It takes about a minute or so for the Generator to warm up, and by that time they'd have detected it and crushed us with their Fleet Resolution Field. You've got to admire their thoroughness."

"*You* admire it," said Palmer. "It scares *me* silly."

"Know thy enemy," said Ortega. "Do you realize that we're now closer to Duglaar than any human beings have ever been before?"

"Bully for us," muttered Palmer. "Somehow, it reminds me of a bunch of guinea pigs sneaking into a laboratory."

Inward they sped, past the tiny, airless outpost rock that was Dugl VI, the outermost planet of the Dugl system. They passed close by to the base, and Palmer could see that a great part of the tiny planet was a deepspace field, thick with hundreds of ships.

Dugl V and Dugl IV were great gas giants, with extensive systems of satellites, much like Jupiter and Saturn. Still they sped inward, ever closer to Duglaar itself, and as they approached the home planet of the Duglaari, Palmer felt his uneasiness growing. At least the Solarians knew what they were going to try to do, once they reached Duglaar. But he knew nothing. The Solarians had one unknown to deal with: the Duglaari. He had two. He felt more estranged from the Solarian Group than at any time since that night with Robin. But he *had* to trust them, or be trapped between two groups of aliens. This was the payoff, the climax of the whole mission. He only wished he knew what the mission was.

Dugl III was an Earth-sized planet, about an A.U. and a half from Dugl, and about the temperature of Mars. Palmer could see that great domed cities were laid out regularly on its surface, making weirdly regular geometric designs. Great green rectangles, hundreds of miles long, alternated on its surface with similar rectangles of what looked like yellow desert. It was as if the entire planet were being farmed according to a single, unified master plan.

As they crossed the orbit of Dugl III, Lingo checked his instrument panel, and looked up with a grim smile.

"Well, they've finally done it," he said to Ortega.

"Done what?" asked Palmer.

Lingo pointed to a series of dials which were fluctuating wildly and glowing red. "Those are our counter-peepers," he said. "According to them, the Doogs are now giving the ship a thorough going-over with radiation detectors. They're making sure we don't have a critical mass of radioactives aboard. Making sure we don't have a fusion bomb."

"They think of everything, don't they?" said Palmer.

"Everything but the unthinkable," Ortega replied enigmatically.

The planet was shrouded in a heavy cloud cover, so heavy that its surface features were almost entirely obscured.

"Solarians!" said the voice of the Doog Commander. "You this ship to the landing place follow must. A thousand lase-cannon trained on you are. Any deviation from approved course your destruction immediately resulting in will."

"His English may be lousy," said Lingo, "but he makes himself *very* clear."

The Doog flagship began to spiral downward into the atmosphere of Duglaar, with the Solarian ship following closely. At about ten thousand feet, they broke through the cloud cover, and the surface of Duglaar was visible to human eyes for the first time in history.

It was, of course, an anti-climax. All inhabited planets look very much alike from ten thousand feet up.

Palmer could see a coast—water looked like water everywhere. The Duglaari ship descended towards a large city on the flat coastal plain. There was something very strange about the city that he could not quite put his finger on. It was somehow too... too geometric. As they got closer, he could see that the city was arranged in inhumanly neat concentric circles, with arterial roadways radiating from the periphery of the smallest and innermost circle at regular intervals, like the degree markings on a compass. It looked more like a diagram of a city than a city itself.

The innermost circle was perhaps a mile or two in radius, and the Duglaari flagship headed straight for it, coming in to a neat landing a few hundred yards from a huge, ugly, boxlike building.

Lingo followed it down, and landed the ship beside it. Human beings had at last reached the surface of Duglaar.

From the ground, the capital of the Duglaari Empire was a singularly ugly and unimpressive sight. Architecture, as an art, seemed totally unknown. They were on a large open landing field, enclosed by a very functional-looking fence running around the entire circumference of the innermost circle.

Within the circle was a gigantic glass box of a building, flanked by accretions of smaller buildings, which varied only in size from the main structure. Scattered among them for variety were several large silvery globes on stilts.

The rest of the large city, stretching out beyond the horizon in all directions, seemed merely an endless repetition of the buildings within the fence. Great glass boxes and silvery globes on stilts, mile upon mile of them, varying only in size, as far as the eye could see, completely uniform in shape and ugliness. The sky was a dull blanket of thick cloud, diffusing the light of Dugl into a dirty, gray, colorless wash.

The whole hideous effect was like the dream of a boorish monomaniac; a painting in dirty and muted pastels by a totally untalented abstract artist. It would've made the worst pre-stellar Terrestrial industrial slum look like a riot of gay spontaneity.

"Welcome to the gay, carefree capital of the Duglaari Empire," groaned Robin Morel. "Ugh! This is enough to justify a war of extermination, all by itself!"

Somehow, the remark seemed no more than a statement of sober fact.

"And here comes the reception committee," said Max Bergstrom.

Squat, tank-like vehicles were pouring out of one of the smaller buildings and racing across the landing field. There must've been nearly two dozen of them, all mounting wicked-looking portable lasecannons. The tanks ringed the ship, trained the muzzles of their lasecannons inward towards it, and ground to a halt.

About a half dozen Duglaari disembarked from one of the vehicles and trotted towards the ship on their long, powerful legs. From this distance, it was hard to make out their features, but easy enough to spot the long-barreled energy rifles that all but the Doog in the lead were carrying.

"Raul, Jay, let's go down to the airlock and greet our guests," Lingo said,

By the time they had reached the airlock, the Doogs had reached the ship and the leader had climbed up to the airlock door on a movable ramp. As soon as they opened the airlock, they found themselves face to face with their first live Duglaari.

The Doog, at first glance, seemed to be all limbs and neck. He was an upright biped, with two arms, two legs, no tail and one head. That seemed to be the extent of his resemblance to a human being.

The legs were long and powerful, and covered, like the rest of the body, with a fine brown fur. They sprouted from a small, spherical body about the size and shape of a large, hairy beachball. Two long, muscular arms grew abruptly from the equator of the spherical body, ending in large, six-digited hands, with two opposable thumbs.

A long, apparently flexible neck supported a large triangular head, which sported two enormous, bat-like ears. The face, the only part of the creature not covered by the fine brown fur, consisted of two large red eyes with black irises on either side of one huge nostril set flush with the leathery brown skin, and a disconcertingly human mouth.

The Doog stood roughly the height of a man, and was dressed in short black boots, and a plain, armless and legless dun-colored smock.

He pushed his way past them and stood to one side while ten more Doogs poured through the airlock. The only noticeable difference between them and the first Doog was that they wore gray smocks and carried ugly-looking energy rifles.

"Who's in charge here?" barked Lingo.

The Doog in the dun smock glared at him unblinkingly; not a difficult task, since his eyes had no lids.

"I am *Haarar* Ralachapki Koris. I am in charge of this squad," said the Doog, in grammatically perfect English, but with a weird lack of regard for syllable stresses.

"You speak quite good English, *Haarar* Koris," admitted Lingo.

"I am a graduate of the Institute of Human Studies. It is part of my function to be able to distort my speech-patterns in the approved human manner," Koris said, pronouncing every syllable independently, clearly and with absolute equality of stress.

Palmer somehow instantly preferred the mangled English of the Fleet commander.

"Is this your largest room?" asked Koris.

"Of course not. Why?"

"This cubicle is too cramped for us to remain for any length of time," Koris said. "As you must know, you vermin have a decidedly unpleasant odor. Prolonged confinement in such close quarters with human vermin would tend to produce in my digestive tract a disturbance analogous to what you call nausea. That would not be desirable."

Palmer clenched and unclenched his fists convulsively, but Lingo and Ortega seemed unruffled.

"As any fool can plainly see," Lingo said dryly, "this *cubicle* is an airlock, designed only for entering and leaving the ship."

"Not being 'any fool,'" said Koris, with utter lack of humor or rancor, "I would not be privy to such data. Let us continue this discussion elsewhere. Already it is possible for me to detect tiny but undesirable tremors beginning in my digestive tract."

"We'll go to the common room, then," said Lingo. "Please do us the courtesy of not vomiting on the rug."

"You are due no courtesy, vermin," said Koris, following Lingo into the corridor and motioning his troops to follow. "Nevertheless, I will endeavor to refrain from emptying my digestive tract. The wasting of nutrients is not desirable."

The other Solarians were already in the common room when they arrived; Lingo, Ortega and Palmer in the lead, Koris and his troops immediately behind. As soon as

Koris had his head inside the room, he shrilled orders to his troops in a language that hurt the ears—tremendous variations in pitch, but absolutely constant in volume and totally devoid of stress differentials.

The ten armed Doogs spread themselves out along all four walls at regular intervals, completely boxing the seven humans in. They trained their energy rifles inward and stood, immobile and ready.

"I was not informed that there were so many of your vermin on this ship," Koris said, in his emotionless monotone. His great membranous ears jiggled convulsively, perhaps a sign of some unreadable emotion.

"It wasn't any of *your* business," Lingo snapped.

"You are on the planet Duglaar, vermin," Koris droned, his voice unchanging, but his ears flapping madly like the wings of a bat. "You are prisoners of the Duglaari Empire. It is not your function to decide what is my business and what is not. It is not your function to dispute the statements, questions or orders of an officer of the Duglaari Empire. You are prisoners. Your functions are to obey my orders and answer my questions; nothing more and nothing less."

"We are *not* prisoners," Lingo said.

Koris screeched something in Duglaari. The guards snapped to full alert, their six-fingered hands tightening on their guns.

"If you try to escape," Koris said, "you will be killed. Should you somehow regain control of this ship, it will be destroyed by the armed vehicles surrounding it. In the statistically improbable event that you manage to get it off the ground, a thousand lasecannon are already zeroed in on it. In the one chance in seven point three that you do reach the upper limits of the atmosphere, the three full Fleets patrolling the planet will surely...."

"That's quite enough," snapped Lingo. "I'm convinced that we can't escape. Spare me the gory details."

"The quantity of gore produced is entirely up to you, vermin," Koris said. "You are to fulfill the proper functions of prisoners or face instant death."

"I *told* you, we're not prisoners. We're a diplomatic mission and we demand to be treated as such."

"You are prisoners," droned Koris. "You are enemies. You are within the territory of the Duglaari Empire. Therefore you are prisoners. There is no other possible classification for you to occupy. I do not comprehend this concept of diplomatic mission."

"I see my error," Lingo said evenly. "I shouldn't have expected you to understand the concept. It is something beyond you. You are a soldier, eh? What is your function?"

"You are right, vermin," said Koris, the motion of his ears dampening somewhat, "I am a soldier of the Duglaari Empire. My function is to cause the enemies of the Empire to suffer defeat and destruction. A soldier's function is to destroy the enemy."

"What's he trying to do," Palmer muttered *sotto voce* to Ortega, "get us killed?"

"Shut up," Ortega hissed. "He knows what he's doing."

"Is it ever a soldier's function to surrender?" asked Lingo.

"I have not been taught the concept," replied Koris.

"I didn't think so," said Lingo. "Surrender means to disarm oneself and give oneself over to the enemy in the hope that the outcome of such action will be preferable to the outcome of continued fighting."

Koris batted his ears furiously. "Only vermin have need of such a concept. Such a concept is superfluous to

the soldiers of the Duglaari Empire, since the only outcome of continued fighting possible is eventual Duglaari
victory. It is undesirable for my proper function to even
possess knowledge of such a concept. Therefore, I shall
have it erased from my memory as soon as this unpleasant task is completed."

That really got him going! Palmer thought. Now he
could sense what Lingo was doing. Logic was the Duglaari strength; might it not also be their weakness?

"So you would say that surrender is something you do
not even wish to consider, something you are not
equipped to comprehend?"

"Surrender is a concept for the use of vermin only, a
derangement of the inferior human brain to which a Duglaari soldier is immune."

"Well," drawled Lingo, "it just so happens that we are
here to surrender the entire Human Confederation to the
Duglaari Empire. Try comprehending *that!*"

Koris said nothing, but his ears suddenly wilted, as if
their supporting cartilage had turned to jelly.

Palmer grinned grimly. Obviously, the creature was
shocked at the concept of surrendering one's entire race
to the enemy. And who could blame him!

"Well," said Lingo, "what's the matter? Aren't you
equipped to consider this proposal?"

"I am not," droned Koris, his ears coming to furious
life.

"You mean to tell me," snapped Lingo, "that all you
Doogs are so stupid that none of you can consider a simple offer of surrender?"

Koris flapped his ears madly. "Cease your arrogance,
vermin," he droned. "The Council of All Wisdom can
comprehend all things. Such alien concepts as you sug-

gest are clearly within the function of the Council of Wisdom to deal with, rather than a soldier such as myself."

"You mean you intend to take us before the Kor and the Council of Wisdom?" Lingo cried, in great mock surprise.

"You are correct, vermin," said Koris, his ears at last at rest. "The Council and the Kor will know how to deal with this bizarre matter."

"I see we have no choice," sighed Lingo. "If you'll give us time to change into the proper clothes...."

"What you are wearing now will be quite sufficient," Koris said.

Lingo shrugged. "Suit yourself," he said. "Of course you must realize that these clothes are full of human microscopic parasites, and the clothes I mentioned are completely sterilized. I admire your courage, if not your prudence."

"You will change into the sterile clothes, vermin."

"Very well. The six of us will be ready in a few minutes."

"I count seven of you, vermin."

"*Please*," whined Lingo, rolling his eyes horribly, "there are only *six* of us — four men and two women."

"You are demented, vermin. There are *three* females: one with brown top-fur, one with red and one with yellow."

All the Solarians except Linda Dortin moaned horribly and wrung their hands.

"What is going on?" demanded Koris.

Lingo sighed, and said to the other Solarians: "He's an alien, after all. What can you expect?" Then he turned to Koris.

"The blond woman you claim to see does not officially exist," he said. "Not for the past two days, and not for two days to come. It is a part of human functioning, but there is an absolute taboo against even mentioning it. The non-existent woman must remain on the ship. To do otherwise would be an unthinkable insult to your Kor, and both we and yourself would have to answer for the terrible consequences."

Koris stood silent for a moment, apparently digesting this new evidence of human illogicality.

"Very well," he finally said. "The yellow-haired female may remain on the ship. Escape is impossible, and in any case, she can be as easily disposed of here as in the Hall of Wisdom."

"Disposed of? What are you talking about?"

"Do not further display your stupidity, vermin," droned Koris. "You have penetrated to the surface of Duglaar itself. You are to actually view the interior of the Hall of Wisdom. Surely you must realize that no human vermin can possibly be permitted to retain the data you now possess. There is, after all, a probability of one in several trillion that you might somehow escape. That probability must be reduced to exactly zero. Therefore, as soon as the Kor and the Council of Wisdom have finished interrogating you, you will of course all be immediately killed."

Chapter VIII

LINGO ducked into his cabin and emerged carrying a pile of clothes. "Here, Jay," he said, "put it on."

"What is it?" Palmer asked dubiously. The clothing seemed to be some kind of garish uniform, all green and scarlet and gold braid.

"Dress uniform," Lingo muttered. "Let's say we... uh... anticipated that you might need it, so we had one made."

Palmer fingered the uniform sourly. "Doesn't look like anything *I've* ever seen."

"Just put the thing on," Lingo said impatiently. "It's been designed for psychological effect, not for elegance. We've got to create a certain impression, and that Ambassador's uniform is part of it. No time to argue about it now. Just hustle it on, and get back to the common room before our Doog friends start getting trigger-happy."

Then Lingo stepped into his cabin and slammed the door behind him.

Palmer stood self-consciously for a moment just outside the common room. He looked and felt like a comic-opera field marshal. The uniform had bright green pants and shirt, heavy gold-braided epaulets, a Sam Browne belt fastened by a gigantic ornate brass buckle, calf-length black boots tooled in gold and green, a snow-white cap with brass braided visor, and a long flaming scarlet cape. A square foot of ribbons adorned the tunic's breast.

Sourly, Palmer wondered why Lingo had failed to supply a ceremonial sword.

The Solarians were already in the common room, and *their* uniforms seemed designed to make Palmer feel even more ludicrous. All but Linda Dortin, who was to remain on the ship, were dressed in black from head to toe, dead, totally unadorned black; plain black boots, black cotton pants, and black leather shirts. They were bareheaded, and the only insignia on them was a tiny golden sunburst on the left breast.

Somehow, the total effect was terribly sinister and infinitely earnest; a uniform that was not quite a uniform — almost a priest's habit. But dark indeed would be the rites led by such priests....

As they looked him over approvingly, it was painfully obvious that the Solarians were suppressing their laughter only by the most heroic efforts.

Even Koris, as he surveyed the peacock in the nest of falcons, seemed moved by some unreadable emotion — his head weaved erratically on the end of his long flexible neck, and his ears twitched convulsively.

"Come, vermin," Koris droned. "We proceed to the Council of Wisdom."

As they stepped down onto the concrete of the field, onto the surface of Duglaar itself, the sheer strangeness of the place hit Palmer with its full force. The city, spread around them as far as the eye could see, glass and metal in the dull gray light, seemed more a gigantic factory or monstrous machine than a city as such — Palmer could not conceive of a park or amusement section, a lake or even a stray blade of grass in that vast, ugly conglomeration of globes and boxes. There was an indefinable humming regularity about the sounds of the city, as if of an enormous engine, with all parts meshing smoothly.

And the smell of the air — a harsh, chemical, disinfectant smell, the odor of hospitals, of dynamos, of great impersonal public buildings. Not merely an artificial smell, but the odor of artificiality itself.

Palmer shivered convulsively, though the air was quite warm and though he was practically trotting to keep up with the strides of the long-legged Doogs. Robin and Fran were looking around with the same disdainful expression. Half of Max' mind seemed back on the ship with Linda. Lingo and Ortega were also elsewhere, wrapped up in their thoughts, and noticing their surroundings only mechanically.

Now they were nearing the entrance to the Hall of Wisdom, itself. The main entrance to what was, in a sense, the capitol building of the entire Duglaari Empire, was simply a large rectangular hole in the smooth plastic wall.

"Enter, vermin," ordered Koris.

Instead of the great open area that one would've expected the entrance of a large public building to open onto, Palmer and the Solarians found themselves in a small sealed chamber. The open entranceway was the rear wall; the two side walls were translucent and featureless plastic.

The wall facing the entranceway consisted of ten closed panels, each with a small light over it, and what looked like the coding board of a small computer.

Koris made straight for the coding board and manipulated the typewriter-like series of buttons built into the console.

"I have coded us into the Council of Wisdom," Koris informed them. "We will now await our directives."

After a few moments, the lights over two of the panels lit up, and the panels slid upward, revealing smooth-walled tunnels, with moving-strips for floors. A quick clatter came from the computer-console, and a few lines of curlicued Duglaari letters appeared on the little screen above the incoding buttons.

Koris glanced at the message on the screen.

"Vermin, take the right-hand input channel," he droned. "Soldiers of the Empire will take the left. We leave you now, vermin. You have been coded into an input channel of the Council of Wisdom. Do not suppose that you may deviate from directives just because you are unguarded. No guards are required once you are incoded. Any attempt to deviate from directives will immediately result in your destruction. Go."

Lingo led them through the open doorway and onto the moving-strip. As the strip bore them on, into the bowels of the Hall of Wisdom, Palmer glanced back and saw that the panel had slid shut behind them.

The strip carried them inward and, every twenty yards or so, it came to an intersection of three to five separate passageways. But there was no question of choosing which passageway to follow; as they approached each intersection, panels slid down blocking off all passageways but one and the strip carried them through the approved tunnel. The Council of Wisdom itself was carrying them inexorably towards whatever fate awaited them.

Palmer felt as if he were a molecule of water caught up in a highly complicated system of piping. Whatever was operating the "pumping system" was controlling their passage through it simply by closing the proper valves. It mattered not at all that the contents of *this* piping system happened to be sentient human beings, for they had no control over their movements whatever.

As they shot past the various intersections, Palmer was able to catch tantalizing glimpses of sections of the building before the panels slid shut. One passageway opened into a large hall filled with machinery where dozens of Duglaari scurried about at unguessable tasks. Another emptied into what seemed to be a storeroom. He caught glimpses of what might've been computer panels; of a commissary; of things completely beyond his experience.

Finally, the moving strip deposited them in what was patently some kind of waiting room or cell: a small, empty cubicle, containing only a flat, hard bench and a speaker grill set high on one smooth wall.

The panel slid shut behind them, and the speaker came on with an audible click.

"Vermin. You will remain here until the Kor sees fit to interview you. Do not attempt to leave."

Then the speaker clicked off, and they were completely isolated, imprisoned somewhere in the vast bowels of the Hall of Wisdom.

Numbly, Palmer sat down on the bench.

"It... it's not like a building at all," he muttered. "It's like being inside of some gigantic machine."

Lingo grinned sardonically and sat down beside him. "Jay," he said, "you don't know the half of it. Not ten percent of the truth. It *is* a machine. A computer."

"*The whole building?* One computer? But I thought this was the Hall of Wisdom, the Kor's palace and the meeting place of the Council of Wisdom."

"Oh, it's that too, in a way," said Ortega. "But it *is* a computer."

"How can the whole building be a computer and be....?"

Lingo laughed hollowly. "Not just the *building*," he said. "The whole *city*. And in a sense, the entire Duglaari Empire."

"*What?*"

"There are things the Confederation doesn't know about the Duglaari Empire," Lingo said, rising to his feet and pacing up and down the small cubicle. "Things it has been much better off not knowing. MacDay found some of them out—in the beginning, you know, every battle was fought to the death, and we did take an occasional Doog prisoner. Some of these things... well, they were one more good reason for isolating Sol from the Confederation. For if the Confederation should ever learn them...." Lingo shrugged bitterly. "The Confederation now despairs knowing only a small part of the truth—if they knew it all, they'd no longer have the will to continue fighting."

Lingo stopped and stared down at Palmer, his great green eyes heavy with the weight of some terrible burden.

"Jay has a right to know the truth," Robin said. "It's his life that's at stake as well as ours."

"You're right, Robin," said Lingo, with a little sigh. "We owe him *that* much. Jay, what do you know of the history of the Duglaari Empire? The Doogs are creatures of perfect logic; hasn't it ever occurred to you to wonder what made them that way?"

"Wasn't it just an accident of evolution?" Palmer said, knowing at once from the look on Lingo's face that he was wrong.

"No," said Lingo. "Life does not evolve along logical lines. Not unless it takes evolution into its own hands. Which is what happened to the Duglaari at least a millenium ago. We don't know the whole story; what we do know was collected piecemeal from less than a dozen Doog prisoners, and there are great gaps in our knowledge. Apparently, the Duglaari had a great leader, perhaps a millenium ago, perhaps even longer. This Doog made himself the first Kor of all the Duglaari—at that time, it would seem that the office was simply that of absolute dictator. This first Kor was a genius. Unfortunately, he was also quite insane, at least by our standards."

Lingo stood up again, and resumed his nervous pacing, bouncing his voice off the walls as if speaking to no one in particular.

"It's so hard for a human being to comprehend what happened," he said. "Even then, the Duglaari were very different from us, with much less individual consciousness, and more of a sense of collective identity. They were alien, and to *really* understand, you'd have to be able to think like a Doog madman, a paranoiac. This first Kor, like all sentient beings, knew he was mortal and doomed to die. But in his madness, he would not accept it. He was insanely determined that even after death, he would continue to rule the Duglaari Empire forever.

"So he built the Council of Wisdom."

"*Built it?* But the Council is...."

"No it isn't!" Lingo snapped savagely. "MacDay thought it wiser to conceal the Council's true nature, once he learned it. For the Council of Wisdom is not some Duglaari legislature, as the Confederation has been led to believe. It is... *this city.* But it is not a city—it is one immense computer. The first Kor built the computer and gave it total power over the entire Duglaari Empire. We think that there are duplicates of the Council scattered throughout the Empire, deactivated, but ready in case this one should be destroyed, but of course, their locations are the Doogs' most closely kept secret.

"But at any rate, we do know that the Empire has no government, as we think of governments. The computer *is* the government. But it is more than that—remember, the Council of Wisdom is not a complex of computers as you have on Olympia IV, it is not merely a machine for deciding policy. It is one huge, integrated computer, and its output circuits do not feed into data boards—it does not advise, for every military move, every economic move, everything, down to the design of hand-weapons, down to the personal lives of every single Duglaari is dictated by the Council of Wisdom.

"No, the computer does not advise—*it commands!*"

Palmer was completely staggered. "You mean... you mean the Kor is just a figurehead for the Council of Wisdom? The Duglaari Empire is ruled by... *by a machine?*"

Lingo laughed darkly, and his face twisted into an ironic grin. "Nothing as simple as that," he said. "It would be impossible—a computer, after all, is only a logic machine. It can only determine the most efficient means to a given end. But a living being must set those ends. The selection of goals is not a matter of logic. And logic must be founded upon *premises*. No system of logic can set its own premises; therefore, no computer can set its own goals. They must be set by intelligence, *arbitrarily.*"

"In other words," said Palmer, "a computer must be *programmed*. It must be given goals, or it will not act."

"Exactly!" said Lingo. "The function of the Kor is to program the computer. He tells the Council of Wisdom what the goals of the Empire are to be, and the computer runs the Empire accordingly."

"But then the Kor really *does* rule. The Council of Wisdom just takes care of the details."

"Ah, but that's where the madness comes in!" said Lingo, slamming his hand down on the bench. "You see it is the *computer* which chooses the new Kor when the old one dies. *The Council of Wisdom selects its own programmer!* And remember, its control over the Empire is absolute. It determines *everything*. Including breeding. That was the madness and the genius of the first Kor. He gave the Council of Wisdom power over everything, total, absolute, complete power. It was the *computer* which made the Duglaari into a completely logical race—by a millenium of training, indoctrination and selective breeding. In a very real sense, all Duglaari have identical personalities — *the personality of the Council of Wisdom itself!*"

"But why? What kind of monster would make his people over in the image of a machine?"

"A most special monster," said Lingo. "A monster craving immortality. Remember, the original computer could do nothing until it was given goals, until it was programmed. And it was the first Kor who set the original premises of the computer. He created its 'personality' and he used his own mind for the blueprint!"

"I don't...."

"Think, man, think!" cried Lingo. "He made the computer into an image of *himself!* An image with the same madness, the same paranoiac goals and fears, but with the resources of an entire race to accomplish them! And infallible logic, one hundred percent efficiency, to boot. And to complete the circle, the Council chooses its own programmer. It chooses a Kor on the basis of how close his personality is to that of the original Kor — and for a thousand years, it has been breeding the Duglaari so that they are *all* as close to the original Kor as possible. Then it just chooses the most perfect duplicate available. Yes, Jay, the Duglaari Empire is made in the image of a machine, but *that machine* is the image of a being dead for over a millenium."

Palmer sat woodenly on the bench, scarcely daring to think. *This,* then was the true nature of the enemy! Not a government, not even a race, but in a very real sense *one integrated immortal organism!* No wonder the Computation Center on Olympia IV was hopelessly outclassed. It computed strategy for the General Staff, but the Council of Wisdom *was* the Duglaari Empire. The Empire was ruled by... by...?

"But then what *does* rule the Duglaari Empire?"

Lingo laughed sharply and shrugged. "You pays your money and you takes your choice," he said. "In a sense, the first Kor actually succeeded in achieving the mad goal of immortality. The computer rules the Empire. The Kor directs the computer. But the computer chooses and molds to its image, the Kor. And the Council was molded in the image of the first Kor. Is the Duglaari Empire ruled by the Kor? By the Council of Wisdom? *Or by the ghost of a Doog dead a thousand years?* Which came first, the chicken or the egg?"

"And this is what you think you can outwit? Six Solarians against an organism that is an entire empire?"

Lingo stopped pacing. He stared directly at Palmer, and there was a fire in his eyes that instantly made Palmer *believe*, though in what he could not tell.

"*Yes,*" Lingo said, in a whisper that was a shout, "we will fight the computer, the Kor and the whole bloody Empire. We will fight, and we will win! Because we *must*. The Duglaari Empire is a thing insane. A malignant cancer that threatens the death of an entire Galaxy. It must be destroyed, for the sake of all sentient beings everywhere! By the memory of MacDay, by the words of The Promise, a promise that was *meant*, Jay. We will destroy it! We must. We...."

Suddenly, the panel slid open.

"Vermin," droned the wall speaker. "Enter the input channel at once. The Kor awaits you."

The input channel emptied into a cavernous rectangular chamber at least fifty yards in width, a hundred yards long and full three stories high. The moving strip continued on down the length of the great chamber, through a living corridor of immobile and fully armed Duglaari soldiers, hundreds of them, shoulder to shoulder down the entire length of the chamber.

The entire rear wall of the chamber—fifty yards wide and three stories high—was the face of a gigantic computer; hundreds of square yards of controls, punchboards, data panels, tended by an army of Duglaari technicians, clambering over its face on many-leveled catwalks.

Directly in front of this huge complex, haloed by the ever-changing light patterns, was a plain throne-like affair, elevated about three feet off the floor. A ring of small data panels formed a semi-circle around its base.

Seated on the throne, and peering downward at the data panels was one lone and ancient Doog, his brown fur grizzled with gray, a microphone held loosely in one hand like a sceptre—the most powerful single individual being in the known Galaxy—the Kor of all the Duglaari!

As the moving strip carried them inexorably towards the throne, Palmer could sense a terrible aura of power emanating from the being on the throne. This was the will, the might, the mind of an entire race channeled into one individual through the face of the giant computer at his back. It shone through all racial barriers, all inscrutability of alien features. Palmer's heart sunk, and he felt like a fool in his comic-opera uniform.

For *this* was Power.

But a glance around him at the Solarians showed him something far more terrible. In the midst of hundreds of Duglaari soldiers, in the face of the Kor, of power personified, Ortega, Max, Robin and Fran rode the moving strip as if it were a special convenience erected for them out of deference—and a rather inferior one at that. In their ominous black uniforms, with thin smiles of amused contempt on their faces, they looked every inch the representatives of the mystical legend that Confederation propaganda had made of Fortress Sol. They walked as if they owned the universe, and the illusion was so complete, that Palmer found himself believing it too.

But if the other Solarians carried themselves like royalty, Lingo was a god. His blazing green eyes raked the faces of the Duglaari soldiers like the muzzles of twin lasecannon; such was the power in his stare that as he passed, each Doog was forced to avert his eyes—dogs stared down by their master. Lingo held his hands loosely at his hips, his mouth twisted in a grin that was light-years beyond contempt, a scorn that transcended defiance.

Even though a part of him knew that there was nothing to back up the facade, Palmer's soul was vitally stirred by the pretense itself. Their glacial pride might be nothing but a facade, but there was truth in its bravery. And that truth made him deeply proud of his humanity, and prouder still that these magnetic beings from Man's home system had accepted *him* as a part of their Group. Somehow, the importance of the fact that he was likely to never leave this chamber alive receded into a far distance, leaving him filled only with the glory of the moment. They would face the Kor, the Council of Wisdom and the whole Duglaari Empire with every ounce of pride the human race could muster, and somehow, that in itself was a kind of terrible victory.

The moving strip deposited them at the foot of the throne.

"All will bow in deference to the will of all-knowing Duglaar," droned the grizzled Kor.

Hundreds of Duglaari soldiers dipped to one knee as a single organism. Lingo hand-signaled to Palmer to follow suit, and, reluctantly and awkwardly, Palmer obeyed.

But the five Solarians, alone in the great chamber, remained standing.

"Kneel, vermin, to the power of Duglaar," droned the Kor, his leathery ears flapping like monstrous bats. "Know that I am Kor of all the Duglaari. Know that by the Microphone of State in my hand and by the Data Panels of Truth at my feet, I am in direct circuit with the Council of Wisdom itself, the will of the entire immortal Duglaari Empire. We are Duglaar. Know and kneel."

Lingo slouched negligently and in a cold voice, filled with infinitely easy arrogance said: "*Animals* kneel to Solarians, and never the reverse."

The nearest guards sprang to their feet, energy rifles at the ready. But the Kor stopped them with one wave of his hand and motioned the rest of the soldiers to their feet.

"We are not illogical human vermin," he droned. "I have been informed that you are here to surrender. That data has been coded into the Council of Wisdom, and the Council has issued the following directive: The surrender is to be accepted. The Council of Wisdom has computed the following terms of surrender: all human forces are to immediately cease hostilities against the forces of the Duglaari Empire. All solar systems now controlled by human vermin, including the home system known as Fortress Sol, are to be immediately occupied by the forces of Duglaari Empire. All vermin in those systems are hereby deprived of any and all rights as sentient beings. All vermin are forbidden to continue breeding. All vermin are forbidden to possess arms or any other form of personal property. All vermin are hereby declared property of the Duglaari Empire. These are the rules of surrender."

Lingo laughed, long, loud and contemptuously, his voice echoing and filling the otherwise silent chamber. He pursed his lips and spat in a lazy, high arc at the foot of the throne.

Instantly, the guards trained their rifles at him; their fingers squeezing the triggers a hair's breath away from the firing point.

But at that instant, their bodies were frozen to living stone. Only their frantically rolling eyes betrayed their intent. Max Bergstrom stared blankly at them, his gaze deceptively remote and placid. But Palmer knew well what that calm, brown stare meant—the guards no longer controlled their own bodies.

"I fear you are mistaken," Lingo said, in a preternaturally hollow voice that made the words a toll of doom.

"The Council of Wisdom does not make mistakes," the Kor droned with a furious snap of his ears. "The Council of Wisdom is perfectly logical. Its nature does not permit incorrect calculations."

Lingo laughed again, this time with the tolerance of a teacher for a not-very-bright child. "Well, then just let's say that the Council of Wisdom has been supplied with incomplete data."

"If you wish to supply additional data," the Kor said, "do so. This chamber is circuited directly into the Council of Wisdom. Every word you say will be coded directly into an input channel of the Council."

"Excellent," smiled Lingo. "I compliment you on your service. I will now supply the missing data—*our* terms. You see before you an Ambassador from the Human Confederation," Lingo said, pointing to Palmer as to a mess on a rug. "Amusing creatures, perhaps, to some tastes, but no longer of concern to us. We have transcended them as our remote ancestors transcended the primates from which they sprang. These primitive humans of the Confederation are yours to do with as you like. They are no longer under the protection of Fortress Sol."

It took long moments for the meaning of Lingo's words to impress themselves on Palmer's stunned mind. It... *it was all a phony!* Everything the Solarians claimed to stand for! The friendship... the.... It was all a monstrous lie! They were nothing but traitors, cowards, miserable, inhuman....

With a savage and wordless growl, Palmer sprang at Lingo, his hand clutching at the Solarian's throat.

But even as his fingers reached around Lingo's neck, he felt himself losing control over his own body; he felt the tendrils of Bergstrom's mind enfold his own, and against his will, his fingers let loose their grip, his arms drifted to his side, and he found that he could no longer move.

"That will be quite enough," Lingo said, with exasperating arrogance. "Either behave yourself, or Max will have to dispose of you immediately."

Palmer realized it was no use — there was no way to fight a telepath. And quite suddenly, it didn't seem to matter any more. The world had collapsed about him. The Solarians had accepted him as a brother — more than a brother — he had felt something within the Solarian Group that he had never felt before, something fine, and proud and loving.... And it had all been a foul lie! A cheap, cowardly trick, in perfect harmony with everything else the Solarians had done. The Solarians were the perfect traitors — false on every level of their beings, false bravery, false Promise, false love....

The fight was all gone out of him. What was the use? He was alone, more alone than any human being had ever been. Caught between Man's mortal enemy, and the most abominable traitors in all history. What hope was there?

And as soon as he felt this defeated resignation, he felt Bergstrom leave his mind, and return control of his body to him. *Why not?* Palmer thought bitterly. He knows what I'm thinking. He knows that I'm beaten....

"As I was saying before this annoying interruption," Lingo continued, with infinitely smooth arrogance, "we will hand over the Human Confederation to the Duglaari Empire, to do with as you see fit. Sol demands but two token conditions in return."

Lingo ticked off his words on his fingers as he spoke, and his voice changed to that of a dry pedant, to match his gestures.

"One: the Duglaari Empire must sign a treaty of eternal fealty to Fortress Sol. Two: once the Duglaari Empire has occupied the Confederation, you must hand over four thousand of your ships to Fortress Sol as a token of your good faith."

Before his words could stop echoing in the vast chamber, Lingo spoke again, and now there was nothing at all of the pedant in his voice.

"Should you be so *stupid* as to refuse these overgenerous terms," he hissed, sneering threateningly at the Kor, "the Duglaari Empire will have but ten years left to exist. At the end of that time, Sol will be more than ready, and the forces of Fortress Sol will fall upon the Duglaari Empire and annihilate it down to the last living creature. The choice is, of course, up to you."

The Kor sat stupefied for a full minute, only his ears moving in a dance of rage.

"Vermin, do you dare to offer such an ultimatum to the Duglaari Empire?" he finally said. "Do you dare to insult the Kor, the Council of Wisdom and the will of all Duglaar with such proposals?"

Lingo smiled wanly, and gave a diffident little shrug. "The terms are far more generous than you deserve," he said. "Do not try my patience."

"Vermin, you are either a fool or completely insane. The Council of Wisdom has calculated that it will be possible to complete the destruction of the Human Confederation within seventy-eight years. At the end of that period, Fortress Sol will have to face the entire might of the Duglaari Empire alone."

"Long before the end of that period," Lingo said, in a perfect and savage imitation of the Kor's drone, "the Duglaari Empire will have ceased to exist. In ten years, *Sol alone* will be able to crush you to atoms. Let the Council of Wisdom digest *this* data: at present, *at present*, mind you, it would take eight thousand Duglaari warships, more than total existing force, to destroy Fortress Sol. I don't need a computer to tell me the significance of *that*. And that is only *now*. By the end of this decade, Sol will have completed development of weapons that your Council of Wisdom can only dream of."

Lingo rattled off the list like some black litany: "Impenetrable screens of force. Explosives based on the total conversion of matter to energy. A means of detecting and locating ships while they are still in Stasis-Space. A ray that can nova suns from light-years away, without having to come anywhere near them, as you must to produce a nova with a Stasis-Field generator. These are only a few of the more mundane examples. If you do not meet my terms, and meet them *now*, the Duglaari Empire will have vanished in ten years. Let the Council of Wisdom calculate its way out of that!" He finished with a peal of staccato laughter that reverberated off the high ceiling like gunshots.

The Kor was silent. Palmer could sense that he was deeply disturbed from the way his ears seemed to wilt. The ancient Doog shrilled orders in Duglaari to the technicians on the network of catwalks covering the great face of the computer behind him. They scurried furiously to their tasks, setting up the new problems for the computer.

The great chamber was utterly silent, save for the padding feet of the technicians, and the muted noises of the great computer in operation, as the Kor sat immobile on his throne, his eyes intent on the data boards in front of him, waiting for a determination from the Council of Wisdom that was both his slave and master.

After silent minutes that dragged on like centuries, the Kor's eyes came to life. The computer's answers were appearing on his data screens.

As the Kor scanned the screens, the cartilage supporting his drooping ears slowly began to stiffen, until the great ears were once again stiff and erect. He lifted his face and stared intently at Lingo, his glaring red eyes meeting the cold green of Lingo's in what seemed a clash of equal demons.

"The Council of Wisdom has completed, its calculations, vermin," he droned. "As I suspected, it is *you* who have calculated incorrectly. The will of Duglaar will prevail." Somehow, devoid of all gloating, all emotion, the dead, flat voice seemed utterly deadly and final.

"The Council of Wisdom has determined," the Kor continued, "that the weapons of which you have spoken are within the range of possible scientific development. Of course, it is not possible to determine whether or not you can actually produce such weapons within ten years. The Council of Wisdom has calculated that if you do produce such weapons within ten years, you will, as you boast, be able to defeat the Duglaari Empire."

Palmer held his breath. Was it really possible that in spite of everything, Sol would be able to save itself at the expense of the Confederation? Would they really be able to callously trade the lives of hundreds of billions of people for the ten years' time needed to develop the superweapons that could save Sol?

If we die, he thought savagely, then let Sol die with us!

Lingo returned the Kor's stare without displaying any more emotion than a Doog.

"However," the Kor said, after a long and ominous pause, "the Council of Wisdom has calculated that at the present, despite your foolish boasting, it is a mathematical impossibility for any single solar system, including Fortress Sol, to be able to withstand the attack of four thousand warships. Vermin, let me remind you that the Duglaari Empire possesses seven thousand warships. The Council of Wisdom has calculated that three thousand ships will be sufficient to maintain our defensive lines against the Human Confederation, with acceptable losses, during the time necessary for our remaining four thousand warships to proceed in one great Fleet to Fortress Sol and annihilate it completely. Your superweapons of the next ten years will never come into being, vermin. Sol will last not another ten weeks. The Council of Wisdom has already given the orders to marshal the necessary four thousand ships. Within months, all Solarians will be dead."

The Kor leaned forward and eyed the five Solarians one by one. His ears twitched in what might've been amusement.

"It will be a source of considerable satisfaction," he droned, "to commence the extermination process immediately, with the five Solarians now present, as well as their tame ambassador from the Human Confederation. You are to be killed at once."

Chapter IX

DIRK LINGO smiled back blandly at the Kor. "I'm afraid not," he said. "Not unless you want to die with us. You and the Council of Wisdom itself."

"What are you talking about, vermin? The Council of Wisdom covers many square miles. It would take a large thermonuclear device to destroy it."

"Exactly," said Lingo. "And of course, we knew that long before we came to Duglaar. *Max!*" He gestured to Bergstrom, who stepped to the foot of the throne.

Bergstrom stared evenly and blankly at the face of the ancient Doog. Mechanically, he began a screeching drone of incomprehensible syllables in a reasonable human approximation of the Duglaari language.

The Kor's ears began to flap crazily. "How can you know that, vermin?" he droned. "You would have to be reading my mind!"

Lingo nodded to Max, who averted his gaze from the Kor and stopped his ear-jarring recital.

"You're a lot smarter than you look," Lingo cracked at the Kor. "Max is a telepath. He *was* reading your mind. Since you were thinking in Duglaari, and since Max doesn't understand the language, all he got was meaningless sounds. But of course, with someone who speaks English, with, for instance, *another* telepath, he could maintain two-way communication over quite a distance."

"Very interesting, vermin. Thank you for providing us with this additional data before your execution. And now...."

"Just a minute!" said Lingo. "You're missing the best part. If you will check with your *Haarar* Koris, you will learn that one of us was permitted to remain on the ship.

A girl by the name of Linda Dortin—another telepath. She is in direct communication with Max at this moment."

"What of it, vermin? You think it possible for her to escape? The lasecannon at the landing field would incinerate your ship before it got off the ground, and...."

"Oh, she has no intention of taking off," Lingo said with a little smile. "Far from it, she'll wait for us to return unharmed to the ship, before we take leave of your hospitality." He laughed sharply, and sneered self-confidently at the Kor. "And you *will* let us go, you know," he said. "You see, our ship contains quite a large thermonuclear bomb, easily large enough to destroy the entire Council of Wisdom. If Max relays my order, or if we should be killed...." Lingo ran his right forefinger across his throat.

The Kor leaned back, unperturbed. "So you take me for a fool, vermin," he said. "Did you really suppose that we would permit your ship to come anywhere near Duglaar without going over it most thoroughly with radiation detectors? I know very well that there cannot be so much as an ounce of radioactive matter on your ship."

"Perhaps," said Lingo blandly. "Nevertheless, if I were you, I'd do the safe thing and run another check."

"You will do anything to prolong your miserable existence another few moments, won't you, vermin? Very well, to be absolutely sure, we will do another check. But it won't give you very much more time, since the vehicles surrounding the ship are equipped with radiation detectors."

The Kor screeched a few words in Duglaari into his microphone, and then concentrated his attention on the data screens before him.

Suddenly, his ears collapsed and his red eyes rolled.

"The detectors show a large concentration of radioactives on your ship," he droned. "How were you able to get it past the detectors? It is impossible."

"Impossible for *you*, perhaps," Lingo said, with a nasty little laugh, "but then, you are merely a *Doog*. Now then, my hairy friend, the situation is quite clear. Let us go, and you live and the Council of Wisdom survives. Kill us, and you die too, and the surrounding hundred square miles are vaporized in the bargain. The choice is yours."

The Kor shrilled orders to the technicians on the catwalk who busied themselves at the face of the computer.

"I have submitted your proposal to the Council of Wisdom," the Kor said. "We will await its calculations,"

After a few minutes, the Kor looked up from his data screens, and his ears were stiffly erect.

"Very well," he droned. "The Council of Wisdom has completed its determination. You are free to go."

"That's very wise of you," drawled Lingo, eying the Kor narrowly. "But I'd *keep* being smart, if I were you. For instance, I wouldn't be so simple-minded as to let us leave the surface of Duglaar and then blast us as soon as we're far out enough in space for the bomb to be harmless. Because at the first hint of a hostile move, once we leave this planet, we'll just turn on our Stasis-Field generator, and Dugl will go nova."

The Kor's ears flapped with thwarted rage. "So you think yourself clever, vermin? So you have guessed the outcome of the Council of Wisdom's calculations. But you have been too clever, for you have pointed out the essential flaw in your plan. What is to prevent you from turning on your Stasis-Field generator as soon as you leave Duglaar, whether you are attacked or not, thus destroying this entire solar system?"

"It would result in our deaths too," said Lingo. "We don't want to die."

"And why should we believe that?" said the Kor. "While it is true that duplicates of the Council of Wisdom are scattered throughout the Empire, in reserve, they are of course all dormant and unprogrammed, and it would take many months to set up a new one, thus setting back the date of Fortress Sol's destruction by a good many months. How can I know that you would not consider the sacrifice of your lives for this delay a reasonable exchange?"

Lingo smiled. "You can't," he said. "You have to take my word for it."

"Why should I?" replied Kor. "Unless you are willing to take my word. I will permit your ship to leave the system of Dugl, but it will be completely surrounded by a Duglaari Fleet until it is safely beyond the point where it could turn Dugl nova by turning on its Stasis-Field generator. The Fleet will be in a position to crush your ship within its Fleet Resolution Field, and of course it will be close enough to do so in the time it takes a Stasis-Field generator to warm up. As you know, it is a simple matter to detect a growing Stasis-Field before it is large enough to do any damage, thus giving our Fleet sufficient time in which to destroy you. But I give you my word that we will not destroy you unless you attempt to turn on your Stasis-Field generator within the Dugl system."

"And how do I know that you won't just destroy us without waiting for us to turn on our generator?"

The Kor twitched his ears convulsively. "You can't. You have to take my word for it," he said.

Lingo frowned. For the first time, he seemed unsure of the next move. It was obvious that he could not trust the Kor. It was equally obvious that the Kor could not trust *him*. Yet one would *have* to trust the other. Palmer grinned to himself. This time, Lingo had outsmarted himself. In fact, he suddenly realized, Lingo had been fouling himself up all along. The Kor hadn't bought the story about Sol's impregnability—the Doogs would soon be attacking Sol in overwhelming force as a direct consequence of Lingo's arrogant boasting. And now, Lingo had painted himself into a corner!

Palmer almost forgot that it was *his* life Dirk Lingo was bargaining for as well.

"Just a minute, Dirk," said Raul Ortega. "Let me take over for a minute."

He turned to the Kor. "The Council of Wisdom is circuited into this?" he asked. "I've got some tricky calculations for it to do."

"It is," the Kor said.

"Okay," said Ortega. "Basically, here's the situation: First of all, we can destroy the Council of Wisdom, provided we are willing to die ourselves, and *you* can destroy us, if you are willing to see yourself killed and the Council of Wisdom destroyed. But I think it safe to assume that you would rather have the Council survive, just as we would rather survive. You'd be willing to let us get safely away into Stasis-Space as long as you had a guarantee that we would not nova Dugl."

"Of course," said Kor. "The death of seven humans is not worth the destruction of the Council of Wisdom, especially since Sol will soon be destroyed in any event."

"*So...*" said Ortega licking his lips. "The problem is simply one of trust. Both of us prefer mutual safety to mutual destruction, at least we *say* we do. The trouble is, you can't trust *us* not to go into Stasis-Space prematurely, sacrificing our lives but destroying Dugl, and we can't trust *you* not to destroy us with your escorting Fleet as soon as you have the chance. In other words, if the Fleet *is* close enough to destroy us before we can go into Stasis-Space, *we* must trust *you*, and if it isn't, *you* must trust us."

"You have stated the dilemma correctly, vermin."

"Ah!" cried Ortega. "But there *is* a way out. A way that does not require trust on *either* side. Let the Council of Wisdom calculate an exact course for our ship, and for your escorting Fleet, so that the relative positions will be such that it would take *exactly* as long for you to destroy us as it would for us to warm up our Stasis-Field generator and nova Dugl. In other words, should either side make a hostile move, the chances of our ship's being destroyed before we can go into Stasis-Space would be exactly equal to the chances of our turning Dugl nova before we were destroyed. We'd of course check the computer's calculations ourselves, so there could be no tricks. This way, it wouldn't pay for either of us to gamble on a hostile move, since our chances of failure would exactly equal our chances of success."

Palmer's head was swimming. Wheels within wheels within wheels…. Yet there seemed to be something Ortega was missing. But it was too much for him, Palmer thought, and from the look of it, too much for the Kor as well. The great ears of the ancient Duglaari were flapping like crazed bats.

But the Kor, unlike Palmer, did not have to rely on his own brain to unravel the implications of Ortega's proposal. He gestured imperiously with the microphone in his hand, and shrieked a few words in Duglaari.

The technicians tending the Council of Wisdom once again sprang to furious life, setting up the new problem for the great computer.

Silence reigned for long minutes in the cavernous chamber, broken only by the muted clickings and whirrings of the Council of Wisdom at work.

Palmer watched the flickering pattern of lights on the great computer-face tensely. He knew that the outcome of the computer's calculations would determine whether he would live or die, but somehow, after the perfidy of the Solarians, this did not seem terribly important—not when the entire human race was doomed in any case. A part of him wanted to live, but another part of him wanted the Solarian strategy to fail. Revenge was a poor satisfaction when it meant your own death, but perhaps it was better than no satisfaction at all.

And there was *something* that Ortega was missing. Palmer could not put his finger on it; it was little more than a feeling in the pit of his stomach. But somehow he just *knew* that Ortega had overlooked some small but vital detail....

Finally, after what seemed like centuries, the Kor began to study his data screens intently. After a few moments, he looked up, his alien face calm and unreadable, his ears still.

"The Council of Wisdom has completed its calculations, vermin," the Kor said. "It accepts your proposition, with the understanding that any attempt to deviate from the agreed upon course will be met by instant destruction."

"Agreed," said Ortega. "With the further understanding that if any of your ships try to inch up on us, we will immediately activate our Stasis-Field Generator."

"Understood, vermin. You will return to your ship immediately. The guards will conduct you to the proper output channel." The Kor screeched an order in Duglaari, and the ten nearest Duglaari soldiers stepped forward and surrounded the humans. The Solarians turned their backs disdainfully on the Kor and stepped towards the moving strip which led out of the chamber. Five of the guards began to walk in front of them.

The other five stepped between Palmer and the Solarians. Two of them grabbed his arms and pulled him to his knees. The other three raised their energy rifles.

Lingo whirled, his huge green eyes blazing. "What is the meaning of this?" he snapped.

"The Confederal officer who accompanied you is about to be executed," the Kor said blandly. "Nothing more. Return to your ship."

"Just a minute," Lingo said, pointing to Palmer as if he were some inanimate object. "*He* goes with us."

"You have declared that the humans of the Confederation are no longer under the protection of Fortress Sol," the Kor said. "Therefore this officer is not under your protection. Therefore he is a prisoner. Therefore he is to be killed."

"Not so fast," Lingo said. "We agreed to withdraw our protection from Fortress Sol *providing* you met our terms. Since you have not met our terms, the offer no longer holds. Or do I misunderstand you? Are you now willing to turn over four thousand ships to us? If you are, why then…."

"Enough, vermin," the Kor said, with a furious snap of his ears. "You are to be permitted to escape with your lives. Do not attempt to set further conditions. Return to your ship, while you can."

"Don't give me orders, *Doog*," Lingo roared. "This officer came here under our jurisdiction, and by damn, he'll *leave* under our jurisdiction, or I'll give the order to detonate the bomb right now!"

The Kor flapped his ears in rage, but the Duglaari penchant for logic prevailed. "Very well," the Kor said. "It is not worth risking the Council of Wisdom over human illogicality. Take the Confederal vermin and go."

Palmer was jerked to his feet and ushered onto the moving strip with the Solarians. He stared at Lingo with unrelieved loathing. The Solarian *had* saved his life, but only to show his superiority over the Kor. Somehow, Palmer felt more sympathy for the Doog who had wanted to kill him than for the human who had saved his life.

"Sorry about this, Jay," Dirk Lingo said, "but we're going to have our hands full, and we can't take the chance of your doing anything foolish."

Palmer convulsed his muscles against the bonds tying him firmly into one of the dummy seats in the Solarian ship's control room.

"Don't give it a second thought, traitor," he snapped. "You've got much more important things to be sorry about."

Lingo was already preparing the ship for lift-off; Fran Shannon was in her control seat; Ortega sat in the other dummy.

"Things aren't always what they seem, Jay," Lingo said, as the great hemispherical viewscreen was activated.

"*They sure aren't!*" Palmer said. "You people *seemed* like decent human beings, friends... more than friends. All that baloney about accepting me as a member of the Group. All that crud about the noble mission of Fortress Sol. And what do you turn out to be? Garden variety cowards and traitors!"

Lingo scanned the gray cloud cover, patently ignoring Palmer. "Should be here any minute," he muttered to himself.

"If you had any guts," Palmer sneered, "you'd detonate that fusion bomb right now, and at least destroy the Council of Wisdom. How can you live with yourself, anyway?"

Lingo, Fran and Ortega burst into laughter.

"*Bomb?*" said Ortega. "Bomb? Didn't you hear what the Kor said? It's impossible to sneak a fusion bomb past radiation detectors. There isn't any bomb."

"What? But... but the second time, the detectors *did* show that there was a bomb...?"

"Oh, use your head!" grinned Lingo. "Remember, *Linda* was on the ship at the time. Thought waves are a form of electromagnetic energy, and a rather gross form, compared to what radiation detectors work on. If telepaths can control other beings' bodies, they surely can create illusions on delicate instruments, create the illusion of radioactives where there are none."

"The whole thing was a fake? Like everything else?"

"Very aptly put, Jay," Lingo said. "Think about it: the bomb was a fake, like everything else. Like *everything* else."

"Here they come!" cried Ortega.

Duglaari warships were breaking through the cloud cover and dropping down towards the ship, ten... twenty... fifty... a hundred, over two hundred ships formed a solid blanket over the landing area, hovering at about two thousand feet.

"Solarian ship to Duglaari commander. Solarian to Duglaari...." Lingo droned into his mike. "We are now lifting off and proceeding as per our agreement."

"Acknowledged."

Lingo turned on the Resolution Drive. The ship began to rise, and the blanket of Duglaari warships above rose at the same rate, keeping the distance between them constant.

As soon as they had emerged from Duglaar's atmosphere and achieved escape velocity, the Duglaari Fleet formed itself into a great hollow hemisphere, concavity forward. The Solarian ship took its position, as calculated, just forward of the lip of the cup-shaped formation and directly in line with its center, and hence with its line of flight, balanced just ahead of the great Duglaari Fleet Resolution Field.

Thus, a slight relative acceleration forward would put it momentarily ahead of the Doog Field, and an equally minimal cut in speed would throw it directly upon the Duglaari Fleet Resolution Field.

The Solarian ship began to accelerate outward, accompanied by its oversize escort which maintained its position nearly, but not quite, surrounding it, like a shock wave pushing a dust mote before it.

Palmer was somehow calmed by the terrible spectacle of the Duglaari warships, filling the viewscreen in all directions save one. Here was raw power; here was death. He remembered that he had faced much the same death with these six Solarians before, not once but three times. He remembered that wonderful comradeship, that unspoken mutual trust that he had felt then, and he perversely found himself mourning for it, like a small boy who has finally discovered that his trusted father is a fallible human being.

He found himself desperately considering Lingo's words: "... the bomb was a fake, like everything else. Like *everything else*." Everything that Lingo had said to the Kor had been a bluff or a lie or a trick: the bomb, the impregnability of Sol, the... Why, even the superweapons might not be real! They *did* sound suspiciously like Human Confederation propaganda…. But…. But why would Lingo have warned the Kor of weapons Sol might or might not have in the next decade? Why had he bragged that it would take eight thousand ships to destroy Fortress Sol, when he must've *known* that it would be impossible to defend against even four thousand? Surely, they must've known that the Council of Wisdom would not be fooled.

There had to be some hidden purpose behind it all, hidden from himself as well as the Duglaari. And if everything else was some kind of elaborate trick, couldn't Lingo's attempt to sacrifice the Confederation be just a trick too? After all, the Kor *hadn't* accepted it…. In fact, he suddenly realized, Lingo had made the proposal in such arrogant terms that he must've *known* that the Kor would turn it down. He must've planned it that way!

As the ship sped outward from Duglaar, balanced precariously on the razor-edge of death, Palmer realized that he wanted very much to be able to trust the Solarians again. For without that trust, all was meaningless, all was hopeless. Whether they escaped alive or not, Fortress Sol was the myth that had sustained the Confederation for three centuries, and if Sol were proved a hideous and traitorous lie, the human race was finished and the paranoiac's nightmare that was the Duglaari Empire was destined to destroy the Galaxy.

Palmer felt a more terrible fear lurking behind the normal fear of death—the fear of dying meaninglessly, alone, confused and betrayed, of dying alone with the awful knowledge that the entire human race would soon follow him into that final oblivion.

And the only thing between him and that most horrible of deaths was belief in six people who were, on the face of it, the blackest traitors in all history.

He desperately wanted to believe in them but he knew all too well *why* he wanted to believe, and so he could not.

"I don't like it…" Ortega muttered, staring out at the great amoeba that was the Duglaari Fleet. "It just doesn't add up. The Kor gave in too quickly. It was all far too easy. It just doesn't make sense that they would let us go like this. There's *got* to be some trick up their sleeves…."

"Oh, come on, Raul," said Lingo, "stop worrying. You should have more confidence in your own Talent. You just outsmarted them, that's all. It's much more logical for them to let us go and not take the chance of losing Dugl than to try and destroy us and risk a nova."

"It's much *more* logical to destroy us *without* risking Dugl," Ortega said uneasily. "That's how the Council *should've* seen it. That's the way *I* would've figured it in their place…."

"But how? That's just it, Raul, they can't try to englobe us without an even chance that we'll be able to activate our Stasis-Field generator before they can crush us in their Fleet Resolution Field. We set things up that way, didn't we? Once we pass the point where we can go safely into Stasis-Space without triggering a nova…."

Lingo's jaw dropped. His face whitened.

"Oh no!" Ortega cried. "*That's it!* Of course! How could I've been so stupid? Sure it isn't worth the risk to try and destroy us while there's a chance for us to nova Dugl. But what's to prevent them from trying to englobe us *after* we cross the point where our Stasis-Field generator won't nova Dugl? And you can be damn sure that the Council of Wisdom has calculated when that distance will be reached, down to the microsecond! They'll try an englobement the moment it's safe for them. If they succeed, we're dead, and if they fail, they've risked nothing. Sure, their chances will still only be fifty-fifty, but they'll have nothing at all to lose!"

"And there's nothing at all we can do about it," Lingo grunted.

"Outsmarted yourself again, eh, traitor?" Palmer gloated. "If you damn Solarians had fought beside us in The War, instead of isolating yourselves, you'd've known that the Doogs are clever tacticians. You'd've known that they don't even make *little* moves unless everything is on their side. Why, in the last battle my Fleet fought with them, we...."

Of course! he thought suddenly. There *was* a way to escape! The Solarians might be big on strategy, but they hadn't fought a battle in centuries. If they had, they'd've seen it too. It didn't require any supercomplicated schemes; it was a standard Confederation escape tactic, and it almost always worked. This case might be slightly different, but....

He grinned sourly. If there was one thing the Confederation forces had plenty of practice at, it was the art of retreat.

"What is it, Jay?" Ortega said, turning to stare at the smirking Palmer.

"Why don't you figure it out yourself, Gamemaster Ortega?" Palmer said. "Any Confederation Fleet Commander would know what to do. Standard tactics. Maybe it's just a little *too* simple for your complicated mind. Too damn bad!"

"You're talking like a fool," Lingo snapped. "Remember, Jay, you're on this ship too. It's your life as well as ours. If you've got a way out, you've nothing to gain by not telling us."

"Nothing but revenge, Lingo," Palmer said.

"Only a madman throws away his own life for mean-ingless revenge. I don't think you're insane, Jay."

It hit home. There was no point in dying, not when your death was meaningless, not when you died not knowing whether you were killing traitors or whether you might be destroying... friends.

"Okay, Lingo," he said. "As usual, you win."

Outward the ship sped, trailed by the Doog Fleet, past the orbit of Dugl V, approaching ever faster the orbit of Dugl VI, Dugl's outermost planet—and the border of Dugl's vulnerability to the Solarian Stasis-Field generator. The border of their safety, as well.

"How close are we, Fran?" Lingo asked, nervously studying the wall of warships behind him.

"About ten minutes to the orbit of Dugl VI," was the reply.

"It's now or never, Lingo," Palmer said. "You've got to do it gradually."

"Are you sure this is going to work? Are you sure they won't detect it?"

"I'm not *sure* of anything," Palmer snapped. "But the chances of their detecting it are very slight. I'd say that the mass of the Duglaari Fleet is at least three hundred times our mass. So our combined speed will decrease only a total of a third of a percent, and if we spread that decrease out over ten minutes, the deceleration will never be more than a thirtieth of a percent. I can't see them de-tecting *that*. Besides, we're doing the exact opposite of what they should be expecting us to do."

"Okay, Jay," Lingo said. "Here goes nothing."

Slowly, minutely, gingerly, Lingo began cutting the power of the ship's Resolution Drive. The ship lost the tiniest fraction of its forward speed and fell back towards the Duglaari Fleet by less than a hundred yards—an imperceptible distance by the standards of interplanetary space.

But that miniscule change in relative position was enough to put the ship within the boundaries of the mighty Duglaar Fleet Resolution Field.

"We're in contact with the Doog Field," Lingo said. "I don't think they've noticed anything."

"So far so good," said Palmer. "Now keep cutting power slowly but steadily. You've got to time it so that our Resolution Field is completely off just as we cross the orbit of Dugl VI."

Palmer watched tensely as Lingo continued cutting the ship's power. It should work, he thought. Their mass is so much greater than ours that they'll never realize that our drive is off and that we're just riding their Fleet Resolution Field. And once we cross the orbit of Dugl VI....

"Eighty percent power...." Lingo droned. "Seventy... sixty... thirty... twenty... ten...."

He lifted his hand and breathed a sigh of relief. "It's working!" he said. "Our Resolution Drive is off, and we're riding their Fleet Field. And I don't think they realize it."

"Good," said Palmer. "Now remember, timing is everything. You've got to turn on the Resolution Drive full power ten seconds before we cross the orbit of Dugl VI, and you've got to go into Stasis-Space exactly ten seconds later. If you turn on the Stasis-Field generator too soon— *blooey!* And if you turn it on too late, the Doogs, with their more powerful Resolution Field, will be able to make up for our sudden burst of speed and englobe us. It all depends on timing. Timing and surprise."

"Don't worry about the timing," Lingo said. "And we can only hope that they'll be surprised, because if they realize what we're doing...."

"Don't even think it!" said Ortega.

"Fran," said Lingo, "I want you to give me two count-downs: first to the ten-second to Dugl VI's orbit position, and then give me another ten-count as soon as our drive is on."

"Right, Dirk."

Outward the convoy continued. We're ready for *our* tactic, Palmer thought. I wonder what the Doog commander is thinking right now....

"We're just about there, Dirk," Fran Shannon said. "Twenty seconds to the ten-second mark. Fifteen... ten...."

Lingo gripped the throttle lever of the Resolution Drive with his right hand; the forefinger of his left hand was poised over the button that would switch on the Sta-sis-Field generator.

"Nine... eight... five... four... three... two... one... now!"

Lingo slammed the throttle lever over. The ship's Resolution Drive went on under full power.

The Solarian ship had been moving forward at the same speed as the Duglaari Fleet, riding the Fleet's powerful Resolution Field. Now it was suddenly given a tremendous additional burst of speed by its *own* Resolution Field — an inertialess drive capable of accelerating the ship to near-light velocities. The ship shot forward, leaving the Resolution Field of the Duglaari Fleet and opening a gap between itself and the Doogs.

"... two... three... four... five..." Fran Shannon began counting.

Palmer watched the receding Duglaari Fleet in the view-screen intently. It was still falling behind... *but it was receding slower now!*

The Duglaari commander had recovered! Now the Doog Fleet was accelerating; the Solarian ship was no longer gaining ground, but the sudden gap it had opened up was too great for the Duglaari Fleet to begin its en-globing action as yet....

"Six... seven... eight..."

Now the Doogs were catching up! The great Fleet Resolution Field was accelerating the warships far faster than the Solarian ship could accelerate, and the gap of safety was rapidly closing.

"... nine... ten... now!"

Lingo pressed the button under his left hand. There was an agonizing minute's delay as the Stasis-Field gen-erator warmed up, as the deadly, clutching amoeba that was the Duglaar Fleet reached out to englobe them in its grip of death....

Then the Doogs, Dugl, and the stars themselves were suddenly gone, replaced by a swirling maelstrom of color. They were safely in Stasis-Space.

Lingo heaved a deep sigh. "We're on our way!" he said.

"On our way where?" Palmer asked sourly.

"Why where else, Jay? *Fortress Sol*, of course!"

Chapter X

LINGO locked the controls and walked over to the dummy pilot's seat into which Palmer was tied.

"I want to thank you, Jay," he said. "We all owe you our lives."

"I don't want your thanks, Lingo," Palmer snapped. "I saved this ship for only one reason—I had the misfortune to be on it. As you pointed out, suicide is an insane act. But as for you traitors, you can go...."

"Don't go off half-cocked," Lingo said with careful mildness. "We're still your friends. We've got a long voyage ahead, and we'd like it to be as pleasant as possible. We don't want you for an enemy, Jay. We want you to feel a part of our Group. You did once before."

"And of course, as a token of your affection, you're keeping me tied in this seat. I'm deeply touched."

"We tied you up only to protect the ship," Lingo said, still patiently. "You've got no weapons, and there's no place for you to go. If you'll promise not to get violent, I'll untie you."

Palmer shrugged as best he could in his bonds. "Okay," he said. "Obviously I can't go all the way to Sol trussed up like a turkey. No rough stuff. But please, no more phony buddy-buddy lies either."

"Have it your own way," Lingo said, untying Palmer. "You'll have a good long time to simmer down."

Palmer stood up shakily, rubbing the circulation back into his limbs. Then he pointedly turned his back on Lingo and started for the control room door.

"Where are you going, Jay?"

"To my cabin, if you don't mind. There seems to be an unpleasant odor in here. As our friend Koris would say, 'I

165

feel undesirable twinges beginning in my digestive tract.'"

Palmer lay on his bunk for hours, staring bleakly at the wall. The trip to Sol would take weeks; it might as well be centuries.

A week in this nest of traitors is as bad as a millenium, he thought bitterly. Why was I such a damned coward? I should've let the Doogs crush this filthy ship like a walnut. It would've been all over in a minute or so. All I did was prolong the agony.

After all, what had he really gained by saving the ship and his own life? A few more weeks cooped up with the Solarian traitors, a few more weeks, maybe, on Earth, and then the Duglaari would descend on Sol in overwhelming numbers. Man's home system would be completely annihilated.

Maybe *that's* something to look forward to, after all, he thought bitterly. The pleasure of seeing Fortress Sol die.

But he knew that it would be a hollow satisfaction indeed, for the death of Sol, in the long run, would be the death of the entire human race. For three centuries, the myth of Fortress Sol had sustained the Human Confederation in the face of defeat after defeat, in the face of computations that promised certain extinction within a century. All the hope of all men everywhere had been placed in Fortress Sol. It was the last and greatest hope of the human race, the bastion, the Rock of Ages, the Citadel of Man.

And Fortress Sol was nothing but a lie.

Palmer felt alone, more finally alone than any other man had ever been. He was alone with the unacceptable truth that Man's last god had died, with the knowledge that that god too, like all the others, had been the bastard child of hope and fear, the futile denial of the final reality — that the human race itself, like all of its members, was mortal and doomed to die.

He thought of the great, dead mass of the Galaxy, through which the ship was hurtling; billions of stars, millions of planets. A cold, dead void ruled with an iron hand by the impersonal laws of physics.

What was Man, what was life itself, but a trace element, an insignificant contaminant in the vast, dead universe? In the whole of the Galaxy, life was statistically insignificant. The total mass of all living protoplasm since the dawn of time did not equal the mass of one unimportant, dead dwarf star. And sentience was but the billionth part of all the life in the universe.

The part that cared, the part that gave the dead rock and the fiery gas meaning.

And the part that clung so madly to each hour of its existence that it would sacrifice anything for a few more months of life.

That was the crime of Fortress Sol.

Dirk Lingo had done the impossible — he had invented a new sin. A sin not against men or gods, but against life itself. The universe, after all, was a vast battlefield where life warred against death, where awareness, sentience, intelligence, fought for survival in an infinite sea of nothingness.

And Fortress Sol had gone over to the enemy. No greater treason was possible. For the Duglaari Empire was not on the side of life; it was an agent of nothingness, of death.

Only now could Palmer understand the true nature of the enemy he had spent his life fighting. The Doogs were a thing insane. They did not fight to extend their territory, or increase their wealth or seed the dead universe with life. Death itself was the only Duglaari goal—the extinction of all other intelligent life. And when that mad goal was finally achieved, would the Doogs themselves have anything left to live for? Might not the Council of Wisdom simply shut itself down, and might not the Doogs themselves follow their computer into the final oblivion?

And nothing would remain anywhere, but flaming gas, and cold, cold rock, and hundreds of trillions of cubic miles of dead nothingness....

Palmer shook himself fearfully. He felt himself teetering on the edge of madness. These waters were too deep for any man to safely fathom alone....

And quite suddenly he knew that whatever his feelings, whatever his hate, he would sooner or later have to make at least a temporary peace with the Solarians. No man could bear to die this way, bereft of all human contact.

The Solarians were cowards, they were traitors, they were things unnamable, but at least they were human beings.

And whatever their sins, whatever hate there might be between them, they might very well be the last human beings he would ever see.

There was a knock on the door.

"Go away!" he snapped.

The knock became insistent.

"Go away, damn you!" Later, he knew, he would have to face them, but now hate was all that he could feel, and he wanted to be alone with the dying embers of his fury.

"It's me," said the voice of Robin Morel.

Who else? he thought grimly. The one he hated most, with the possible exception of Lingo, and of course the one he would be least able to turn away.

"All right, all right," he muttered, "come on in."

Robin kicked open the door and stood there, with an unbearable look of understanding and compassion on her face and a drink in either hand.

"Raul mixed us a couple of Supernovas," she said, sitting down on the bed beside him. "Have one. It'll make you feel a lot better." She held out the small glass of blue liquid in her right hand.

"How do I know it's not poison?" Palmer snapped sullenly.

"Don't be juvenile, Jay. If we wanted to kill you, we wouldn't have to resort to trickery to do it."

"I've learned not to think I can understand the Solarian mind," he said bitterly.

"Jay...." she sighed resignedly, and then gave a little laugh. "An old, old Terran toast," she said, switching glasses. "If there be poison in thy wine, let my life pay for thine."

Smiling, she downed the drink she had first offered him.

Palmer felt infinitely foolish and embarrassed, but also, somehow, quite touched. Wordlessly, he took the second glass.

Remembering the Nine Planets he had drunk, he was prepared for almost anything as he drank the clear blue liquid—anything but what it turned out to be like. It had no taste at all; it was exactly like a cool drink of water.

It glided tastelessly down his throat and into his belly. Suddenly he felt a strange sensation, as if a part of him were diffusing into the drink, rather than the drink diffusing into his bloodstream. He felt his emotions, his hate and fear and fury being leached from him, being compacted into an insufferable, dense, massive ball of emotional turmoil which seemed to be located in the pit of his stomach.

The rest of him, his freshly purged mind, now seemed cool, detached, insanely unemotional and objective, observing the burning, seething miniature sun that his emotions had become from an outside point of view, as a half-amused and half-repelled bystander.

As he watched the seething, churning, glowing ball of hate and fury and fear that was his own emotions, it seemed a thing apart, something alien and ludicrous.

Then it exploded.

For one terrible, nauseating instant, he felt the awful, monstrous, irresistible blast of his own hate sheer through his being like hard radiation through paper. Then it was past him and it was gone.

Completely gone. He felt cleansed by the fire of its passing; cleansed and tranquil and open. The hate had not been a part of himself; it had been the product of the confluence of outside forces beyond his control, and when it had exploded in a blast of cleansing fire, it had expended itself and left him a creature of his own ego and will once more.

Robin laughed softly.

"And *that*," she said, "is why it's called a Supernova."

He looked at her with his calm new eyes, and he saw not a traitor, but simply a human being, a woman. She too might've been in the thrall of outside forces somehow lodged, horrid and alien and inescapable within her, but whatever she and the other Solarians had done, however black their crime, they too were in a sense victims. Victims and victimizers in one body, light and darkness in one mind—they were human beings, after all.

"I guess I've been acting pretty melodramatically," Palmer said, rather sheepishly.

"No more than we have been," she answered. "The difference is that we were doing it for a reason. But then part of the reason was so that you would act the way you did."

"This thing must've *really* made me drunk. I don't understand you at all."

She laughed, but there was something sad behind it. "No, Jay," she said. "You're not drunk. A Supernova doesn't get you drunk; what it does is let you see your emotions as something apart from the rest of you for a while. It sort of lets you see them from the outside, as if your mind were a detached observer. It isolates your emotions and calms you down. If anything, you're *more* sober now than before you drank it."

"If I'm *not* drunk, then what in blazes *did* you mean about your doing what you did so that I'd do what I did? Sounds like a lot of doubletalk to me."

She seemed to be studying him carefully, almost clinically. "I guess you're ready to hear the truth," she said. "At least part of it."

"That's all I get around here," he snapped. "Little pieces of the truth and great big slices of lies."

She smiled sardonically. "I see that the drink is already beginning to wear off," she said. "Too bad the effects can't be made permanent. Just try to remember how you felt without your emotions clouding your mind."

Suddenly Palmer realized that he *did* feel different again. He was no longer completely and coldly rational. Once more, he felt the old mixture of confusion, fury and hate. But it was different now; it could never again be completely the same. He had seen that there was another side to his feelings, that the situation did look different when he saw it completely stripped of his emotions. And even though his emotions were fast returning, he realized that the memory of that other, now-alien, point of view had muted and softened them permanently.

"You've been playing games with my mind all along, haven't you?" he said. "From the first minute I boarded this ship. Why? What do you have to gain?"

Robin sighed deeply, and her face and posture seemed to relax, as if a great burden had at last been lifted from her.

"Yes..." she murmured. "In a way we have been... changing you. But largely for *your* gain, not ours. Try to think of yourself as you were at the beginning, before you met us, and then compare that memory with what you are now. Don't you *approve* of the changes?"

He thought back... and the weeks seemed as years. He realized that he had expanded his mental universe; experienced more, in terms of new human relationships, learned more, deepened more, grown more, in these few weeks than he had in the entire previous decade. He felt ten years older; not ten years more tired, but ten years more mature. Though he had been brevetted to the largely meaningless rank of general, he had still had the mentality of a Fleet Commander. Now he understood things about the Duglaari, The War, the human mind, Sol, that not even a Confederal High Marshal could fathom. The rank of general was no longer an empty mockery; it was now merely his due.

He *had* changed, and he found that he did approve of the changes, for the changes had been growth.

"It startles you, when you turn around and look behind you, doesn't it?" Robin said. "You really are a better man now than the one you started as. For instance, you would not have doubts about your fitness now, were you to become Confederation Commander-in-Chief, as you someday may. Because you know that you're a big enough man for the job now. If anything, the job is too small for *you*."

"What does that matter now, even if it is true?" he snapped. "The War's lost. Sol is about to be destroyed, and when that news gets to the Confederation, there won't be any will to fight left. Thanks to you."

"You don't know it all yet, Jay. I think you're ready for the rest—at least a good part of it. It's time you spoke to Dirk. He's got an apology to make."

"An *apology?* How do you apologize for treason?"

She shrugged. "Go on up to the control room and find out," she said.

Lingo was alone in the control room, staring out into the meaningless swirl of Stasis-Space, a strange half-bitter, half-triumphant smile on his face.

"Sit down, Jay," he said, easing himself into his pilot's seat.

Palmer sat down next to Lingo. "Robin said you had an apology to make," he said tonelessly. "I suppose you know where you can stick your apology. How can you apologize for your stupidity—trying to sell out the human race?"

Lingo laughed harshly. "Traitor, I can understand…" he said, "but I'm injured when you accuse me of stupidity."

"Come off it, Lingo!" Palmer snapped. "You know damn well you blew it. I can understand what you were trying to do, even if it does turn my stomach. Bluff the Duglaari into leaving Sol alone, even using the entire Human Confederation as a kind of consolation prize to the Doogs. Then, if those super-weapons do have time to be developed, when all mankind is dead but you…. But you were a little *too* smart, weren't you? You got the Doogs a little *too* scared, didn't you? And now you'll never have a chance to build any superweapons."

Lingo turned to Palmer, his face convulsed with laughter. "So you believed it too!" he finally said. "Let me congratulate myself! Jay, weren't all those superweapons somehow familiar? Didn't they sound terribly like the sort of nonsense the Confederation propaganda section is always churning out? They should, you know, since they were lifted verbatim from Confederation propaganda. Each and every one of them was a lie. No one will be able to build weapons like those for centuries, if ever. Let me tell you, Jay, four *hundred* Duglaari warships would have little trouble defeating the forces of Fortress Sol, let alone four *thousand*."

"Then what in blazes can you find to laugh about? So it was *all* a bluff to make the Doogs think Sol was too tough a nut to crack, and it backfired! Now the Duglaari will attack Sol with *ten times* the force necessary to wipe you out. By your own admission, you've outsmarted yourself!"

Lingo shook his head. "Ah, Jay," he said, "surely you are capable of more subtlety than that! Haven't you ever heard of Brer Rabbit?"

"*Who?*"

"*Brer Rabbit.* An ancient Terran folk legend. Brer Rabbit was a Machiavellian little bunny who lived in a thorny briar patch. One careless day, he was captured by his arch-enemy, Brer Fox. Brer Fox amused himself by reciting a long catalogue of atrocities he was going to inflict on his victim. But instead of the expected reaction—fear and hate—poor Brer Fox found himself being thanked by Brer Rabbit for his infinite mercy. Finally, Brer Fox demanded to know *why* he was being thanked for his promise to skin Brer Rabbit alive and boil him in oil. To which our hero replied: You promised you'd only boil me in oil, skin me alive, and eat me. But thank you, Brer Fox! At least you're not going to throw me into that awful briar patch."

"So? What does that have to do with....?"

"Really, Jay!" sighed Lingo. "Can't you guess what Brer Fox did then? He threw Brer Rabbit into the briar patch, of course! Exactly what our clever little bunny was angling for all along."

Palmer's jaw fell. "You mean....?"

"What else?" said Lingo, with a shrug and a grin. "From beginning to end, *everything went exactly according to plan.*"

He sighed, frowned, and stared at Palmer with a sad, contrite expression.

"And *that's* what I want to ask you to forgive me for, Jay," Lingo said. "You were *used. You* were part of the plan too. Did you ever ask yourself what in blazes we needed a so-called Ambassador from the Confederation for? After all, if, as we told Kurowski, the whole surrender business was simply a ruse to get to see the Kor, we could've faked an ambassador too, couldn't we?"

"But it wasn't! You really *did* plan to surrender the Confederation, so you did need an Ambassador."

Lingo shook his head. "Don't be juvenile!" he said sharply. "Do you really suppose the Confederation would've honored any surrender you made? Of course not, not in a million years! And do you think *we* would be so stupid as to think that you'd agree to a surrender in the first place? Jay, we needed you along to do *exactly as you did.*"

"*What?* You needed someone to try to kill you?"

"Precisely. It made the whole thing credible. We had to make sure that the Doogs *really* believed that we were throwing the Confederation to the wolves. And the only way to convince them of *that*, was to have *you* believe it too, and act accordingly. Let me congratulate you, Jay. You played the part of the betrayed Confederation Ambassador perfectly."

"Believe me, Lingo," Palmer snapped, "I wasn't acting!"

"Of course you weren't. That's the whole point. You would never have been able to fool the Doogs if you were. You had to really believe that you were being betrayed."

"But why?"

"To make the whole thing credible," Lingo said patiently. "Your attack on me convinced the Kor that we really *were* ready to hand over the Human Confederation. And once he was convinced of that—or I should say, once the Council of Wisdom was convinced—the rest followed logically: Fortress Sol is no longer protecting the Confederation. Therefore Sol is using the Confederation to buy time. Therefore, Fortress Sol expects to have *use* for that time. Therefore the superweapons that I told them about may actually be in the process of being built. Therefore, it behooves the Duglaari Empire to take no chances, alter its plans and attack Sol *now*, rather than after the Confederation is destroyed."

"You.... you mean the whole thing, the whole purpose of the mission, was to get the Duglaari Empire to attack Fortress Sol?"

"To be more precise," Lingo said dryly, "our purpose was to get the Doogs to attack Fortress Sol in *overwhelming force.*"

It explained everything! Palmer was staggered. All the inconsistencies fell into place. The Solarians had told the General Staff one improbable story so that they could get a Confederal Ambassador. They needed an Ambassador so that they could convince the Kor of still another lie.

The Kor and the Council of Wisdom had to believe that lie about superweapons so that they would immediately attack Fortress Sol!

It all added up, in logical sequence. But the sum total was *madness!*

"But why, Lingo, why?" he exclaimed. "What've you accomplished? Only the destruction of Fortress Sol!"

Lingo smiled slyly. "What've we accomplished? Only what no one has been able to do in three centuries! Think man, think! For three hundred years, the Duglaari have been fighting the War *their* way. They started out with an advantage in ships, and they've been very careful never to risk losing it. They've *never* risked more than three hundred ships in a single battle."

"Of course not. Neither have we, for that matter. No single solar system is worth risking three hundred ships. It's *ships* that count in a war like this."

"Exactly, Jay, exactly. The Doogs have been having everything their way: this is a war of attrition, a war where relative numbers of ships is what counts, a war where they started out with a sizeable advantage. And so our completely logical friends have never risked endangering that advantage. It's been their war, on their terms, all the way. Until now, that is!"

"I still don't understand. Having four thousand Duglaari ships attack Fortress Sol is somehow one for *our* side?"

"Come on, Jay, use your head!" Lingo said. "Never before have the Doogs risked a *tenth* of what they're risking now. For the first time in the history of The War, we've forced them into fighting on *our* terms. It's no longer a war of attrition, a war we had to lose. We've maneuvered them into staking the entire outcome of The War on one single battle! What would happen if that entire fleet of four thousand Doog warships attacking Sol were to be completely wiped out?"

"Why... why... the entire course of The War would be changed! It'd be turned around. We'd have the advantage in ships. It'd be *our* war!"

Suddenly, he realized the enormity of what had happened. The fate of the entire human race would depend on what happened when the huge Doog armada attacked Fortress Sol. If Sol were destroyed, the fight would go completely out of the Confederation, and the Duglaari would be left with only a simple mop-up operation. But if the Duglaari fleet were destroyed by the Solarian superweapons... superweapons? *Superweapons?* But... but....

"But the superweapons don't exist!" he exclaimed. "It was all a lie! You said so yourself. There aren't any superweapons. Why... why you said that four hundred Doog ships could easily defeat the forces of Sol!"

"So I did," said Lingo. "And that was a pretty conservative figure."

"But then all you've done is insure our defeat! The Doogs will annihilate Sol, and...."

"Ah," said Lingo with an enigmatic smile that contained both a trace of triumph and one of... almost regret, "but there is *one* weapon you have overlooked. One weapon the Kor has not considered. One weapon that we've had all along."

"All along? But what is it?"

Lingo turned, and stared off into the enigmatic maelstrom of Stasis-Space, through which the ship was hurtling at many times the objective speed of light towards its rendezvous with Armageddon. His face seemed to drain of all color, and when he spoke, the words were somehow leaden with bitterness.

"What else?" Lingo said, withdrawing into his own thoughts.

"What else but Fortress Sol?"

Chapter XI

MAX AND LINDA were fooling around listlessly with the telepathy table. Robin and Dirk were off together in the control room, withdrawing into each other, as they had been doing more and more of the time in the past week or so.

Fran Shannon was slumped in a chair, half-reading a book of poetry. Ortega diddled aimlessly about the bar.

The total effect was a combination of impatience and foreboding, like a man with a toothache waiting in a dentist's office. The pattern of life in the Solarian Organic Group had changed, had adapted itself to the new moody feeling in the air.

It was hard for Palmer to put his finger on the individual differences — it was a total effect compounded out of dozens of subtle changes: the way Max and Linda spent more and more time staring silently at each other, communicating wordlessly and deeply in the intertwining of their minds; the way Robin and Lingo went off for longer and more frequent periods to be alone together; the way Fran Shannon was trying, largely unsuccessfully, to withdraw into the books; the way Ortega seemed overstuffed with directionless nervous energy.

And yet, the Solarians were still very much a Group. Somehow, their individual psychic needs had changed, and the patterns within the Group had altered themselves in response. The communal spirit was still there, but now it was closer akin to the togetherness of an old couple, sharing silences more than words.

To an outsider, the effect was somehow maddening, and Palmer felt his nerves drawing even tighter.

"Damn it, Raul," he said, picking up a glass nervously from the bar and ringing it with his thumbnail, "what's going on?"

"Huh?" muttered Ortega, withdrawing suddenly from some private reverie. "Oh, nothing much, Jay... just thinking."

"That's not what I mean, and you know it. Everyone's so keyed up, so wrapped up in themselves."

"You're not exactly loose as a goose yourself, you know," Ortega said.

"Well after all, the fate of the entire human race is going to be decided in a few weeks or so," Palmer said. "It's pretty hard to accept—*the* decisive battle. After you've been conditioned to believe that The War would last at least another century...."

"It still may," said Ortega, pouring himself a small shot of whiskey. "In fact, it almost certainly will, no matter what happens. Even if the Doogs lose four thousand ships, they'll still have three thousand left, after all. The Duglaari Empire just won't dry up and blow away. They'll be in the same position the Confederation is in now—fighting a hopeless holding action in a war they can't win, losing solar systems, one by one.... It'd probably go on for at least another century. The big difference would be that *we'd* be the ones assured of eventual victory."

"And if the Doogs wipe out Sol," Palmer said, "the Confederation won't be any worse off, militarily speaking, than it is right now. The defeat'll be purely psychological, and they'll fight on listlessly for a few more decades."

"*They?*" said Ortega, arching his eyebrows. "They, not *we?*"

"Pour me one too, Raul," Palmer said. "Yes, I said *they*. As for me, I don't know who or what I am any more. I've spent too much time with your people. I know too much about the real nature of the Doogs and The War to feel like just another Confederal citizen."

He sipped moodily at his drink. "Robin told me I'd changed, and when I took a good look at myself, I was really surprised. I hate to admit it, but there's something... incomplete and naive about the Confederation. I can't feel completely a part of it any more."

"Pentagon City," Ortega mumbled.

"What?"

"Pentagon City. It sums up what's wrong with the whole Human Confederation. Doesn't it remind you of someplace else, now?"

"Why... it does. It... it somehow reminds me of Duglaar! Of the Hall of Wisdom! In a less thorough way, it's just as ugly, just as functional, and..."

"And just as much a dead end," Ortega said. "Specialization, Jay, specialization. A law of evolution: the more specialized a species becomes, the closer it is to extinction. What happens when The War is over, assuming that the Doogs are wiped out? What then? Like a cheap imitation of the Duglaari Empire, the Human Confederation is specialized for war in every way: economically, scientifically, psychologically. Even religiously—the only 'religion' of the Confederation is the myth of Fortress Sol; strictly a warrior's religion. The only thing holding the Confederation together is The War. There isn't even a Confederal government as such, just the Combined Human Military Command. It can't survive peace."

Palmer drained his glass. "It's true," he said. "The future of the human race is Fortress Sol, if there *is* a future. I've been feeling it all along, but I've been afraid to admit it to myself. You people have *something*.... A new kind of humanity, based on what's *human* about the human race. The Confederation *is* a dead end, a denial of what makes a man a man. I only wish...."

"You only wish what, Jay?"

Palmer sighed. A dam within him seemed to burst, and deep waters indeed flowed forth. "I only wish I could be a part of it, Raul. I know that you've tried to help me become a part of it, and now I can at least appreciate what you've tried to do. But it can't work; I'm too much a part of the Confederation. I've got too many years of a different culture behind me. I can't be a part of what you are....

"And yet, now that I've had a taste of something better, I can't be a part of what the Confederation is either. I'm alone, Raul. I'm the most alone human being in the Galaxy. I know too much, and I know too little.... Hell, pour me another drink. A big one."

Ortega filled Palmer's glass up to the rim and then refilled his own.

"No, Jay," he said, staring into the depths of his glass, "you're wrong again. We're not the future. We can't be. There are only five billion of us, and two hundred billion people in the Confederation. We can only be a seed, a germ, the beginning of something. We must be absorbed into the totality of the human race, like any other favorable mutation. We're not the human race of the future; we're a new thing that must become *part* of the human race."

He drained his glass and stared at Palmer. There was something in his eyes that seemed almost envy.

"*You're* the future, Jay," he said.

"*Me?* I'm not part of *anything*. I'm not a Solarian, and I'm no longer part of the Confederation either. I'm nowhere."

"The future is always nowhere, Jay. It's the creatures who are ousted from their familiar environments who have always been forced to evolve. And the future is always alone. The first fish to be flung up on the land and live long enough to breed was alone. The first monkey to come down from the trees was alone. The first men to colonize the stars were alone. There couldn't be *any* change if there weren't someone who couldn't feel a part of everything else that already was."

"That's not a very comfortable view of the universe, Raul."

"It's not a very comfortable universe! It wasn't designed by you or me or by the first Kor of the Duglaari, either. The universe couldn't care less about your comfort, Jay. And if you'll forgive me—and even if you won't—neither do we."

"What do you mean? How is it *your* fault?"

"You think it *isn't?*" sighed Ortega. "Jay, when we decided to take along an Ambassador from the Confederation, we wanted more than just a dupe. Hell, as far as that goes, Kurowski would've played the part better than you. And don't think we couldn't have bulldozed Kurowski into coming along, if we had wanted to. But we didn't want a Kurowski. Remember, way back when we first landed on Olympia III, how Max and Linda went through everyone's minds? It wasn't idle curiosity; they were looking for something. They were looking for *you*, in effect. They were looking for a potential that had been thwarted. They were looking for a man capable of meaningful change—and you must realize by now that that's not so common in the Confederation. To be blunt, they were looking for the right guinea pig. You were an experiment, Jay. If it's any consolation to you, we consider the experiment a success."

Ortega's words bit into Palmer like the cold of space itself. "What are you talking about?" he said sharply. But he knew, and he knew he knew.

Ortega nodded, as if in response to Palmer's thoughts, rather than his words. He seemed unable to meet Palmer's eyes.

"We had to know whether the humans of the Confederation were capable of change, capable of accepting that new thing which we had become as a part of the whole of mankind," Ortega said slowly.

"If the human race were ever to become whole again, there would have to be men who could stand apart from both the Confederation and Sol, men who would be neither Solarians, nor trapped in the dead end that the Confederation had become. Men like you, Jay. A bridge between us and the rest of the human race. The Organic Group is the social unit of the future—but people who are too deeply a part of one can't bring it to people who are not. And someone who is part of the Confederation cannot understand that the Confederation *must* change. Yes... that's what you are Jay: a bridge. A bridge between the past and the future. Whether you're happy about it or not, that's what we made of you."

"I suppose I should hate you," Palmer said. "But I really can't do that any more. I understand you too well. Fortress Sol itself is an experiment too, isn't it? MacDay's experiment. And if you ask me, MacDay was crueler to you than you've been to me. Because he didn't even know what he was trying to achieve. He forced you to change, but he didn't know to *what*. You were guinea pigs too, Raul."

Ortega laughed. "I suppose so," he said. "Maybe all human beings are guinea pigs, one way or another. If not ours, or MacDay's, then evolution's. Welcome to the club, fellow guinea pig!"

He held out his hand.

Palmer took it.

Ortega refilled the glasses. "Let's drink to all guinea pigs," he said, "past, present and future."

"If there *is* a future," Palmer said, draining his glass. He took the bottle and poured another round.

"One more toast," he said, hoisting his glass. "To home, wherever that may be."

Ortega slammed his glass down on the bar. A dark shadow crossed his face. "I don't want to drink to *that*" he said coldly.

"What's the matter? You're going home, aren't you? Home to Sol, home to Earth. I wish...."

"Don't wish!" Ortega snapped. "Don't wish when you don't know what you're wishing for. I wish I *weren't* going home. I wish I were going anywhere but Sol. Home.... You're better off without a home, Jay. Home is only someplace you have to leave."

"You mean the Duglaari fleet? But you're the ones who made the Duglaari decide to attack Sol in the first place. Lingo said something about one real super-weapon...."

Ortega snorted. "Yeah, the weapon..." he said bitterly. "Only there's nothing super about it, Jay. You don't get something for nothing. Every victory has a price, and the greater the victory, the bigger the price. And sometimes, you have to pay the price in advance, and hope that the goods are delivered."

He finished his drink, and got out from behind the bar.

"All of a sudden, I don't feel very sociable," he said. "I think I'll go check in the control room."

And he left Palmer staring confusedly at the empty glasses.

There was something wrong, something strange beyond the usual strangeness of the Solarians, which Palmer had more or less gotten used to, going on.

Palmer was sure of it, as he made his way from his cabin to the common room. With every day, the ship was getting closer and closer to Sol. Yet, instead of the spirits of the Solarians becoming ever more buoyant as they approached their home sun, a strange ominous brooding had slowly but steadily come over them.

It showed in a hundred little things: the subdued and trivial talk at meals, the choice of music played on the hi-fi, the way they seemed to become upset at the most inexplicable times, the way Ortega had that time in the common room....

Whatever it was, it was something they could not, or would not share with him. It was a wall between them, and every attempt he had made to break through it had been met by a gentle rebuff.

For reasons of their own, the Solarians were keeping something else from him.

Well, he thought, as he entered the common room, whatever it is, it can't last much longer. We're only a day or so from Sol itself.

He looked around the common room. The lighting seemed to be strangely subdued. Max and Linda were seated together on the couch, communing wordlessly with each other. Fran Shannon was puttering listlessly about the bookcases. Robin was standing next to the hi-fi. She nodded to him, turned on the hi-fi and sat down in a lounge chair. Palmer sat down next to her.

He was about to say something trivial when the music she had put on caught his ear. It was like nothing he had ever heard before, a crazy jumping from theme to theme, melody to melody, style to style. Even the instruments playing the music seemed to change every few bars: traditional strings to guitar-and-banjo, to primitive drums, to a full orchestral percussion section, to flute-and-drum, to sounds and instruments he had never heard before.

The mood, the tone, the whole feeling of the piece seemed to change every few seconds. It was orchestral, folk, electronic... every kind of music Palmer could remember hearing and more. Yet there was an uncanny unity to it, as if all the diverse elements were still part of some all-embracing whole.

"What *is* that?" he asked Robin.

She appeared lost in the music, staring moodily off into space.

"Robin," he said. "Robin, what is that?"

She turned to him slowly, as if she were reluctantly rousing from some powerful, all-embracing dream.

"That was composed not too long ago. A few months before we left Sol. It's called the *Song of Earth*."

The music went on, and now Palmer began to understand it. The composer, for reasons of his own, had tried to capture all the music of Man's home planet, the music of all times and all places, and put in into one kaleidoscopic piece that would capture the entire musical heritage of a variegated planet whole.

It seemed that, to a remarkable degree, he had succeeded.

As the music skittered about like a nervous chameleon, Fran Shannon walked over to the smell-organ and began to play, matching odor with melody, smell-chords with the ever-changing style of the music, so that the effect was as of an aural and olfactory odyssey through the endless panoply of cultures, races and peoples that through the millenia had shared the planet called Earth.

Palmer had never thought very much about music or odor symphonies, but he found himself transported, taken over entirely by the mingling flux of sound and smell. Flutes and oak forests... bagpipes and heather... guitars and castanets and the smell of garlic and saffron.... Ever-changing, faster and faster, now flowing into one another, merging, combining, recombining.

Palmer looked at Max and Linda. They had come out of their telepathic communion, and they were listening to the joyous music, the music and smells of Earth, the distillations of millenia of history and thousands of cultures, a heritage that was richer and more convoluted than the cultures of all planets in the Confederation combined. But the expressions on their faces were not in keeping with the scintillating patterns of smell and sound. Their mouths were grim and drawn, and their eyes were wet with tears....

Palmer turned to Robin. She was biting her lower lip with her upper teeth. Her hands were balled into tight fists, and she was crying.

And then the music began to subtly change, and the smells began to change with it.

It was impossible for Palmer to tell just when the change had begun or what precisely it was. The shifts in styles and instruments and cultures began to speed up gradually. At some indefinable point, the music and the smells, the quick flux of the patterns crossed the threshold between the scintillating and the frantic.

The quality of the tape changed too: it was as if it had been recorded at one speed, re-recorded at a faster speed, and then slowed down again. The effect was thinness, frenzy and an almost forlorn wailing quality.

Fran had changed her style on the smell-organ to fit the change. The smells were coming far too fast now; they were mingling with each other in strange and nauseating combinations. Common, innocuous, even pleasant odors were combining into one pervasive, awful stench—the odor of decay, the stink of loss, the reek of death.

Somehow, the gay kaleidoscopic sounds and smells had been transmitted into a frantic, forlorn, mournful dirge played at triple time. The entire composition now seemed like the final moments of a drowning man—a lifetime of impressions, sensations, memories trying hopelessly to crowd themselves into a few transitory moments.

Faster and faster the music and the odors swirled, mounting into a hideous cry of mortal terror and loss, a choking, all-enveloping stench of destruction and lost civilizations, till Palmer could no longer stand it, till his ears ached and his stomach quivered.

And then, suddenly, abruptly, without warning— *silence.*

Utter silence, a silence so heavy, so deadening, so loud that it seemed the voice of death itself.

For long moments, Palmer sat, stupefied. What would cause anyone to write a thing like *that*, he wondered numbly. It was a work of unbelievable genius but of equally unbelievable horror. And what was it called? *The Song of Earth!*

Finally, Palmer turned to Robin. "What..." he muttered, "why...?"

She turned to him, tears streaming down her cheeks. "Jay..." she said, "in a million years, I wouldn't be able to find the words to tell you. In a...."

Suddenly, Raul Ortega stuck his head into the control room. "Come on, everyone!" he shouted. "Come on up to the control room. "We're there! It's time to come out of Stasis-Space!"

Palmer got up and, along with Max and Linda and Robin, tensely followed Ortega down the corridor. The six Solarians were merely going home—although it had become obvious that, for some dark reason, they felt little joy in the homecoming.

But he was about to see that which no living human of the Confederation had ever set eyes upon: Man's original solar system, Sol; Man's maternal planet, the Earth.

Not for over two hundred and fifty years had a Confederal expedition even tried to penetrate the limits of the Sol system. That last expedition, two and a half centuries ago, had run into a vast minefield enclosing the system just beyond the orbit of Pluto with a globe of certain death: automated lase-cannon mines, like those the Doogs used; thousand megaton fusion bombs with five hundred mile radius proximity fuses; fragmentation mines that could fill ten cubic miles of space with near-microscopic, metal-eroding carborundum particles.

Half that expedition had been destroyed trying to go through the minefield. The rest had finally turned back before reaching the orbit of Pluto, but not before catching glimpses of the Solarian armada waiting to destroy any ship that by crazy luck might penetrate the minefield. The Solarian ships had obviously been constructed without Stasis-Field generators, for they were so huge that it was mathematically impossible to construct a Stasis-Field big enough to contain them. In fact, they were probably little more than huge Resolution Field Generators, which could be built virtually any size—the perfect defensive weapon.

Destined never to leave their own systems, there was no need to limit the size of the ships or their Resolution Field generators to that which could be encompassed by a Stasis-Field. Together with the minefields, the monster ships had made Sol virtually impregnable to Confederal forces.

And now, at last, a Confederal general would penetrate to the heart of Fortress Sol, to Earth itself, unmolested.

Palmer grimaced ironically to himself as he entered the control room. A few weeks ago, he would've given anything for this opportunity. Now it was essentially meaningless. The fate of the human race would be decided right here, and not by the Confederation, but by Solarians. If he lived to carry back word of any of the secrets he was about to learn, those secrets would have already become quite meaningless. And if the Confederation would still have use for such secrets, it would mean that he wouldn't be around to tell anyone....

"Well, Jay," said Lingo, "in about one minute, you'll see Sol itself. I suppose that's a sight you never thought to see."

"Not under *these* circumstances, anyway," Palmer said.

"Thirty seconds, Dirk," Fran Shannon said. "Twenty... ten... five... four... three... two... one... *now!*"

Lingo pressed the button. The swirl of Stasis-Space disappeared, and the stars came out, red, blue, yellow.

Centered in the red circle indicating the ship's line of flight was a bright yellow star, at this distance, the brightest thing in the viewscreen.

A curious, unanimous sigh came from the throats of the Solarians as they stared somehow forlornly at that yellow sun.

And Palmer gazed for the first time on Man's home sun, the forlorn hope of a war-torn humanity, Fortress Sol.

It was just another G-type star; in fact it could just as well have been Dugl. There was no way of telling, at this distance, and far-off Sirius was almost as bright. An obscure, medium-sized yellow star in an out-of-the-way part of the Galaxy, lost in a vast sea of similar balls of gas.

But it was home.

Palmer was astonished at what he felt. He had never seen this yellow sun; he had never even been within seventy light-years of it before. He had been born on the fourth planet of Brycion, a sun not even visible from Earth. Not one atom of his body had ever felt the heat of Sol.

Yet somehow, the ordinary, middle-sized sun seemed far brighter than it should have; its light seemed somehow richer, somehow more benign, as if Sol itself were welcoming its long-lost son home.

"It's... it's beautiful..." he muttered inanely.

"It's just another G-type star," Lingo snapped unexpectedly, his voice heavy with bitterness. "Just another ball of gas."

"How can you say that, man?" Palmer exclaimed. "It's *Sol!* It's the home system of the human race. It's your home sun. Don't you have any feeling at all?"

"Don't I...?" Lingo fell silent, and no one else seemed willing to speak. The seven of them stared for long minutes at Sol, and Palmer thought he saw a tear form on Linda Dortin's cheek. Max squeezed her hand and Robin leaned on Lingo's shoulder.

"Just another G-type sun," Lingo finally repeated, with unnatural harshness. "There are a billion others just like it, so let's stop mooning over it." His voice quavered slightly.

"Resolution Field on," he said coldly. "We'll soon be crossing the orbit of Pluto. Watch out for military secrets, Jay." The joke fell very flat.

As the ship began to accelerate faster and faster, Palmer saw that the nearby space was filled with mines — there must've been close to a billion of them surrounding Sol, for even in the limited field of vision of the viewscreen, he could see perhaps a dozen.

As they passed close by one of the mines, Palmer could see that it was lasecannon type: muzzles projecting in all directions, and antennae of all kinds sprouting all over the globular mine. Of course the mine would not open fire — it would naturally be programmed to distinguish and pass Solarian ships. But....

There was something very wrong. The various sensing devices and antennae were mounted on universal joints so that they could monitor space in all directions, sweeping their laser and radar beams in regular patterns through all quadrants, gathering data from all directions.

But the antennae were not moving. They remained stationary. The mine was dead, deactivated.

"That one's defective," he muttered to Lingo. "You ought to report it."

Lingo said nothing.

As they neared the orbit of Pluto, they passed close to another mine. This one too was dead.

"Another dead one!" Palmer exclaimed. "What's wrong?"

"Nothing's wrong, Jay," Lingo said. "They're not defective. They've all been deactivated, except for tell-tale camera satellites scattered through the system to give us visual pickups from anywhere we want to see close up."

"What? But the Doogs...."

Lingo grimaced. "This minefield was never designed to ward off a concentrated attack by four thousand warships," he said. "There are several ways for that many ships to find a way through. That's what the Council of Wisdom meant by it being mathematically impossible for any solar system to withstand attack by four thousand ships."

"We're crossing the orbit of Pluto now," Fran Shannon announced.

"Okay, give me an indicator around Saturn."

A small circle appeared around a barely visible point of light. Lingo maneuvered the ship so that the smaller circle was centered in the larger one indicating the ship's line of flight.

"Why are we going to Saturn?" Palmer asked.

"We're not," said Lingo. "I thought we'd give you the Grand Tour on the way in, Jay. The Rings of Saturn, Jupiter, Mars.... You've never seen any of it, and old Sol has some pretty interesting children, for an ordinary G-type sun. I thought... er... I thought you might like to see the sights, since... er...."

Palmer studied the faces of the Solarians, and he thought he understood. They might pretend that the tour was for him, and he saw no reason to deny them the comfortable self-deception, but this might very well be the last chance they would ever have to see the planets of their own solar system.... In a few weeks this system, or what was left of it, might very well be just another part of the ever-growing Duglaari Empire....

"Saturn," said Lingo, in a tone of almost boyish pride, "the largest ringed planet in the known Galaxy, in fact one of only three such planets. Totally useless itself, but with a moon bigger than a lot of planets — Titan, one of the few satellites in the Galaxy with an atmosphere."

Palmer stared in wonder at the great gas giant surrounded by its rings of ice particles, like planet-wide rainbows shimmering in the black of space. Surely, one of the most beautiful sights in the Galaxy.

"It's beautiful," he said, unable to express any less banal a thought. Then a dark cloud crossed his mind.

"The Doogs don't even have the concept of beauty, do they?" he said. "It'd be just another uninhabitable gas giant to them, wouldn't it? Just another piece of useless booty."

"The Doogs don't even have the concept of *booty*," Lingo said. "But I promise you one thing: one way or another, they'll never occupy *this* system.

"*Never!*" he hissed savagely.

Onward they sped, past Jupiter, the giant of the Sol system, a gas giant so huge that Man came close to never being born. For had Jupiter been a magnitude or two bigger, had the birth of Sol gone just slightly different, Jupiter might've become a small star itself, combining its radiation with that of Sol to make Earth a planet where nothing organic could live.

As they passed Mars, where a race that had died while Earth's life was still confined to the oceans had futilely girdled a whole planet with canals to preserve an inexorably dwindling water supply, Palmer first realized that something was very wrong.

Mars had been the first planet men had ever colonized; the colonization of Mars was the basis for countless plays, novels and other works of historical fiction. The surface of Mars had been speckled with domed cities for many centuries. Mars was Sol's second most populous body.

But the cities showed no lights. The skies showed no aircraft, and the space around Mars was totally devoid of ships.

"What's wrong?" Palmer asked. "The whole planet's dead! The Doogs couldn't have gotten here already, could they?"

"Of course not," said Lingo. "Calm down. The planet's been evacuated. Remember, we *planned* for a Duglaari attack on Sol. We knew it would happen months, even years in advance, so…."

"And Mars was too vulnerable, with all the breathable air confined in domed cities! Of course! The domed cities are sitting ducks."

"Uh, huh…" Lingo grunted non-committally.

Palmer was beginning to wonder. There was something very peculiar going on. The mines deactivated… no ships sighted… Mars evacuated… the Solarians sullen and uncommunicative, touring the planets as if they were sure they would never see them again….

Could…? No, it was impossible! No one could be willing to settle for that—let the Duglaari have every planet in the Sol system except Earth itself, every planet in the entire Galaxy save one. Have the pitiful remnants of the human race voluntarily confine themselves to Earth alone, give up even the planets of Man's home system in the wild hope that the Doogs would let one planet survive as a kind of reservation.

Condemn the human race to live in… *in a zoo!*

It was unthinkable! Even for Solarians! And yet, it *did* add up… the apparent lack of resistance, the evacuation of Mars….

Did the Doogs have zoos? Might they be interested in preserving a small remnant of a defeated human race as an exhibit?

Or as a source of subjects for unusually unpleasant experiments?

"Next stop, Earth," Lingo said, snapping Palmer out of his troubled reverie.

Ridiculous! Palmer told himself. I've no reason to think that of them; they've proved that they care about the survival of the human race.

But might they care *too* much? Might not survival be Sol's *only goal?*

Survival at *any* price.

He saw it first as a bright blue star, brighter than Venus as seen from its own surface. From just sunward of Mars, it was the fourth brightest object in space, outshone only by Mars, Jupiter and Sol itself.

But as soon as he was able to distinguish it with his eye, it outshone all else in his soul.

It was Earth.

Earth, the original Earth-type planet; Earth, the planet of the original 1-gee gravitational field, which all other gravitational fields were defined in terms of; Earth, whose very name meant simply "*the* ground", "*the* world"; Earth, the only 1.000 Earth-normal planet.

Earth, the ancestral home of Man.

The sight of that sapphire point of light, waxing into a disc as they sped towards it, released a torrent of associations, of primal emotions in Palmer, to whom the planet was little more than a legend; a man whose body contained not an atom of Earth, but who was a son of Man's home planet nevertheless.

For though he had never seen the Earth, the planet was inextricably a part of him, of his mind, of his way of thinking, of the very language he spoke. "Earth-normal... Earth-like... extraterrestrial... the good earth... brought to earth... unearthly... earthy...."A thousand words and phrases that he had used casually all his life now became pregnant with new meaning in the light of the blue planet.

As the disc grew larger and larger, Palmer knew that though Man might survive The War, though the human race live a billion years, spreading its seed throughout the Galaxy, even to Andromeda, begetting its kind on a million planets of a million suns, Man could never forget the small third planet of an insignificant yellow sun in the outer boondocks of the Galaxy that had given him birth. As a salmon somehow blindly negotiates a thousand miles of hostile waters to return to the pool where he was born, so men everywhere would always, in their hearts and minds and souls, in their languages, in their criteria of the universe, in the depths of their being, turn to this one small planet.

For it was home.

Not a word was spoken as the ship sped straight toward Earth; for no words were needed and none could be adequate.

In his three decades of life, Palmer had never felt what he was feeling now. He was coming home....

Now the ship crossed the orbit of Luna, that one moon in all the Galaxy known simply as *the* Moon. From Luna's orbit, the sunlit portion of the Earth presented a spectacle that moved Palmer almost to tears.

The outlines of North and South America were clearly visible; greens and browns softened by the white fleece of cloud cover and surrounded by the luminous blue seas that gave the planet its brilliant sapphire sparkle as seen from Mars, the seas that were the ultimate womb of all life.

And Palmer knew that across those seas, over those continents, a wind blew that was clean and fresh and somehow *right* in the way that the wind of no other planet could be, no matter how... how *Earthlike.*

Home.

The ship spiraled Earthward, nearing the fuzzy line of Earth's atmosphere-blurred terminator as it approached. Apparently, Lingo was going to land the ship somewhere on the night side.

Soon I'll be standing on the surf ace of the Earth, Palmer thought, looking up at the stars as the first men must've seen them, never dreaming that someday their children would live on hundreds of alien worlds circling those far-off points of cold light.

The ship crossed the terminator and the night side of the Earth passed beneath them. Soon the jeweled lights of a thousand cities would appear like a terrestrial mirror of the stars.

But... but....

Palmer stared numbly at the night side of the Earth in uncomprehending horror. It was dark; it was totally dark, unlit by the light of a single city.

The lights of Earth's cities were out.

And suddenly Palmer realized that Lingo was swinging the ship in a great parabola past Earth. The darkened disc was no longer waxing, it was waning. They were swinging around the Earth and continuing sunward.

"What... what are you doing? *What's happened to Earth's cities?* Wha...?"

"Nothing's happened to Earth's cities," Lingo said. "Not yet, anyway. They've been evacuated."

"Evacuated? But why?"

"That should be obvious, shouldn't it, Jay?" Lingo said. "Earth is *the* prime target. Lighted, inhabited cities would be sitting ducks."

"You mean you *expect* the Doogs to get through to Earth? You goaded them into an attack *knowing* you couldn't stop them short of Earth? Why, that's... that's...."

Lingo laughed humorlessly. "*Inhuman*?" he suggested. "Sacrilegious? Jay, you've come a long, long way from the man you were when we left Olympia III, but don't make the mistake of thinking you've come *all* the way yet. The last step is the biggest and the hardest, because no one can lead you by the hand, no one can tell you. Some things you just have to *live*. Man or Duglaari will survive The War, one or the other, and not both. The primary goal of the human race," Lingo said, with cruel emphasis, as if trying to convince not Palmer but himself, "must be to *survive*. To survive, no matter *what*, no matter how terrible the price, no matter what must be risked."

He stared at Palmer, and, strangely, his eyes seemed to be pleading for approval. "If it was crucial to survival," Lingo said, "if it meant the outcome of The War, one way or the other, you'd risk Olympia III, wouldn't you?"

"Of course," said Palmer. "But Olympia III is just another planet, even if it is the capital of the Confederation. This is *Earth*, you're talking about, man! *Earth*...."

Lingo turned and stared stonily at the waning disc of the Earth. "It's just another planet too, Jay," he said oversharply, obviously not quite believing it himself. "Just another planet. Man is more important than any planet, even this one. But I can't expect you to *feel* that, not now. You think you've come a long way, Jay, and you have. But the final step is the biggest, and the most painful. And you'll have to take it all at once, whether you like it or not. They'll be no considering, no weighing, no...."

Lingo laughed bitterly. "I was going to say I pity you, Jay, but I really don't. In a way, I envy you."

"But... but why aren't we landing on Earth?" Palmer muttered.

"Because our mission is elsewhere," Lingo said, suddenly distant. "We're going to Mercury."

Although the lens of the viewscreen camera was covered with a heavy filter, the image was still blurred and overexposed, for Sol was a great ball of fire, completely dominating the sky of Mercury.

Why land here? Palmer knew that there had always been an outpost station or two in Mercury's twilight zone, ever since the early days of interplanetary travel, but no one had ever thought seriously of colonizing Mercury. It was a half-molten ball of slag on the sunside, space-cold on the dark-side, totally devoid of atmosphere, bathed constantly in solar radiation — just about as useless a piece of real estate as a planet could possibly be.

Then Palmer saw that Lingo apparently had no intention of landing on Mercury. After much maneuvering, he put the ship into a low, precise polar orbit so that it would remain in the twilight zone throughout its orbital period.

"Lock us in on the station, Fran," he said.

Fran Shannon busied herself with the radio. After a few minutes, s e looked up. "I've locked us in on the beacon," she said. "We're in range now, Dirk. Start broadcasting."

Lingo activated his microphone.

"Phoenix... phoenix... phoenix..." he said, repeating the word over and over again.

Finally, a signal came in, blurred by the intense solar static, but readable. "Acknowledged... acknowledged... acknowledged…" droned a patently mechanical voice.

Lingo nodded and shut off the radio.

"Let's get out of here," he said. "Too hot for comfort. Raul, start dropping tell-tales."

Lingo broke orbit, and set the ship on a strange course, not outward but upward, perpendicular to the ecliptic. As the ship accelerated faster and faster, further away from the ecliptic, Palmer could see something small and metallic being dropped astern.

'Tell-tale?" he asked.

"Yes," said Ortega. "Just a camera and a transmitter. I think Dirk told you we've got them scattered throughout the system. Just dropping a few more for good measure. They can all be fed directly into the main viewscreen, so we can get close-ups of just about any location in the Sol system we want."

"But where are we going?"

"*Nowhere*" Lingo replied, "absolutely nowhere."

For hours, the ship kept accelerating, farther and farther above the ecliptic, pushed to near-light velocity by the Resolution Drive.

Finally, when Sol no longer showed a disc, when it was merely a bright star, Fran Shannon said: "We're far enough now, Dirk. We could safely go into Stasis-Space any time."

"Stasis-Space?" exclaimed Palmer. "Where are we going? Back to Olympia?"

"I told you," said Lingo, "we're not going anywhere."

Instead of punching the Stasis-Space generator button, Lingo cut the Resolution Drive and locked the controls.

The ship floated dead in interstellar space.

"End of the line," Lingo said. "We'll wait here."

"For *what*?" asked Palmer.

"What else?" replied Lingo. "For the Doogs, of course."

Chapter XII

"DAMN IT, Dirk, why won't any of you tell me what's going on?" Palmer said, pounding his fist on the bartop. "We've been sitting out here in the middle of nowhere for over two weeks now, and no one will tell me a thing. Why, man, *why?*"

Lingo sighed and drummed his fingers in a little puddle of liquid that had been spilled on the bartop.

"Jay," he said, slowly and hesitantly, as if groping for words, "we didn't tell you what we were doing before we went before the Kor, and as you later learned, we had a good reason. We needed a certain reaction from you, and we wanted you to learn certain things in certain ways...."

"So? So what does that have to do with it?"

"So we had good reasons then," Lingo said. "We have good reasons now."

"That sounds pretty lame to me."

Lingo grimaced. "I suppose I can understand that," he admitted. "But the point is that there are some things which... well, which just *are*. Things which must be learned, but cannot be taught. You know, the best way to teach someone to swim is still throwing him in the water. You are the future, Jay, and if that future is to be anything but madness, you've got to become a bridge between Solarians and the Confederation. But you know all that by now.... You've come a long, long way, Jay, and we're proud of you... and to be honest about it, a little proud of ourselves, too. You've proved that a man of the Confederation can at least come to understand Solarians. But that's not enough. You've got to somehow become a real part of our Organic Group, emotionally, viscerally, or the whole thing is pointless."

"But what's that got to do with all this secrecy? For that matter, I'm perfectly willing to become part of the Group right now. Just tell me how."

"Jay, Jay," Lingo sighed. "I *can't* tell you how. No one can really tell you how. How do you think a Group is formed in the first place? By drawing lots? By accident of birth? By a Master Computer like the Council of Wisdom? An Organic Group is a bunch of people who have shared enough deep and meaningful experiences so that they come to *feel* they are a Group. 'Organic' is the key word, Jay. It *grows*, like an organism, in a sense it *is* an organism. It isn't formed, like some government. For instance, take us: Max and Linda happened to grow up together, close as only telepaths can be. I once saved Raul's life. Robin saved mine. Robin and Raul were together in those days, and Raul became my enemy, briefly. But that passed, and we became friends. Fran and I worked together in something like a local government, for *years* before the Group was formed…. Max and Raul…. but it's pointless to go on. The point is that the formation of a Group is a slow, complex, arbitrary, essentially alogical business, like any other natural process. It involves shared emotions, good and bad, shared moments of fear and…."

Lingo paused, trying to grope for words which would not come.

"I just can't find the words to tell you," he finally said. "Because the whole concept is essentially non-verbal. All I can do is tell you a long series of half-truths, semi-truths and near-lies. I promise you one thing, Jay—if you do live through this, you'll *know* what I'm talking about. I won't tell you, and neither will anyone else, but you'll know it because you'll have *lived* it."

"But *why* can't you tell me what's going on?"

"Because... because if I told you, you could never understand. You'd... you'd think we were monsters. You'd be too biased by foreknowledge to learn what you *should* learn from the experience."

"I don't understand."

Lingo sighed heavily. "Of course you don't," he said. "I guess I can tell you this much, though—even if everything goes exactly as we've planned, even if we've figured the Doogs' reactions correctly down to the tenth decimal place, something terrible is going to happen, something more terrible than any wild suspicion you can dream up. *That's* why I can't tell you what it is—because it's worse than any fantasy secrecy could possibly create in your mind. I know, Jay, and believe me, I'd give almost anything to be able to change places with you."

"But if it's so horrible, then why...?"

"Why?" snapped Lingo. "Because it has to be done! The Organic Group has given men new levels of awareness, but don't make the mistake of believing that increased awareness is always pleasant. Sometimes... well, just think of poor Douglas MacDay. He had a choice to make: do nothing, sit tight and live for today, and know that the human race will surely perish. Or plunge a solar system into chaos, into agony, into terror, in the hope that some day, somehow, *something* would emerge from the madness that *might* be able to save the human race. MacDay chose, and he chose well. What would *you* have done had you been Douglas MacDay?"

"I... I... I honestly don't know, Dirk," Palmer said.

"Nor do I..." said Lingo quietly. "Nor do I. I like to think I would've been man enough to do what he did, but maybe I'm just kidding myself... who knows? Who in hell knows...?"

Palmer eyed Lingo narrowly. "There's something else, isn't there?" he said. "Something personal."

Lingo stared downward at the bartop, not looking at Palmer, and when he spoke his voice was strangely constricted.

"Yes…" he mumbled, "I suppose there is…. Jay, sometimes, perhaps more often than not; men must choose, not between good and evil but between two different evils. Even if things work out well, when you make that kind of choice, one way or the other, you know it will haunt you for the rest of your life…. Douglas MacDay had that kind of choice to make, and so did we. MacDay chose, and he chose right, but he never lived to *know* whether he had been right. We've chosen too, but…. Well, there aren't many Douglas MacDays. Jay, I think one of Man's most basic and perverse needs is the need to be *judged*, to have some outside opinion on whether you've been right or wrong—whether you end up accepting that judgment or not. And I suppose that's what we really need you for—to judge us. An unbiased, unprejudiced, un-preinforrried judge…."

"But not unsympathetic, Dirk," Palmer said, trying instinctively to console Lingo for he knew not what.

Lingo looked up and laughed sardonically. "No, not unsympathetic," he said. "Old homo sapiens has always believed in loading the deck. I suppose…."

"Dirk! Dirk!" Raul Ortega ran into the common room. "Come on! Come on! Up to the control room! They're here! The Doogs are here!"

"I don't see anything," Palmer said, as he, Ortega and Lingo burst into the control room, where the other Solarians were already staring transfixedly out at the great vista of stars in the huge hemispherical viewscreen.

"Over there!" cried Ortega, pointing towards what looked like a miniature comet just approaching the Sol system. "The screen is set at normal view now. We're seeing what the ship's own cameras are picking up. Let's switch over to one of the tell-tale satellites.... There's one just within the orbit of Pluto."

Ortega went over to a large jury-rigged console and threw one of several dozen switches. The image on the great view-screen blurred, flickered out, and was replaced by a closer view, with Sol the brightest thing in the viewscreen and... *and*....

"Lord!" gasped Palmer. "I never realized there could be so many ships in one place at one time!"

What had appeared to be a comet, tail facing away from Sol, in the previous view was now revealed as a monstrous cone-formation of Duglaari warships, hurtling towards Sol, base forward. The eye simply could not encompass the vastness of the Duglaari Fleet. The base of the cone seemed a solid wall of ships, miles in diameter; the apex of the cone was a good twenty miles behind the base and all the intervening space was packed with warships. The total mass of the gigantic Fleet must've exceeded that of a major asteroid.

"I don't believe it," Palmer muttered. "I see it, but I just don't believe it...."

"It's there all right," said Lingo, his face an impassive mask. "Better than half the strength of the entire Duglaari Empire."

Now the Duglaari Fleet was approaching the outskirts of Sol's minefield. The seven humans stared into the viewscreen, birds transfixed by a cobra.

The base of the Duglaari formation seemed to blur for a moment, as if the ships had all suddenly begun to fall apart. Flashes of fire seemed to spread throughout the forward wall of ships. Had the forces of Sol somehow already...?

Then Palmer realized what was happening.

The flashes of fire were rockets; the "fragments" of Duglaari ships were a gigantic fusillade of missiles, thousands upon thousands of them.

Adding the acceleration of their rockets to the forward thrust of the great Duglaari Fleet Resolution Field, the formation of missiles shot ahead of the warships and into the Solarian minefield.

There was a terrible flash of light that momentarily outshone everything else in space combined; a flash of light that could only last for a moment—the deadly brilliance of a titanic thermonuclear explosion. But, incredibly, the explosion did not flare for a moment and then go out. It continued to outshine the rest of the heavens for impossibly long minutes. It elongated, it began to grow Sol-ward, an immense advancing lance of thermonuclear fire, a hell scores of miles in diameter and straight as an arrow.

"Wha... *what is it?*" cried Robin.

"They're... they're blasting a 'tunnel' through the minefield!" Palmer replied. "It's... it's unbelievable! Thousands of thermonuclear missiles, timed to go off one after the other as they cross the orbit of Pluto and pass through the minefield so that the effect is one gigantic, continuous explosion! And each missile must have close to a thousand-megaton warhead, from the look of it... *a multi-million-megaton explosion!*"

Now the terrible cylinder of fire, thousands of miles long, advanced past the orbit of Pluto. It began to gutter and die at the end nearest the Duglaari Fleet. It shortened, like an immense flame extinguishing itself, and in a few minutes the last missile had exploded and the lance of thermonuclear destruction was gone.

And the great Duglaari Fleet had a perfectly clear, arrow-straight path through the minefield, and into the Sol system.

The Doog Fleet began to accelerate Solward through its invisible lane of safety. It reached the orbit of Pluto and suddenly changed course ninety degrees.

"What are they doing?"

"They're headed for Pluto," Ortega said. "The Doogs are *thorough*. I think they plan to sterilize every habitable body in the system!"

The base of the Duglaari formation was obscured by flashes of rocket exhaust once more. A great barrage of missiles sped along in Pluto's orbit straight for Sol's outermost planet. Even as thermonuclear destruction hurtled towards Pluto, the Duglaari Fleet changed course again, and resumed its Solward journey.

"But Pluto's a dead world...." Palmer muttered. "Why...?"

"*Thoroughness,*" said Ortega. "That Fleet has enough firepower to blast everything in the system to a cinder, and they fully intend to do just that. After all, there might be a few dozen humans on Pluto, and their goal is *total* extermination. And the Doogs always mean everything they say quite literally."

Suddenly Pluto erupted in a sheet of fire. The planet almost seemed to quiver in its orbit, as thousands of huge fusion warheads blasted its surface simultaneously. Its long-dead surface flowed in rivers of molten rock; miles-deep layers of frozen gases were vaporized, and in its death-throes, Pluto was shrouded by what it had never had before — an atmosphere.

Even as Pluto's now-molten surface was enveloped in clouds of volatilized ice, the great Duglaari Fleet zigged and zagged, launching missile barrages at the moons of Neptune and Uranus.

Then the Doogs changed course again and headed for Saturn.

"Every habitable moon!" Lingo said. "They're going to blast every habitable moon!" He nodded to Ortega, who threw another switch on the console, changing cameras again. This tell-tale must've been located near the Rings of Saturn, for Titan, the system's largest satellite dominated the view as the Doogs approached it.

Instead of a missile barrage, the Duglaari went into a low orbit around Titan. Sporadically but methodically, great beams of coherent light, the searing power of thousands of lasecannon, raked the surface of Titan.

"What are they doing?" Palmer muttered. "Why aren't they using missiles?"

"Another Doog virtue," said Ortega, "*economy*. Titan's few cities are all domed and very conspicuous. So they're just cracking the domes open with lasecannon, like so many walnuts. They don't need missiles. Titan's poisonous atmosphere will do the job for them, once the domes are holed."

Now the Duglaari Fleet broke orbit and changed course, headed straight across the lane of the ecliptic towards Jupiter.

"Where in hell are your ships?" demanded Palmer. "Why don't they counterattack? Why doesn't Sol *do* something?"

But the Solarians ignored him, their full attention riveted on the Duglaari Fleet as it split into several smaller-but-still-immense sections and attacked the habitable moons of Jupiter. This time the Duglaari followed up

their lasecannon attacks with "dirty" thermonuclear missiles, since all the moons of Jupiter were airless.

As the Duglaari Fleet completed its deadly work and
began to reform itself into one huge cone formation,
Palmer kept shouting over and over again: "Where are
your ships? Why don't they attack?"

Lingo turned from the terrible spectacle for a moment.
"Please, Jay," he said, "stop shouting. How can you expect anyone to defend the Outer Satellites against *that*?"

"But those are millions of people dying, Lingo! How
can you just let them die without at least trying to....?"

"The Outer Satellites have been evacuated," Lingo said
coldly. He turned back to the viewscreen, Ortega threw a
switch, and the scene changed again. This time the tell-
tale was located above the plane of the ecliptic, looking
down on the heart of the Asteroid Belt.

"The Belt should be next..." Ortega muttered. "Ceres...
Vesta... Pallas...."

But the Duglaari Fleet did not appear in the
viewscreen.

"What's happening?" exclaimed Lingo. "Where in
space are they?"

"I don't know," said Ortega. "They should've reached
the Belt by now. Let's try a long view."

He switched over to the ship's own cameras. The Duglaari Fleet appeared as a comet in miniature once more.
But it was not headed for the inhabited asteroids of the
Belt; it had zigged again and was bypassing the Asteroids.

It was heading straight for Mars, Sol's second most
populous planet, Man's second oldest domain. Surely,
thought Palmer, Sol will at last counterattack to defend
Mars!

"What in blazes are they doing?" muttered Ortega. "Why should they bypass the Belt?"

He switched over to a tell-tale just beyond the orbit of Mars. The red planet loomed in the viewscreen twice the size of the Moon as seen from Earth. The image was large enough to show the miles-wide strips of native vegetation growing along the ancient canals and the cultivated and regular fields of mutated terrestrial plants as well. Unlike the Outer Satellites, Mars, even from this distance, looked unmistakably inhabited, domesticated. Palmer even thought he could see a glint from one of the great Martian domes, covering cities bigger than many on Earth itself.

Which made the sight of the monstrous Duglaari Fleet bearing down on the planet infinitely more horrible.

Still uncontested, the Duglaari made orbit around Mars. The Doogs broke formation and spread out, girdling the Martian surface like a great globular net of metal.

And still there was not the slightest sign of resistance from the forces of Sol. Not so much as a single Solarian ship had yet appeared, and the Duglaari warships were unopposed, even by ground fire.

The Duglaari attack began.

Lances of lasecannon fire from four thousand warships raked the Martian surface, holing every dome, scorching the cultivated fields and the native vegetation alike.

Missiles struck the Martian surface, but they did not explode. Apparently, their warheads contained not fusion bombs but deadly gases and perhaps plague bacteria adapted to the Martian air.

Then the nuclear bombardment began. Both polar ice caps were volatized in minutes and the dry atmosphere at least temporarily contained significant amounts of water vapor, for the first time in billions of years. But this was not a rain of life, but of death, for the vaporized ice was contaminated with millions of tons of lethal radioactive fallout. Ominous mists began to enfold the planet spreading towards the equator from both poles.

Still the missiles fell, now exploding in the iron oxide deserts, dotting them with lakes of molten steel, over which hovered clouds of radioactive dust, and, ironically, large quantities of liberated oxygen.

In a matter of half an hour, Mars was transformed into a nightmare of radioactive clouds, lakes of molten steel and deadly rain, where nothing organic could survive.

In a matter of half an hour, a whole planet died.

And still the forces of Sol had not appeared.

The Duglaari ships surveyed their monstrous handiwork and then broke orbit, reforming their massive cone formation. The next stop would be Earth itself!

But....

"Look!" cried Palmer, waving his arms wildly. "Look! Look! Look! They're turning back! They're retreating!"

Amazingly, inexplicably, the Duglaari Fleet was not continuing sunwards toward Earth. Back outward they went instead, away from Earth, away from the corpse of Mars.

"Lingo, I take back everything I ever thought or said!" Palmer exclaimed. "I don't know how you did it, but man, you did it! They're retreating! Without a shot being fired at them, they're turning back!"

But the Solarians were not shouting. Their faces were perplexed, confused, frightened.

"That makes two of us, Jay," Lingo said softly. "I don't know why they're retreating either. *We* haven't done anything to stop them."

The Duglaari Fleet arced obliquely back, across the ecliptic towards the heart of the Asteroid Belt. Small squadrons detached themselves from the main Fleet and began bombarding the few settled asteroids.

Meanwhile, the main Fleet continued out to the outer fringes of the Belt and then stopped dead in space.

"What are they doing?" asked Palmer.

"I haven't the slightest idea," said Ortega. "It doesn't make sense. Why didn't they attack the Belt before? Why Mars first?"

Now the destruction of the habitable asteroids was completed. The detached squadrons rejoined the main formation.

And the fleet began to move again.

Slowly it began to move, base forward as always, parallel to the edge of the Belt. It continued on that course for a while, then stopped and reversed direction a hundred and eighty degrees. Again it grazed along the margin of the Belt, and again it reversed itself, cutting slightly deeper into the Belt with each reversal.

"Oh my God!" cried Ortega as the Duglaari Fleet made yet another reversal. "Of course! That's four thousand ships there, four thousand ships in one Fleet Resolution Field. The biggest Resolution Field that ever existed. It's powerful enough to move small planetoids! Look... just ahead of the Doog Fleet!"

Now the reason for the Doogs' strange maneuvers became apparent. Just ahead of the fleet, well within the huge Resolution Field, a mass of rocks and small planetoids was accreting, with every pass that the Fleet made into the Belt. The Doogs were collecting a huge screen of rocks, a gigantic and deadly artificial meteor swarm.

Back and forth like a pendulum the Duglaari Fleet swung, each swing adding still more rocks to the ever-growing shield of meteors.

Finally, slowed considerably by the additional mass it was propelling, the Duglaari Fleet rose high above the ecliptic, and changed course again, crossing above the Asteroid Belt, and resuming its sunward course.

The Duglaari Fleet pushed before it the largest swarm of meteors the Sol system had ever seen; the Doogs were going to use a chunk of the Asteroid Belt itself to hurl at the Earth!

Earthward, behind its huge screen of rock, the Duglaari Fleet sped, back across the orbit of Mars, further and further sunward....

"Damn clever!" muttered Ortega, in grudging admiration. "Look how they keep the asteroids between them and Earth. The perfect shield—it'll detonate any missiles that try to go through it, and even lasecannon fire would simply be deflected. They're practically invulnerable now."

Lingo shook his fist at the image of the Doog Fleet in the viewscreen. "A lot of good it'll do you, damn you!" he swore.

Now the Duglaari Fleet was approaching Luna, the first extraterrestrial body that men had ever stood on. Surely Earth's moon would be armed to the teeth, thought Palmer. At last, the counter-attack would begin.

The Duglaari Fleet made orbit around Luna, and they threw the great meteor swarm into orbit with them but slightly below them, so that they were completely screened from surface fire.

In fat, lazy arcs, they launched nuclear missiles into polar orbits, at right angles to the orbit of the fleet, over and around the orbiting shield of rocks.

Unerringly, the missiles began to drop, one by one, onto the domed cities of the Moon.

"Thermal differential fuses," said Ortega. "On the dark side, Luna is so cold that our cities stick out like sore thumbs, and on the other side of the terminator, they can home in on the comparative lack of heat."

Nuclear explosions tattooed the surface of the Moon with pinpoint accuracy.

"Like shooting fish in a barrel!" cried Palmer. "Where in blazes are your fleets? Why don't they *do* something?"

"Luna has been evacuated," Lingo said coldly. "We're not going to waste the effort to try to defend it."

"But *Earth* is next!" Palmer said. "Less than a quarter of a million miles away."

"I know my astrogation as well as you do, Jay," Lingo said, quietly and somehow finally. He nodded to Ortega, who switched the viewscreen over to a tell-tale about fifty thousand miles from Earth itself.

Earth hung huge, green and brown and blue and peaceful in the viewscreen. And now, like a swarm of ugly black flies spying a particularly lush and ripe piece of fruit, the Duglaari Fleet streamed towards Earth.

Cautiously, the Doogs advanced on Earth, keeping the screen of artificial meteors between them and Man's home planet. They eased into a polar orbit, with the meteor screen directly below them, so that they would eventually pass over every point on the planet.

Twice they orbited, under full power and at a speed far greater than orbital velocity, apparently trying to draw out Earth's defenses.

But nothing happened. Not a single ship rose to do battle, not lasecannon beam tried to penetrate the meteor screen.

The Duglaari Fleet seemed to hesitate, as if uncertain and puzzled, as well they might be.

Then they stopped dead in space for a moment, while their meteor screen passed beneath them. They rose to a slightly higher orbit, accelerated at full power; caught up to the meteor screen, reversed direction and dropped down in front of it for a brief moment, facing the meteors head-on. Then they rose above the meteors again, and returned to their original polar orbit.

"What's going on?" said Lingo. "What are they doing?"

"I think I can tell you that," Palmer said grimly. "They've slowed down the orbits of the meteors so that they're now travelling at less orbital velocity. They've put them into decaying orbits.... *Look. Look!*"

By the thousands, by the tens of thousands, the asteroids were falling to the surface of the Earth, their deadly paths ignited into fiery tracers by the heat of their passage.

Randomly, the Earth revolved under their decaying orbits. Thousands of the meteors burned up the atmosphere, but thousands more fell over the entire surface of the Earth, millions of tons of red-hot rock falling on cities, countryside, deserts, seas. The oceans hissed steam and swallowed their share of the meteors, but the land blossomed in craters, pockmarked and tortured now like the Moon—in the desert, on the land, and smoldering holes where cities had been, all with dreadful impartiality.

What had taken ages on the Moon was accomplished in minutes on the Earth—the face of the Earth was transformed into a skin pitted with huge smoldering pockmarks, like a human face ravaged by an impossibly rapid and virulent case of small pox.

And still the Duglaari Fleet orbited, unopposed.

Palmer was too numbed with horror to speak. Where were the forces of Sol? Why weren't they fighting to save Man's home planet? What could they be waiting for?

Now the Duglaari Fleet let loose a tremendous barrage of thousands of thermonuclear missiles. Palmer's heart sank... and then rose, as he saw how badly the Doogs had aimed.

For the great fusillade had missed the continents entirely! Unexploded, harmlessly, they were falling into the depths of the Pacific Ocean, off the western coast of the Americas, around the great eastern crescent of Asia. The Pacific swallowed them all with barely a ripple.

Had the Solarians some fantastic defensive weapon that had caused it? Did they have some unimaginable way of protecting the continents from bombardments?

Suddenly, the Pacific Ocean, in a great semi-circle arcing up the Asiatic coast, across the Bearing Straight and down the western coast of the Americas, seemed to rise in a titanic ridge. Monstrous clouds of radioactive steam shot forth as if every volcano in Earth's great Pacific ring had erupted at once, as if the molten bowels of the Earth were pouring forth, deep below the ocean, in the great fault that rimmed the Pacific, as if....

"Lord!" whispered Ortega. "The Pacific fault! They're bombing the Pacific fault underwater!"

As the clouds of steam mounted like a forest of malignant toadstools into the stratosphere, the entire Pacific coast of the Americas seemed to shudder, to shiver like a great beast awakening after an aeons-long sleep. The entire Pacific fault was shifting!

With calm and horrid majesty, the Pacific coasts, to the very slopes of the Rockies and the Andes, began to slide down under the steaming waters of the Pacific.

And across the vast mother of oceans, the islands of Japan began to break up and subside into the deeps. Indonesia, the Philippines, the Malay Peninsula, slid downward into the Pacific. Every volcanic island in the vast Pacific erupted rivers of lava, boiling the already-tortured Pacific into new clouds of steam.

The entire Pacific basin was a hell of subsiding land, flowing lava and quaking chaos, veiled in all-encompassing clouds of billowing steam.

The Duglaari Fleet fired two more barrages, in opposite directions at the poles. The polar icecaps vaporized into great radioactive mists as thousands of thousand-megaton thermonuclear explosions rocked them in minutes.

Four times the Duglaari Fleet orbited the steaming, erupting, quaking that was Earth, surveying their dreadful handiwork.

Then they began to fire missiles again, thousands upon tens of thousands, wave after wave.

These missiles never reached the tortured surface of the Earth. Instead, they exploded at all levels throughout the atmosphere, releasing tens of thousands of huge clouds of deadly radioactive elements: sodium, cobalt, carbon 14. Radioactive elements with half-lives of decades, centuries, millenia, spreading throughout the Earth's atmosphere, mixing with the all-encompassing clouds of super-heated steam.

Perhaps it was possible that there were living creatures down there which had unhappily survived the holocaust. Unhappily, because their deaths would be the worst of all.

Both of Earth's icecaps had been vaporized. Cubic miles of the Pacific had been steamed into the atmosphere. As the heat of the explosions dissipated and Earth began to regain its temperature equilibrium, all that vapor would condense and fall back to Earth as rain.

Already, the rain was beginning to fall, all over the Earth, with unbelievable fury. The rain would last for months, perhaps for years. It would rain until the Pacific regained the waters it had given up; until the great polar icecaps reformed. All over the Earth the rain fell and would continue to fall.

And it was a rain of death.

It was a rain permeated with radioactive isotopes of cobalt, sodium, carbon and dozens of other elements. It was a planet-wide bath of radioactivity from which there could be no escape. It would continue for months; it would drench every square inch of the planet with radioactive death. Nothing organic could survive and nothing organic would be able to exist on the planet for a thousand years.

Earth was dead.

Only slowly could that enormity burn its way into Palmer's consciousness. *Earth was dead.* Man's home planet was no more.

There was no way to comprehend it. It was the end of everything. It was as if he had lost his father, his mother, his family unto its ultimate ancestors, everything he had ever loved or cared for in one gross and terrible instant. It was that, and it was more.

It was the death of a religion, a hope, a Promise. It was the death of all Man had ever fought for and the triumph of evil incarnate. It was the death that could not be — the death of the human race itself.

It was the midnight of the soul.

Palmer was dimly aware that his body was wracked with sobs. The tiny fragment of his mind that still bothered to think noted without comment that tears were streaming down his cheeks, the first tears that he had shed in two and a half decades.

Earth was dead. He stared transfixed at the steaming ball of destruction, floating like the decomposing corpse it was in the viewscreen. Earth was dead, and something within him had died with it—hope, meaning, the future, all that made life matter. It was over... *everything* was over....

He forced his eyes away from that terrible sight and looked at the Solarians.

They stared stonily at the spectacle, but their cheeks were wet with tears.

With the last bit of rage left within him, with the waning dregs of his caring, he shouted at the Solarians:

"Monsters! Fiends! Beasts! Madmen! *You* did this! You killed the human race! You...."

"*Shut up!*" Lingo roared, with unbelievable fury, with the full power of his trained voice of command. "*Shut up!*"

Such was the power in that terrible voice that Palmer instantly fell silent, the last measure of defiance, of caring leached from him.

Like a man in some nightmare, who emotionlessly observes a wall about to fall on him, Palmer was incuriously aware that the Duglaari Fleet, filled to overflowing with its triumph, was breaking orbit.

Slowly, majestically, as if savoring each moment to the fullest the Duglaari Fleet left the scene of carnage and made its way Solward once more, going forth to complete the destruction of the Sol system, to wipe out what pitiful remnants might remain on Venus and Mercury.

Without taking his eyes from the viewscreen, Ortega switched cameras to a tell-tale just beyond the orbit of Venus. From this point of view, the corpse of Earth was only a bright blue star, the same bright blue star it had been for billions of years. The heavens would not erect a monument to Earth's passing.

And then a great cloud of black ships appeared on the viewscreen. The Duglaari Fleet was approaching Venus.

But what does it matter? Palmer thought, staring numbly at the viewscreen, which now showed Venus, the Doogs, and the flaming ball of gas that was Sol itself. What does anything matter?

The Duglaari Fleet arced arrogantly towards Venus.

Woodenly, Palmer glanced away from the viewscreen at the hateful figures of the Solarians. Suddenly he noticed, in uncomprehending confusion, that the Solarians were watching neither the Duglaari Fleet nor Venus.

They were staring stonily and tight-lipped at Sol itself. And their faces were not softened by despair, but hardened into granite as if with some terrible triumph.

He followed their gaze, and at first he was puzzled. There was nothing to see save the globe of incandescent gas that was Sol, seen through the heavy filter of the tell-tale camera.

Then a curious optical illusion seemed to occur. The image of Sol in the viewscreen seemed to shimmer momentarily, as if something had jarred the tell-tale camera out of focus. Then, incredibly, Sol seemed to contract, to shrink for an instant, to fall in on itself, reducing its diameter by a noticeable fraction.

As it happened, Palmer suddenly realized what was happening; and as he realized, he began to understand.

And as he understood, he and the universe were transformed....

For another moment, Sol continued to contract. Then some kind of equilibrium point seemed to be reached.

But the equilibrium lasted less than a second. Suddenly monstrous prominences of flaming gas and plasma shot spaceward from the entire surface of Sol. The whole surface of Sol seemed to suck up into the forest of prominences, and in moments, the prominences *were* the surface, expanding spaceward with terrible speed and force.

That too happened in instants. Then, suddenly, finally, in one incredible, unimaginable, soundless explosion, Sol shed its surface like the skin of a bursting balloon. Trillions of tons of flaming holocaust, travelling at incredible speed, roared off into space, an ever-expanding globe of destruction....

Sol went nova.

Mercury was engulfed in seconds and vaporized like a snowflake in a blast furnace. Venus was vaporized moments later, and still the globular wave front of destruction, monstrous and hot beyond comprehension, grew and expanded like an opening into hell.

And as it grew, the full, total truth grew in Palmer, with that strange, manic calmness that turns seconds into hours—The War had turned around at the moment of that titanic explosion.

For the Duglaari Fleet was trapped.

The holocaust that had been Sol expanded outward towards the huge Duglaari Fleet far faster than their Fleet Resolution Field could possibly propel them. Only by going into Stasis-Space could the four thousand Duglaari warships flee fast enough to save themselves.

But they could not go into Stasis-Space. They were far too close to the nova that had been Sol. Their Stasis-Field generators would explode, leaving the fragments that would be all that would be left of the Doog ships trapped in the nothingness of Stasis-Space forever.

The four thousand Duglaari warships were doomed. The only choice open to the Doogs was which terrible death they would die.

In one instant of massive destruction whose echoes would resound for a thousand years, the human race had been saved. Now it was *Man* who had the superiority in ships; now it was the *Doogs* who faced inexorable extermination.

Even as the realization that The War had just been won dawned on Palmer, the wave front of the stellar explosion vaporized the Duglaari Fleet like a swarm of moths caught in a flamethrower.

Man was saved; man was saved, but the price was incredible.

The price was Man's home solar system. The price was the planet that had given him birth. The price was Fortress Sol itself.

And five billion lives.

Palmer could not pull his eyes away from the terrible spectacle in the viewscreen, a solar system consuming itself, Sol the source of all life transforming into a flaming, irresistible pyre of death.

More was being consumed in that awful funeral pyre than five billion human beings or four thousand Duglaari warships. As he watched, transfixed, he remembered, with terrible immediacy, the music-odor composition that Robin had called the *Song of Earth. The Composer must've known*, Palmer suddenly realized. He must've known this was going to happen.

For now Palmer completely understood the meaning of the composition. It had spoken for the Solarians then; it spoke for all men everywhere now. It spoke of a loss so great that it would take centuries for its full extent to become fully known. It spoke of a million cities, rich to bursting with history and memories, a thousand cultures seething for millenia in fecund ferment, incandescent gas now, and lost forever.

The human race had been saved from the greatest menace in all its history, but the price was equal to the prize. Man would survive, but his primal home, the greater part of his history and culture, his most basic and fundamental roots, and the last and greatest of his sustaining myths, Fortress Sol, had been torn from him.

The price of survival, Palmer thought grimly, is always the loss of illusions. The human race has left its childhood things behind it. We are now on our own.

And now he understood, he understood so much. *This* was the secret weapon Lingo had spoken of. "Fortress Sol itself..." he had said, but who could've thought he had meant it so literally?

And *this* was why Lingo had refused to tell him anything in advance, *this* was why Lingo had so desperately wanted to be judged. But who am I, Palmer thought, to judge him? How does one weigh five billion lives and the youth of a race against survival itself?

He was ashamed of how glad he felt that no part of such a decision had been his. Now he understood the final dimension of the *humanness* that the Solarians had tried to explain to him with mere words. Such was the humanity of the Solarians that they could weigh the life of Fortress Sol against the fate of the human race, come to the right decision, and yet still care enough about one human being to spare him the awful guilt of sharing, however remotely and indirectly, in it.

Now Palmer knew that the Solarians had kept the secret from him, not to tantalize him, but to spare him.

How can I judge these people? Palmer thought. No one has a right to judge them! No one *will* judge them, if I have anything to say about it!

Quite suddenly, and with no surprise, Palmer realized that at that moment, he had *really* joined the Solarian Group. He was one of them, with no doubts, no reservations.

If they would have him.

Chapter XIII

FOR LONG silent silent moments the seven of them stared at the expanding globular maelstrom of gas that had been Sol—from the point of view of a tell-tale camera far outside the Solar System, for the Solar System was now no more.

Finally, Palmer turned away from the hypnotic spectacle and looked at the Solarians. Robin and Fran and Linda were crying soundlessly, almost tearlessly. Max was staring woodenly at the viewscreen as if turned to stone. Ortega was grinding his teeth and pummeling his left palm with his right fist.

Lingo's face was set in a grim, impassive, controlled mask. Only the corners of his mouth, twitching downward, convulsively, displayed any emotion. Then he realized that Palmer was looking at him.

He turned to stare directly at Palmer. His large green eyes seemed like openings into some bottomless abyss. He grinned at Palmer mirthlessly. "Now you know, Jay...." he said softly, "now you know."

Palmer stared back at Lingo. "Now I know, Dirk," he said. "Now I *really* know. The whole thing, every step of the way, was just to lead up to *this*. The greatest trap in all history. But... just how was it sprung, anyway?"

Lingo sighed heavily. "That was the simplest part," he said. "The *only* simple part. The station on Mercury was nothing but a Stasis-Field Generator with a proximity fuse. The code word 'phoenix' armed the fuse so that the next time any ship approached the orbit of Venus...." He let the sentence hang, there was no need to complete it.

"We built a better mousetrap, that's all..." Ortega said, with bitter, exaggerated harshness. "Biggest and best damned mousetrap in all history."

"With the most valuable bait!" Palmer said.

"Jay, there's one thing you're just going to have to accept," Lingo snapped. "One thing we're *all* going to have to accept. One way or another, Fortress Sol had to die. Sooner or later, Doogs or no Doogs. The future of the human race is out *there*, in the Galaxy, not in the past, not in the womb. The Confederation is the future of the human race, or rather what the Confederation is now free to become. Fortress Sol... The Promise... all legends... once they did serve a purpose, once the human race did need comfortable illusions, mythical outside forces, just to keep going. But we're not children any more. We're winning The War, and we're going to expand out into an entire Galaxy and there's no place in a future like that for myths. Man must finally get it through his thick skull that there is only one thing in the Universe that will ever be worthy of his belief—*himself.* For unless Man learns to put his faith in his own greatness, we will remain children forever. The myth of Fortress Sol, like all the other myths, was a fairy story for children, something to scare away bogey men. It *had* to go if Man was ever to grow up. We haven't lost the past; we've gained the future."

"That's a very pretty speech, Dirk," Palmer said quietly. "Who are you trying to convince—me or yourself?"

Lingo forced a smile. "Again I underestimate you, Jay," he said. "When you make a decision like this, between two terrible alternatives, no matter how right you *know* you have been, you can never quite convince yourself.... Jay, did I ever tell you how Douglas MacDay finally died, years after he had made *his* terrible decision, the decision to plunge Sol into chaos, the most important and the *rightest* decision a man ever made?"

"No."

Lingo turned to stare once more at the holocaust in the viewscreen. "Even though he knew he was right," Lingo said, not looking at Palmer, "even though he knew that he had given the human race the only chance it could have, he couldn't live with it. He killed himself, Jay, he finally killed himself."

"What do you want from me, Dirk?" Palmer said quietly.

Lingo turned to face him, his eyes hollow and burning. "What do I want, Jay? I want you to tell me something. Tell me we were right, or tell me that we were wrong. I want to *know*, Jay. I suppose I want to be judged."

"This is why you refused to tell me what was going to happen, isn't it, Dirk?" Palmer said. "You didn't want me to have to live with what you're living with now."

"Yes. Of course. The fewer heads a thing like this is on, the better all around."

"I can't judge you, Dirk," Palmer said. "I can't judge you because I can't imagine what I would've done in your place. No one can judge you. No one has the right. But I respect you, Dirk, the way you respect MacDay. That should be enough for anyone."

Lingo smiled grimly. "You're right, Jay," he said. "That's all we can ever expect, and all that we should ever want. Thanks."

"One thing that *can* be said for sure," Ortega said, glancing at the viewscreen. "We had better get out of here fast, before that wavefront hits."

Lingo sat down in the pilot's seat. "Take a good look at what's left of Sol," he said. "It's the last anyone will ever see of it."

Then he pressed the button, and they were in Stasis-Space.

Palmer had been lying on his bunk for hours, trying to digest what had been, what would be. Three centuries of history had been turned around in an instant, three centuries of history and three decades of his life.

Man was master now. Though they did not know it yet, though the blaze of light that was the only monument Man's home system would ever have would not reach the worlds of the Confederation for decades, the people of the Confederation had inherited the Galaxy. And *inherited* was the right word.

For it had taken a great death to destroy the power of the Duglaari Empire — the death of Sol and the death of five billion Solarians. The price of life was, as always, death.

Despite anything he had told Lingo, Jay Palmer felt the weight of those deaths. For it was up to him, and men like him, to give them meaning, to see to it that they were not in vain.

Fortress Sol had met the test of history. Now it was up to the rest of the human race to justify that greatest of all sacrifices. Fortress Sol was dead, and now the Confederation too must die a death of a kind. It must give way to a new order, an order where men ruled themselves and were not ruled by machines, an order where men gloried in their humanness and did not deny it out of fear.

"This too shall pass away," was the only universal truth of history. But a corollary must now be added to that ancient law: *This too shall pass away, but Man shall prevail.*

There were no more Solarians, and there must be no more men of the Confederation, either. Only Man.

There....

"Come on up to the control room," said Robin Morel, sticking her head into his cabin. "We're coming out of Stasis-Space."

They were still in Stasis-Space when Palmer reached the control room. Everyone else was already there.

"Why are we coming out of Stasis-Space *now?*" Palmer asked. "We've only been in for a few hours. This is the middle of nowhere."

"So it is," Lingo replied, with much of the old jauntiness returned to his voice, "so it is." The rest of the Solarians seemed to have recovered also, and seemed to be almost grinning to each other.

Yet hours before, five billion people had died.

Fran Shannon nodded to Lingo, and Lingo turned off the Stasis-Field Generator. The chaotic maelstrom of Stasis-Space flickered and was gone. The stars came out. They were in normal space, in the vast, lightless dead space between the suns, almost midway between Sol and Centaurus. There was nothing here, nothing at all. Even nova Sol was not visible—for the image of that terrible event was travelling outward only at the speed of light, and would not reach this point in space for another two years. Sol was just another point of light among the thousands of anonymous stars speckling the empty blackness.

Palmer stared out into the endless darkness. Why did they come out of Stasis-Space here? he wondered. There was something about the very *nowhereness* of this empty void that chilled him to the core of his being. Why....?

"Over there," Fran Shannon said, throwing a red indicator circle around a cluster of five specks of light that just barely showed discs.

But that's impossible! Palmer thought. Nothing can be showing a disc out here!

For they were two light years from Sol, and Sol was the nearest star. There could be nothing close enough, out here in the space between the stars, to show a disc! There couldn't be! Yet there were five discs clearly visible within the indicator circle on the viewscreen.

"What are they?" Palmer murmured. "There *can't* be planets out here...."

"They're not planets," Lingo said, changing the ship's attitude in space so that the discs in the indicator circle were centered in the ship's line-of-flight indicator.

"But we're nowhere near any multiple star system like that!" Palmer exclaimed.

"They're not stars either," Lingo said, turning on the ship's Resolution Drive. "And they're a lot closer than you seem to think. Watch."

Faster and faster they accelerated towards the enigmatic bodies, and the five closely clustered discs grew and grew, until they became globes, until detail was visible, until the five discs became five globes, until it became clear that the things were... *what?*

Palmer saw, but he did not comprehend.

They were far too small to be planets, but they were globes. Five small planetoids, in tight formation, each one perhaps ten miles in diameter.

As they moved ever closer, Palmer realized that these globes were like no planetoids he had ever heard of. All five of them were absolutely regular, perfect spheres, five perfect spheres floating together in the middle of nowhere.

They approached to within a mile or two of the formation.

Palmer's jaw dropped. He gaped in amazement.

They were metal.

Not metallic rock, but *metal*. Metal plates. They were artificial. They were five identical metal globes. They had no markings, no external features except... except what looked disconcertingly like Resolution Field antennae distributed evenly about their equators. They were patently manufactured!

"What... what in space are they?"

Lingo laughed. "Someone, in a black mood, dubbed them 'Meatwagons.' The name sort of stuck. They're spaceships."

"*Spaceships...?*" exclaimed Palmer. "But it can't be! I'm no mathematician, but I know that there's something called the Hayakawa equation which limits the size of Stasis-Fields to bubbles with fifteen hundred foot diameters. Otherwise, everything would be very different.... We could build ships as big as we wanted, since there's no limit to the theoretical size of Resolution Fields. Why, theoretically, you could fly a *planet*, I suppose. But it's simply *impossible* to throw up Stasis-Fields big enough to take things like those... those 'Meatwagons,' whatever they are, from star to star!"

"You're right all the way, Jay," Lingo said. "Nevertheless, the Meatwagons *are* spaceships. After all, what do you think happened to the population of Fortress Sol?"

Palmer stared dully at Lingo. The price that Man had paid, that Sol had paid, for victory was something he had tried hard to forget. Now Lingo had brought it back, and he was reliving those terrible moments once more.

"I... I thought there was no point in saying anything about that, Dirk," he said softly. "I understand that the sacrifice had to be made, if the human race was to survive, but even so...."

Lingo stared at him incredulously for a long moment. Then comprehension came into his face, followed by surprise, then by a strange, almost stunned look that was unreadable.

"Once again, I've underestimated you, Jay," he said. "When you were so willing to forgive and understand, I naturally thought you realized.... But you seem to have seen more deeply into our minds than we have ourselves. Yes, we would've sacrificed five billion Solarians to save the human race, if that had been the only choice. Now I realize that; if we had had to do it, we would've. Even that's a horrible thought to have to face. But Jay, don't you remember, I told you that the outer satellites, Mars, the Moon, had all been evacuated?"

"Yes, but to where else but Earth? And Earth...."

"You don't understand, Jay. *The whole Sol system* was evacuated. Every last human being on every last inhabited body, *including* Earth."

"But how? To where?"

"There," said Lingo, pointing to the five huge metal globes floating in space. "There, in the Meatwagons."

"What! But as big as those things are, five billion people can't live on them. They could never carry enough food or water or air. And even if they could, the people on them would die of old age before they reached the planets of the Confederation. Those things can't go into Stasis-Space."

"You're right and you're wrong, Jay," Lingo said. "You're right—the Meatwagons can't travel faster than light. You're right, they can't carry enough food or water or air for five billion people. And you're right, they'll take so long to reach the Confederation that people living in them would die of old age. *But*, Jay, but! Remember your ancient history. Men *did* go to the stars before the Stasis-Field was discovered, at least to the nearer stars. And how did they do it?"

"Why, they used some kind of suspended animation, didn't they? Deep Sleep they called it?"

"I don't know what they called it, but I know how they did it. They simply froze themselves in liquid helium. Since they were traveling only through interstellar space while frozen, the cold of space kept the helium at near-absolute-zero, and they remained in suspended animation until they reached their destination."

"You mean....?"

"Yes, Jay," Lingo said. "The Meatwagons are little more than tanks of liquid helium, with Resolution Drives attached. Don't forget, we knew what was going to happen years ago. So the entire population of the Sol system was frozen in liquid helium two years ago, and the Meatwagons were given long head starts. You know, people in suspended animation require no food, water, air or even space to move around in. And five spheres, each ten miles in diameter, can hold a hell of a lot of people when they're all in suspended animation and stacked like cordwood.

"But... but... where are the Meatwagons going? What are you going to do with... *with five billion supermen?*"

"Not supermen, Jay!" Lingo snapped. "Men, Jay, men. Not *superhuman*, but *totally* human. Those five billion people represent about a billion Organic Groups. And as long as the Organic Groups are kept together, there'll be no need to thaw out all five billion people at any one place. As you well know, an Organic Group is a complete unit, a little culture in itself. Every one of those people has at least one Talent. Don't think of the Meatwagons as *problems*, Jay. They're not. They're the greatest storehouses of treasure in the history of the human race—the kind of treasure that really counts: *people*. There are hundreds of planets in the Confederation. Each one can easily accommodate a few million more people. Those five billion Solarians will be spread throughout the entire Confederation. They'll become one with the rest of humanity, five billion merging with hundreds of billions, like a drop of water into the sea."

"Not exactly a valid analogy," Palmer said dryly. "They aren't five billion ordinary people, Dirk, no matter what you say. They're different, and as I have to admit, they're *better*. They'll transform the human race completely... *if* the human race will let them survive."

Lingo smiled slowly. "You're right," he said. "But is that something to be afraid of? What we have learned, what we have become, will be the heritage of the entire human race. Intrinsically, there is no difference between the people of Sol and the people of the Confederation. The people of the Confederation have potential Talents too, but they've not been developed. You, Jay, for example, are probably a latent Game-master and Leader as well. Kurowski is a latent Leader, or he could never have become a High Marshal. Yes, Man is going to change—he is going to *awaken*. He is going to awaken to the full potential of his humanness, he is going to become something beyond his wildest dreams. And you, Jay, are the key."

"Me?"

"Yes, you. You've proven that it can be done, that a man of the Confederation can become integrated into a Solarian Organic Group. You were an experiment, and the experiment has been a success. Now you know the full significance of the experiment. For in the decades to come, all mankind will organize itself into Organic Groups. You were the first, but you will not be the last. The great unknown in our plan has been resolved: the people of the Confederation *are* capable of change, of growth. The history of the human race is just beginning. What we will eventually become, no man alive can imagine. But one thing is certain, Jay: it will be men like you who will lead your people... *our* people. Men who can stand apart from both the Confederation and the memory of lost Sol, and be simply human beings.... Which, of course, is not a simple thing at all."

And Palmer knew deep within him that it was so. Together, he and the Solarians had fought and won. Together, in that no-longer-distant day when the human race would be united and whole, they would go forth, Solarians and men of the Confederation alike, to meet the future.

Palmer gazed off into space, at that insignificant point of light that was Sol, at a Sol whose image was almost two years old, the light of whose passing would not illumine the worlds of the Confederation for decades.

Arid when at last the light of nova Sol would reach the worlds of the Confederation to shine for a few brief days in the heavens, men would recognize it not as the funeral pyre of the human race, but as the dawning light of a brave tomorrow.

A light that would never die.

ABOUT THE AUTHOR

Norman Spinrad is the author of over twenty novels, including the acclaimed BUG JACK BARRON.

He is a multiple nominee for both the Hugo and Nebula Awards for science fiction achievement, an American Book Award Nominee writer, and winner of the Prix Apollo. He has written scripts for Star Trek and produced two feature films. He has also published over 60 short stories collected in half a dozen volumes, and his novels and stories have been published in over a dozen languages.

He has been President of Science Fiction Writers of America, Inc. (SFWA) three times.

He is a tireless campaigner for authors' rights and is the creator of the "model contract" now in use by several writers' organizations. He's been a literary agent, President of World SF, briefly a radio phone show host, has appeared as a vocal artist on three albums, and occasionally performs live. He is a long time literary critic, sometime film critic, perpetual political analyst, and sometime songwriter.

He grew up in New York, has lived in Los Angeles, San Francisco, London, and Paris, and travelled widely in Europe and less so in Latin America, Asia, and Oceania.

ReAnimus Press

Breathing Life into Great Books

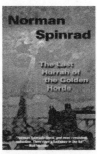

The Last Hurrah of the Golden Horde,
by Norman Spinrad

The Children of Hamelin,
by Norman Spinrad

Passing Through the Flame,
by Norman Spinrad

Fragments of America,
by Norman Spinrad

Experiment Perilous: The Bug Jack Barron Papers by Norman Spinrad

Staying Alive - A Writer's Guide,
by Norman Spinrad

The Exiles Trilogy, by Ben Bova

The Star Conquerors, by Ben Bova
(Standard Edition and
Special Collector's Edition)

Test of Fire, by Ben Bova

The Kinsman Saga, by Ben Bova

Shadrach in the Furnace,
by Robert Silverberg

The Transcendent Man, by Jerry Sohl

Night Slaves, by Jerry Sohl

Bloom, by Wil McCarthy

The Craft of Writing Science Fiction that Sells, by Ben Bova

Space Travel — A Guide for Writers,
by Ben Bova

Side Effects, by Harvey Jacobs

American Goliath, by Harvey Jacobs

"An inspired novel" – *TIME Magazine*
"A masterpiece… year's best novel" – *Kirkus Reviews*

The Sigil Trilogy (Omnibus vol.1-3), by (*Nature* Editor) Henry Gee

Made in the USA
Coppell, TX
25 March 2023